# Deadly Dungeon

MADCAP ADVENTURES

RENE VECKA

RVAELLC

To Rusty Hayes—for shining a light on the way out of my earthly dungeon

# Mid Dreki Realm Map

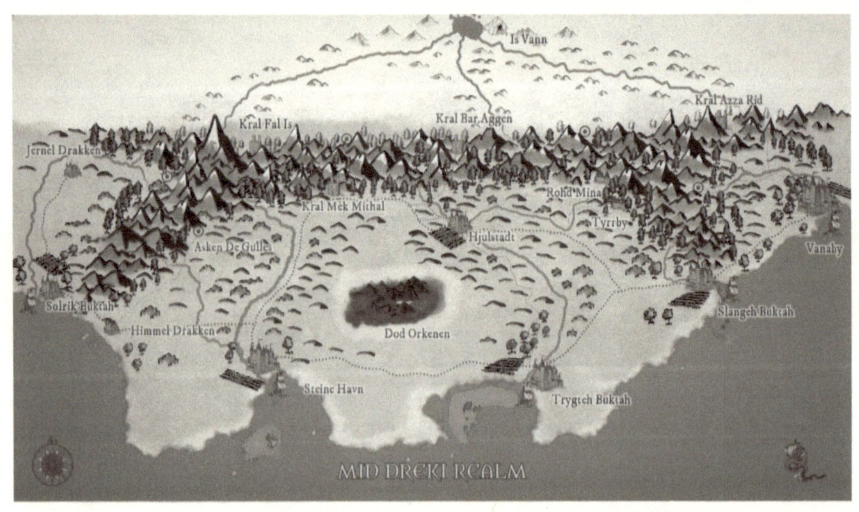

# Contents

# Chapter One

# MESSENGER BIRD

## INGEFÆR

Rory and I rode our mounts through the city of Slangeh Buktah, which straddles the Slangeh River as it flows into the Mid Dreki Ocean. Our mounts' hooves clopped on the cobblestone street as we headed for the docks. We planned to build a new home on his family's land to the north and needed to secure tents and food by the barrel and crate for the field hands we'd hired the day before.

After our escapades in Vanaby and—ahem—an extended honeymoon, we'd returned to Rory's boyhood home, expecting to settle in comfortably as newlyweds. Instead, we found...squatters. For the past six moons, we had haggled with the city authorities as to the proper ownership of Rory's plot of land. By the time we prevailed, we'd missed the planting season altogether.

While coming to get supplies for the workers—and to hire an artisan to design and construct the new home—were the next steps of our joint journey, it wasn't what excited me most about visiting the city. We were here to advertise our new venture, Injustices Righted: inquisitors for hire for tasks such as catching criminals and retrieving lost or stolen property. Lucky for us, there were times the local militia or the high and mighty Order of Gixus—the military faction which served as a city's law enforcement—just didn't want to be bothered.

But after all the legal brouhaha, I sensed Rory had become more interested in defending his family home—a fallow hundred acres with fallen-over structures—than roaming the Realm to capture criminals and stolen goods. The last six moons had worn out Rory's last nerve.

Despite the distractions, we stayed in the throes of wedded bliss—mostly by taking long horseback rides up the western slopes of the southern branch of the Mid Dreki Mountains. Picturesque and peaceful.

While we agreed on most things, Rory's newfound prioritization of farm life over our long-planned bounty hunting adventure stuck out like a lone reed in an otherwise clear pond. If it wasn't dealt with quickly, the mere would soon cloud over.

It's not that I minded farm life—my childhood years were spent on a horse ranch. But I still had so much of the Realm to explore. Besides, it was my heart's passion to help those in need of justice, and the farm didn't have such folk, what with the squatters finally evicted.

As we approached the city, young boys hollered from our lefthand side, selling grilled meat on a stick. Next to them, pretty lasses held up bouquets and candles. Behind them stood a row of storefronts. Various merchants hawked their wares, from food to clothing, to trades like glasswork, furniture, pottery, and jewelry.

We trotted past the throng, heading for the harbor, the smell of the ocean growing with each horse's stride.

Rory clenched his jaw and muttered his distaste. "Foul-smelling fish."

After an overnight gale, the stench was thick this morning. We'd had our fill of fish in Vanaby, and in sailing the seas.

From above came a screeching sound. A crow circled and dove at Rory. He waved his hand at it as the crow dipped and dodged.

I spotted a carrier pouch attached to the bird's leg. "Hold, Rory. It's a messenger bird."

He had started to draw his sword and now shoved the hilt back into place. "What a nuisance."

The messenger bird wasn't what irked him. I asked, "You haven't been practicing your summoning spell, have you?"

He grumbled. "Ah, it's all a waste of time with me. I'm not sensing any of those gold hues from the Aether."

The return of magic fifteen months ago had gifted some with arcane power, and he'd been looking toward developing magical talents. To no avail.

Rory was a farmer by birth and a hunter and tracker by training, becoming an expert marksman with both the bow and crossbow. However, he had one magical gift I've yet to see in another.

His feet.

Rory could outrun a galloping horse...for a little while. Maybe five minutes before he got tired. Acquiring the ability had come at a significant cost.

"You'd think with me seeing a fylgjæ, I'd have arcane talents." Rory groused as he held out an arm, inviting the bird to come back with its message.

When circumstances merited, his fast feet were augmented by a sparkling spirit, Roskva, also known as a fylgjæ. Rory could run four times as fast as any human without tiring when the elemental spirit was present. Alas, she only showed up when his life was in danger. One of those *thanks, but no thanks* gifts.

"The fates toy with all of us," I said.

I was a swordswoman, trained years ago by the Order of Gixus. Yet Rory's foot and blade work now exceeded mine, for he'd been trained by an evil spirit, Laehvateinn. She had possessed his mind and controlled his body for a time. Ridding her from his head had almost killed him.

The crow swooped near and settled on Rory's outstretched arm. I untied the pouch and shoo'ed the bird away before Rory could wring its neck.

Unrolling the parchment, I read. "Dear Master Belkin and Miss vod Renku, I spotted your poster this morning. I am in need of your services—if you can be discreet."

Rory and I eyed each other. He mumbled with a twist to his lips. "Discreet?"

Our first job since our return to Slangeh Buktah. I raised a fist high in the air and laughed. "The poster worked!" And so fast, too.

We had hung several posters yesterday. One by the Order of Gixus, with their permission. Another had been pasted on the wall of a building by the Merchants' Quarter near the center of town, and a third had been tacked up near a minstrel's stage halfway between the Mayor's Hall and the docks.

Rory scoffed. "Doubtless a pickpocket wants something retrieved from another thief." He turned into a curmudgeon when his plans were interrupted.

I ignored his mood and read on. "Upon receipt, please find me at the Temple of Fraegah. The matter is urgent. Signed, Conjuror Elise."

Rory's mouth puckered in distaste, but there was a glint in his eyes. "See. I told you. Thieves."

The mystery we had solved in Vanaby centered on mages. And I had been locked up for most of it. Not an experience for the faint of heart.

I sighed. That was a year ago. Almost to the day.

Time to sever the reed and clear the waters. Turning to Rory, I said, "Now, husband, we had an agreement."

Rory spat at the ground and deflected. "What does the Temple of Fraegah want with us? Better put. Do we want anything to do with them?"

"It would be rude of us to not answer her plea. Our reputation is important...and we had a deal."

Rory's eyes sparkled at me. "We have no reputation. But aye, our agreement stands."

He wheeled his roan mare about, and I followed him on Thunder. Rory knew the location of the Fraegah Temple. He used to travel to the city as a boy with his father, mother, and sister when they were alive.

I caught up on my gelding. "Don't say anything rash. I want to hear her out."

Rory smiled at me. "I am wrongly convicted of a crime I have yet to commit."

"Yes, my dear husband. Alas, your reputation precedes you."

Five minutes later, we arrived at the four-story stone building obstructing two major thoroughfares, forcing the streets and the foot traffic on them to bend to the structure's will. Not another building dared to be within thirty feet of it. That spoke to the Temple's age. However, its outer façade was freshly painted in gaudy black and red. Funeral parlors looked more inviting.

I took a deep breath and dismounted. *Our first official job.* I hoped it would pay well. The legal expenses over Rory's land had put a dent in our savings...and the new home construction and field hands had almost depleted the rest. Money aside, I wanted our names on the tips of tongues for anyone who needed aid.

I straightened the straps over Rory's leathers. "Behave."

He pulled me tight to him. "That's not what you said last night."

I kissed him. I tugged at his lower lip with my teeth, then went deep with my teasing tongue.

# CHAPTER TWO

# THE FRAEGAH TEMPLE

## RORY

Still savoring Ingefær's luscious lips, I followed her into the Fraegah Temple. I scanned the room. It was cast in shadows. The meager light came from four small, squarish windows high on the south wall. The other walls had a series of paintings depicting various mages. At least, I assumed they possessed arcane talents as they wore funny hats and robes of bright colors—some yellow, a few green, one red, and the rest a combination of blues and purples. Each depicted figure was old, with gray hair, most of it worn long and disheveled. Each frowned, the men with dipped mouths and unkempt beards, and the women with crow-like eyes and pinched lips.

The center of the room had a statue made of marble standing six feet high. I detected an age to it and a certain lack of care: rounded corners, chips along the extremities, and a gray to the base of the rock upon which the miniature, red-scaled dreki Goddess Fraegah stood with her wings folded in. Her rock black eyes stared at the door while one of her taloned hands splayed high and wide, holding a golden orb.

In my humble opinion, the flying and fire-breathing scaled winged-lizard wasn't so much casting a spell as it was grappling with shame that came from losing power over the course of a thousand years.

And now the gods—in their true Jotunn-like forms—were locked away in Asagard.

Ever since the avoidance of a second Divine Reckoning fifteen moons ago, everyone had to deal with the return of magic. The fallout from the epic conflict involving the gods had yet to fully rumble through the various governmental, cultural, and religious institutions. Many individuals continued to supplicate to the now-departed gods, and it caused much tension amongst the masses.

I sniffed. The place smelled of dirty socks and wyrms.

Ingefær and I had a lot of work to do, what with the construction of the new home and the weeding of the fields that had lain untilled for a decade. And while I was interested in helping those in need of justice, and in roaming the Realm, the timing was off.

My biggest concern was what Conjuror Elise wanted with us. She was a mage. What couldn't she do that we could? It didn't help that the Fraegah Temple had a poor reputation...well, that was before the return of magic. But how much could be fixed in a year?

Dismissing the first response from a potential customer wasn't the right thing to do as a husband, a partner, and friend. I loved Ingefær and her passion for justice. Best to find out what sort of chicanery the mages of Fraegah were up to and look for a good reason to turn down the job.

Walking around the statue—half the size of any other dreki gods worshiped by others—I spotted a half-alvae sitting behind a weathered desk, playing with something atop it. Something thin, long, and moving.

Striding toward the green-hued female, I introduced myself and Ingefær as I studied her full-length robe of many colors. Had it been splattered with paint by a toddler with no attention to patterns, balance, or harmony? Or was she mocking her own profession? She didn't get up nor offer her hand as she introduced herself as Elementalist Raemoni.

Ingefær had explained the ranking system to me once. Mage was used as a general indicator of anyone with the ability to tap the arcane powers.

An enchanter or enchantress dabbled with one of the five elemental planes. An elementalist was proficient in one, which meant an ability to cast at least two invocations. Conjurors did at least one plane well and dabbled in another, often well, sometimes like an enchanter. Sorcerers and sorceresses played with three, and wizards and wizardesses, four. There wasn't a title for someone who'd mastered all five, as no one had ever showed the competency. Certainly not in the last thousand years.

Ingefær was by official definition a sorceress, as she could channel fire, air, and the Aether. But it's a more prestigious title to be called a battle mage, which indicated control of the planes of fire and air...the two most powerful elements used in combat.

Hmm. Now that I thought about it, Conjuror Elise wasn't at the same skill level as my wife. Maybe I'd been wrong. Perhaps we could be of service.

My thoughts halted when my eyes landed on the pink, crawling creatures covering Raemoni's decrepit oak desk. Each creature was as thick as my pinky and thrice as long. They were wyrms and much of the stink emanated from them.

I waved the crow's message at her. "Conjurer Elise wants to see us."

Reamoni's jaw dropped. "Wow. So fast. She sent the message less than an hour ago."

Ingefær fingered the ice-white snowflake affixed to a choker chain, right above the collar of her chain mail. She'd taken to doing so ever since we'd shaved our heads last year. It had broken her habit of twirling her long red locks.

Since then, Ingefær's hair had regrown into a bob, coming past her ears. She was beautiful with no hair, gorgeous with short hair, and mind-numbing, tongue-drooling with a full head of fiery red hair when it draped past her shoulders. But I was biased.

The snowflake pendant was a magical artifact received as a thank you for a job well done. It had a pearl-like luminescence, and the center was streaked with red, like a distant fire. We had its powers tested upon our return from our honeymoon. It warded against frost-based spells. Not something we would see...ever. Though it was theoretically possible, Ingefær didn't know of any mage who controlled both the air and water planes.

She answered Reamoni's surprise at our promptness. "We were in town. Good fortune."

I wouldn't have used those words. We hadn't completed our dock business yet. And now our work was delayed. Losing an hour of time wasn't a big deal, but getting roped into a week-long affair posed a problem...for me.

I glanced around a third time. Being inside the Fraegah Temple bothered me. A bunch of sorry mages. Less than two years ago, prostitutes had been more welcome amongst the citizenry. And here we were, mucking it up with them.

Our adventures in Vanaby last year did little to improve my opinion of mages. One out of ten had proved helpful and worth working with. The rest had their noses high in the air, not caring one ounce about justice.

Raemoni whispered to the pink creatures, and the wyrms crawled into a wide-mouthed cup half full of dirt, one she'd pulled from a hidden pouch in her cloak. She set the cup on the floor beside her desk. Dipping her light-green chin at us, she disappeared through a door opening covered with burgundy drapes made of a heavy woolen material.

Several minutes later, she brushed the curtains to one side. "Conjuror Elise will see you."

I nodded thanks and followed Ingefær after she stepped through. Behind me, the drapes swished into place. We walked to the rear of a much smaller and very cluttered room.

Conjurer Elise was tall, thin of frame, and had tawny hair draping to her shoulders. I placed her at approaching forty. There were deep wrinkles around her eyes that didn't come from laughter. Her mouth drooped to complete the picture of a dour-mood individual. She wore a half black and half red robe, the two colors split at the waist with the darker color flowing to the floor. An emblem of Fraegah was sewn onto the robe's bosom. The mock-dreki shooting forth yellow stars from its mouth could have used some embroidery work.

The room smelled of oil, mold, and must, like month-old laundry needed doing. The windows on either side of the room were paneled over, allowing no natural light to enter. Instead, the room was lit by a series of brasiers hanging from the beamed ceiling. Wisps of smoke trailed off.

We stood in a combination office and storage room, with much of the space a series of piles: trunks, boxes, and loose mounds of various oddities, like beads, jars and vases, discolored robes, and bent and tarnished silverware. Trash to most folk; treasure to the homeless, of which the city boasted its fair share.

To my right was a closed door. The room behind would be narrow. Maybe it was a pantry or linen closet. A landing and stairs, going up, stood to my left at the back of the Temple.

Elise smiled, but it didn't make it to her eyes. She waved us up the wooden stairs.

I stood still. I wasn't ready to follow, as I wanted to hear more information first. Ingefær nudged me. I felt no itch on my back and Roskva hadn't shown. If I quit before finding out whatever it was Elise wanted, Ingefær and I would do marital battle, which was a risk worse than death.

And I would be in the wrong.

So I would keep the peace until I had a good reason to quit the job. With a heavy sigh, I stepped up the stairs, which creaked their objection. I grunted in agreement. At the top, there stood a wooden door. Elise pushed down on the handle.

The doorway opened into a classroom. At least that was my first impression. Four individuals in white robes sat behind long workbenches.

A middle-aged man wearing clothes similar to Elise's stopped talking, his hands pausing mid-wave and relaxing at his sides. Everyone turned their heads to stare at us.

Elise said, "Continue your lesson, Conjuror Maerek. We're just passing through."

We would have received the same bug-eyed stares and slack jaws from the quintet before us if we'd been trolls carrying trunks full of gold. The two young men—students, I think—dropped their jaws as their wide eyes danced over my wife. I glared at them until they turned around.

The classroom arrangement took up the part of the room nearest the door. The balance was in shadows, but I spotted buckets, brooms, and a mound of rags behind Conjuror Maerek. What lay behind that remained hidden by the dark or was walled off by two bookcases standing side by side. They didn't hold books; they held jars, vials, vases, and jugs.

Elise moved through a second door and had us follow up another set of stairs.

I said, "Wait a moment. Why are the stairs on the inside, when they should wind their way up along the outside?"

Elise's brown eyes flashed at me. "I wouldn't know. The Temple was built before my time. But my guess is, the upper floors were later additions."

I scrunched my brows. Did that make sense?

Ingefær gave me an elbow. She whispered. "Behave."

Elise continued her way up. This time, when we reached the landing, she waved a hand and mumbled under her breath. The door swung open of its own accord.

I eyed the wood door as I passed over the jamb. It was an inch thick and made of solid oak. It had opened like it weighed the same as a feather. And silently, too.

We entered a room a couple of strides smaller on a side, but it mimicked the layout of the temple's first floor. Except there weren't any walls between the two rooms, and no statue of Fraegah. Unlike the second floor, the front half was well lit, and everything was bathed in an amber hue.

My gaze swept the third-floor area. Here and there, objects gleamed and sparkled, reflecting amber light from the sconces above. There was no scent, nor smoke, that I could see.

I glanced at Ingefær and mouthed *magic*?

She nodded and whispered, "Though I'd have to cast—"

Elise interrupted. "Yes. The entire Temple is magicked. Protection spells abound. I won't reveal them to you. You should understand why."

Coming from someone who wanted our help, her words scraped across my back like the edge of a knife. I narrowed my eyes at her. "*You* sent the crow. What's this all about?"

Ingefær jabbed me with her elbow. Her message was clear. *Be nice.*

The funny thing? I was being nicer than I wanted.

Elise cleared her throat. "There was a robbery two nights ago. It is my good fortune I spotted your poster, and that you arrived in such short order."

She hadn't apologized for her thinly-veiled insult. Maybe she was direct, which I could appreciate. Or maybe she was tart by nature. I knew which way I would bet. "You said the place had protection spells?"

A twitch of her eyes. "There are ways to disrupt them."

Had she stopped herself from rolling them at me?

I ignored her and inspected the third floor. Closest to me was a stand with four blades, each a different length, and each made of a different metallic mixture. What they had in common was their golden glow. I suspected they were magicked. The sight warmed the pit of my stomach, and not for the first time, I wished I wielded a similar weapon.

The sword stand created a bifurcation marker with an aisle on either side. Just past the swords was another stand, upon which three weapons were displayed: a mace atop a four-foot handle, a spiked flail attached to a two-foot chain and three-foot handle, and a halberd that came within an inch of stabbing the beamed ceiling. These weapons glinted as well, hinting at their enchanted power.

To my right, across the aisle, was a set of plate mail armor on a dummy. While black, the metal sparkled like it was encrusted with diamonds. On either side of it was a leather jerkin and matching pants mounted on more dummies. Gold studs gleamed from the leather armor set on the right. The armor on the left seemed to operate in reverse. It soaked up the radiance around it and reflected no light at all. How was it magicked?

I closed my mouth, lest I drool. I'd seen a charmed weapon twice before. For a time, I wielded one. They are rare. And here was a room with a dozen. This room piqued my interest more than anything Elise could have said.

With all this wealth at her disposal, why would she need our help?

Perhaps I was swayed by all the magic flouncing around, but I desired to learn more.

To my left, against the wall, were three walnut cabinets with glass set in the doors. Each held four shelves and displayed an array of jewels, necklaces, rings, and other valuables. The center most cabinet had a gleaming crown of rose gold—the most valuable metal in the Realm. Beyond the display cases and stands, the second half of the room stood empty, and as no magic candles lit the area, it was an eerie shadow I peered into.

It appeared as a black mist without end, something I could walk into and through for a league and more. Yet where the shadows evaporated for an instant, there stood the wall.

Deep in the gloom, I thought I glimpsed the outline of a head—a tusked beast with fangs a foot long shimmered into sight, then an eye blink later, it disappeared. I rubbed my eyes and told myself to get a hold of myself. Elise wouldn't be so nonchalant if there was danger about. Perhaps it was one of her wards.

I shifted my gaze to all the shiny stuff before me. “I never knew the Temple had such wealth.”

Elise chuckled. True mirth this time. “We don’t advertise.”

Ingefær whistled. “You have treasures jarls would drool over.”

Magic was rare, and few possessed any valuable items. Yet before me stood vast riches. And I thought the Temple was poor.

Elise said, “Jarls and wealthy merchants entrust their valuable or enchanted possessions, handed down over generations, to us for safekeeping. There are other reasons the items are here, but I’m not at liberty to say. This chamber has the most wards on it of any abode in the city, including the mayor’s villa.”

I shuddered. Glyphs reminded me of the monsters and traps that sigils summoned when the protection spells were violated.

Ingefær placed a hand on my arm. “This place bothers me, too.”

Conjuror Elise’s fancy collection of armor and weaponry piqued my interest. I wanted to hear about the job she had for us. And as long as the job didn’t take too long, maybe we could help her...for the proper fee.

I took a deep breath to level out my tone. “So, what was stolen?”

## Chapter Three

# BYPASSED SIGIL

## RORY

In answer, Elise waved an arm, and we traipsed up to the fourth floor. She was wearing out my last nerve with her spoon-feeding-a-toddler approach.

I stopped halfway. "Wait a minute. More stairs inside. That doesn't make sense. The building is the same width and depth on all four levels."

Or so my eyes said.

Elise sighed. "Not everything is as it appears."

Without another word, she turned and hiked up the last of the steps. With yet another flourish of her hand, the fourth-floor door opened.

The light on the fourth floor came from a series of open and un-shuttered windows, each three feet long and a foot high. There were four windows per side, sixteen in total, and none bigger than the width of a man. Of all the rooms in the Temple, it was the brightest, lit by the sun's light.

The room held glass cases, oak cupboards, coat and hat stands, and open shelving mounted on the walls. Lots and lots of open shelves. Though I saw an attempt at organization, the place looked disorderly. Maybe not as much as the piles of stuff on the first floor, but a close second.

"What's here?" Ingefær asked.

"The items may or may not belong to the owner who brought it in." Elise pointed with a long, bony finger. "Most of it comes from honest work, retrieved by adventurers who stumble across a lost or buried item, and bring it to us for coin. Some of it is enchanted." She wet her lips. "As you know, the ability to use magic was lost to most until a year ago."

Fifteen moons, by my reckoning. And I damn well knew. But I didn't say anything. Most folks were ignorant of what Vidarr Allefar had done for the Realm. The d'oglemann, a scaled wingless and breathless cousin to the dreki, had led the charge to stop Ragnarök from destroying the Realm. In the process, he'd banished the gods to their own plane of existence. I struggled to believe...and I was there when Vidarr used the two most powerful artifacts in the Realm to make it so.

There were rampant stories about the heinous acts taken to banish the gods. Much of the citizenry had been incensed. But others, realizing magic had returned—along with a handful of real giant drekis—understood the possibilities. Foremost Aerica, the head of the Tyrrby Order, had held a convocation with the various city-state leaders while Ingefær and I had honeymooned. From what I'd heard since, half the citizens didn't believe that circumstances had changed.

I suspected Elise and the Temple of Fraegah were the beneficiaries of the subsequent turmoil. For once, she had students. But, in my opinion, their reputation as inept crystal gazers would take a while to overcome.

I surveyed the room and wondered why we were up here. What did she have to show us she couldn't say downstairs? Then again, it had done my heart good to see the contents of the third floor.

Ingefær asked, "And all of this belongs to you?"

"No, no." Elise shook her head. "It belongs to Fraegah. This is one of her nine temples in the Realm." Her eyes narrowed at us. "Surely, you don't believe the stories being told?"

Ingefær, the diplomat, shrugged.

I cleared my throat and hedged. "The gods being banned to Asagard has a ring of truth to it."

Her lips twisted in disapproval. "Well, here we pledge fealty to Fraegah. We're not like the followers of Fraedra, either." She shuddered. "The Væniere Goddess is the weaker sister."

Eh. Humans and alvaes never saw eye to eye on the gods even before they were banished.

Elise finished her soliloquy. "I am but a steward on this Realm, bound by my oath."

"So, what would you like us to do?" Ingefær asked.

Elise said, "First, I need your assurances that you will be discreet."

I groused under my breath. She summoned us here to help her and she stipulated rules? Ingefær gave me her 'you're wearing out my nerves' glare.

I softened my mouth. I couldn't turn something down without learning about it first. Though in truth, I had become interested...as long as the job didn't take up too much time. Which, I was sure, left but a little window for our interests to align. "Aye. My wife and I can do that. Yet, it depends on what the task is and what we find out in the process."

Elise scowled at me like I'd compared her mother to a sow.

Ingefær interceded on my behalf before I spoke my mind in earnest. "What Rory means is that if you ask us to help brigands and murderers, then we'll report to the Order of Gixus the first chance we get. We want to bring any miscreants to justice."

"That's what I don't want." Elise crossed her arms under her bosom.

"What?" Ingefær crossed her arms mimicking the conjurer, her brows knitting tight.

Here *I'd* been looking for a reason to turn the job down, and Elise's flippant manner of dealing with miscreants would lead Ingefær to quit the job before we started.

"The Temple has a reputation to uphold," Elise said.

I stifled a laugh. Maggots were better thought of, for at least they had a place in the circle of life. Mages mucked things up. Well, the mages who weren't my wife.

"If my customers hear of a theft, then all these magical items on the floor below will get cleared out overnight." Elise waved a hand at the stored goods to the side of the room. "And our major source of revenue disappears like vapor in the sun."

But they had adherents now. Folks paying good coin to be trained in the arcane arts. It wasn't as bad as Elise painted, though I saw her point.

I said, "I understand." Else, she would have gone to the militia, or the Order of Gixus, and word would spread faster than a bolt of lightning ripping through the air. "So, how do we, assuming we catch him or her, bring the thief to justice?"

Elise frowned, and I saw where most of the wrinkles came from. "I'm not as interested in justice as I am in the recovery of the stolen items."

Ingefær scowled at me and gave the subtlest shake of her head. She wanted out.

I asked, "Why seek the items' retrieval, then? Why not let the theft go?"

Elise paced for a long minute. "Because of my sworn oath to Fraegah. Because one item has a buyer who is keenly interested in its acquisition. And last, because I have the means of finding the individual who bypassed the wards on this level."

What? Then why hadn't she retrieved the stolen items?

"Which are what?" Ingefær asked, her tone suitable for speaking to a dog who had just relieved itself on the family rug.

"The windows are open to the outside air." Elise pointed. "But no bird, spider, or wyrm can pass the threshold."

"Yet somebody did?" I asked. She had me confused.

Elise nodded.

We were four stories up and, from what I remembered of the building from the outside, there were no handholds or gutters. Just a massive overhanging roof. The thief would have had to dangle from the roof and swing for the window, a leap of eight feet or more. Never mind how they climbed up there to begin with.

"How can you be so sure?" I persisted.

"Because the ward on the window was dispelled." Elise stepped toward us, closing the gap. "When the thief picked up the stolen items, a second glyph went off and woke me. By the time I ran up here, the thief was gone, along with four items I had set aside that morning. Pieces I was considering selling to pay Temple expenses." She forced a smile. "We're expanding."

"So, the items were set aside and out in the open?" Ingefær did a slow turn. "Was that wise?"

Elise sighed. "In hindsight? No. I had pulled them out of the protected cupboard and relied on this floor being so high up and on the sigils on the doors and windows. Leaving them lying loose on the glass case with a simple 'screaming banshee' glyph was an error on my part."

"Who knew?" I asked.

"Besides Raemoni, Maerek, and me? No one."

Ingefær and I exchanged glances. Her gaze floated toward the door. Yep, she was ready to go.

But I was puzzled. Either Elise was lying, or she wasn't very bright.

I understood her reasoning for not informing the Order of Gixus, as doing so would impinge upon her business. But I didn't care for the required pledge of secrecy. Elise's inability, or perhaps it was a lack of effort, to retrieve what had been stolen, made no sense to me.

Ingefær said, "I'm sorry, but I don't think this job is right for us."

I scratched the back of my neck. "Yeah. You ask a lot. We're officers of the law." There were shades of gray when it came to justice, and while I could let a thief off with a broken nose, a cut off finger, or similar, Ingefær wouldn't agree as easily.

Elise reached out with a hand and placed it on my arm. “Please. I have nowhere else to turn.”

## Chapter Four

# A PLEDGE IN BLOOD

## INGEFÆR

My desire to aid others stilled my feet, and I turned to face Elise. The woman vexed me with all her clandestine mannerisms. Her uncaring attitude toward justice was like a swarm of redbugs digging into my skin. Yet she'd spent time wowing us with magical artifacts, and her tone begged us to help her. "You don't think Raemoni or Maerek took the items?"

"No." Elise's voice sounded firm. "They have taken the same vow as I have. It is impossible to bring shame upon Fraegah once the ceremony is complete. There is magic involved."

I wasn't so sure. The gods were frauds. But her certainty left an enormous question.

"So, who?" Rory asked, leaning over the diminutive woman.

He hated being led by the nose, one step at a time. And Elise had done just that. Her secretive approach was almost as off-putting as her scoffing at justice.

From within the pocket of her black and red robe, Elise pulled out a glass ball, maybe two inches in diameter. She held it aloft in her palm. I could see something inside of it floating about, like it was on the surface of a pond.

I peered closer. "Is that a nail?"

"Made of silver," Elise replied.

Rory asked, "What's it do?"

"I will cast a spell on the orb. Well, on the nail contained within the liquid inside the orb. It will point in the direction the thief has gone."

Again, my husband got straight to the point. "So, why don't you catch the thief yourself? Why have you waited two days?"

I mumbled my agreement. The conjurer had skills and an artifact to aid her. Something was off about her need for our aid.

"Discretion is one reason." Elise shrugged, her eyes dancing off to the ceiling. "My face is known. And I do not want to be associated with the retrieval of the items. Not publicly. Besides, I am not as skilled as I would like. In the event of resistance, say with a blade or sorcery, I would fail."

Rory chuckled, but turned it into a throat clearing.

Elise looked away as color rose up her neck.

Was she being evasive? Or was she ashamed? My gut told me she was hiding something. But what?

Rory scratched the back of his head, the muscles in his jaw tight. He'd seen the tell, too.

Elise was a conjuror. Why was she asking us for help? I pointed at the orb. "You are not without talent."

"Esoteric spells. Not combat or anything to subdue an individual." Elise stood straight, but her eyes looked at my feet. "The delay is due to my attempt at a quiet recovery, which took most of my time yesterday. While I got close several times, each time, the individual spotted me and raced off. After my failure last evening, I feared further delays would allow the miscreant to dispose of the items and then their recovery would be difficult."

Plausible. Yet the lack of eye contact worried me. As did her words—which implied she knew the thief by sight...and he knew her. She wasn't being forthright.

"What was stolen?" Rory asked. "Be specific."

We hadn't acceded to her pledge of secrecy yet. But I, too, wanted to know what we were in for before agreeing.

She hemmed and hawed. After pacing back and forth, she said, "A blue topaz jewel, about the size of a marble children play with. An elixir of potent healing. I cast the divination spell on it myself. It would be handy for any adventurer. It is valuable. I paid a hundred silver coins for it two years ago. It's worth twice as much. Another item is a signet ring that once belonged to a wealthy family. The owner of a manor outside of the city sold it to the Temple many decades ago. It is valuable as a piece of jewelry with its gold band and ruby stone. The engraved 'R' in the ruby detracts. It is magical, though. My predecessor said it provides the wielder a source of power for casting magic. Very useful, if one could ever get it to work."

She grimaced. "I have tried. Jarl Retzlaff the fifth, the current jarl of the Mansion Hexerei, expressed an interest in the item when we bumped into each other at the Spring Equinox ball. Now that magic has returned, if he doesn't buy it back, I can seek other interested parties."

"And the fourth item?" I asked.

"A very fine dagger." Elise swallowed with difficulty. "It's been in our possession for a century. It is bejeweled along its hilt. The blade runs a foot long with a slight curve. It is forever sharp. Magicked to never fail to penetrate armor."

Belkin whistled. "What's it worth?"

"Four thousand dreki."

That was a lot of dreki coins.

"I like the idea of piercing through armor." Rory mimicked stabbing the air off to the side.

Of course, my husband was drawn to the notion of a magic blade. On our prior excursions, before we fell in love, we had more than once run into *something* that resisted a normal blade's sharpness.

"Ah, but getting close enough with it is the hard part," Elise said with a bite to her voice. The pride of a mage. I knew magic wasn't a cure-all. Stamina failed many who thought themselves all-powerful.

Besides, she didn't know Rory. He could get close enough in an eye blink.

"That's quite the haul," Rory said.

"How much is the reward?" I asked.

"A thousand dreki pieces." Elise flipped an empty hand over. "Or the blue topaz jewel and the vial of potent healing, which together have about the equivalent worth. Recover the dagger and the signet ring, and the other two items are yours."

Tugging at my silver-white snowflake, I said, "Give us a moment to confer."

Rory and I moved to a corner formed by two curio shelves filled with such things as silver and gold thimbles, ivory unicorns, and drekis hewn from amethyst and garnet. We dipped our heads together.

I said, "A thousand silver should pay for the extra expenses to build the home right." We'd downsized our house plans by half after talking with the master carpenter.

He waggled his head. "We have enough coin for a decent-sized house."

His motto was bigger wasn't always better. But I was thinking a decade ahead. Maybe one day there would be children.

He looked at the door. "My concern is how long the job will take."

"The thief is in the city," I replied. "With her magic orb, I'm guessing it won't take long."

He grunted. "Maybe. I'm ok with not reporting the thief. You?"

I groused. "No. I don't think she's being forthright with us either. She knows the thief, and he knows her. I'm guessing it's family. That's why she doesn't want him to hang."

I paused for a moment. Family. My parents were killed when I was ten, and my sister almost two years ago. With a heavy sigh, I said, "Only one thing trumps justice...blood relations."

Rory nodded. "Aye. I agree."

"We'll recover the stolen items and see if we can make things right without arresting the criminal."

Rory asked, with a slight twist to his lips, "What if he resists arrest? I'll not risk our lives to save his."

"It's a concern of mine, too."

Rory said, "I'm alright to try, if we put a time frame on it. Three days. Tops."

I squinted an eye at him. "That may be enough. But what if it isn't?" I put a hand on his arm. "Once we give our word to try, I'm not for quitting."

It was Rory's turn to bark. "There's a house to build and fields to clear."

I smiled. "Both can wait a week or more. The goods and equipment will take that long to show up at the farm."

Rory's lips twitched. "But we haven't ordered them yet."

I nodded. "Alright. We take the job for three days, then take a break to order them if we haven't yet succeeded."

That shouldn't take more than half a day.

My shoulders heaved. "Maybe we'll get the chance to stop by the docks while we're searching for the thief?"

"Ah, the aligning of stars." But he winked at me. "Fine. Let's try it. But let's also keep an open mind."

I locked eyes with him. I needed him to agree to the true reason—our agreement to start Injustices Righted. And as much as I hated keeping a thief's identity secret, our reputation was important to our long-term success. "We talked about this. We agreed we would hunt evil and help those who need aid."

His brown eyes went soft, and he smiled. “Oh, love of my life, I’m agreeing.”

I kissed him on the cheek. Despite Elise’s mannerisms, the thrill of the hunt and the joy of revealing mysteries excited me. I took a deep breath to settle myself.

We walked back to Elise. “We’ll do it,” I said.

Elise said, “But first, I must have your pledge of discretion.”

Rory sighed.

I nodded. “You have it.”

Out of her red and black cloak, Elise pulled a dirk about the length of a dinner knife, one with a narrow, serrated blade. “In blood.”

Rory cocked his head at her. There was an edge to his voice. “You’re going to cast an incantation on us?”

Elise smiled, confusing the worry lines around her eyes. In all her descriptions of the stored goods, she had shown little humor. “You won’t reveal the theft or the thief’s identity to the Order of Gixus without my consent. Nor will you kill him.”

This was a twist I hadn’t expected. My guts jangled. I was alright with letting the thief go. But I had hoped to teach him a lesson. And what if he tried to kill us?

I closed my eyes and took a deep breath. “Um, I don’t care for your restriction. At least the way you phrased it.”

Rory’s lips twitched and his jaw muscles spasmed. “Besides, it’s unnecessary. I am a man of my word. And Ingefær is a former Ære Warrior.”

“Key word is *former*,“ Elise said.

Rory growled low in his throat. She’d thrown the first insult.

I put a hand on his arm. Elise needed our help, and I had an idea why. “We agree if you modify the terms. We must be able to defend ourselves if we’re attacked.”

Rory ground his molars as he paced back and forth. "Yeah. Tell us the words first. Then we'll think about giving you a drop of blood. I want to make sure it isn't necromancy. My wife will monitor your incantation."

Elise paled. "I guess I deserved that. I agree with the modification."

She spoke the words. I knew they were foreign to Rory, who understood but a smattering of Varanusian, the language of magic.

Translating her words, I got, '*Find the thief and goods and be silent about the act.*'

I narrowed my eyes. "It sounds alright. There's nothing there about not killing the thief."

She nodded. "I understand your concern. Just give me your word you won't harm him if at all possible."

I said, "Of course. You have my word."

"And mine," Rory said.

Using her dagger, she took a drop of our blood and uttered the incantation sealing our pledge.

She cast her spell. But she slipped in three extra words.

"Why did you add...*Fraegah compel them*?" I asked.

"In case you tire of the chase."

Rory and I exchanged glances.

I glowered at her. "That was unnecessary."

Rory added, "And deceitful."

Elise shrugged. "I don't know you beyond the poster, do I?"

I sighed. "And we don't know you, either. It would have been right to warn us." Based on the Code of Sorcery, it was required. Who were we dealing with?

Elise shrugged and cast a spell on the glass orb with the silver nail. She paled; her eyes blinked fast. "You have...three days...before the...spell wears—"

She swooned.

Rory used his augmented speed and caught her under her arm, and slowly lowered her to the floor.

Elise's eyes cleared. A hand went to her forehead. "See what I mean. I have no stamina. Retzlaff's ring would come in handy for me."

Two spells and she fainted? I was still mad at her for her deception, but I held back from gloating. Her need for our aid screamed at me.

I was the more powerful mage...at least in terms of fortitude. Knowledge of arcane spells could tip the balance of power her way. An ability to draw more power, infusing each spell with more energy, was yet a third distinction between mages. And the talent to think creatively was another differentiating factor.

With Elise fluttering a hand in front of her face, a smile fixed on mine. Our first assignment. Despite the odd conditions, I was excited. Rory would come around. He always did.

## Chapter Five

# THE SUDS AND SPUDS

## INGEFÆR

Rory and I walked out of the Temple and collected our horses.

I looked at the orb full of liquid and the silver nail floating in it. It pointed south, toward the docks. We rode side by side, headed toward the smell of fish.

Much like in Vanaby, here in Slangeh Buktah, the closer we rode toward the docks, the dirtier, grimier, and poorer the crowd and our surroundings got. And the more the stench of fish entrails filled the air.

I glanced at the sun in the sky. It was almost midday. We had spent more time in the Temple than I realized.

Rory said, "We've taken on a job with troll shit smeared all over it."

I disagreed. Well, not fully. Helping others get justice flowed in my blood. But he was right in that Elise's compel spell was akin to a hammer hanging over our heads, and I didn't enjoy being her nail.

I grumbled. "The pledge to keep our mouths shut doesn't sit well with me."

I hoped for a loophole—a way to turn in the thief despite the spell.

Rory scowled as we rode south. The street merchants near the center of town had been replaced by a host of old and frail women sweeping their porches and thwacking dirty rugs. Passersby dwindled in number.

I checked the floating silver nail. "The nail has been pointing south. But it's drifting to the right."

Rory said, "I suspect it will do more swinging the closer we get to the target."

It would. I scowled at the horizon. Not because of his comment, but at my suspicions over the artifact in my hand. Should I keep them from Rory?

We clopped along.

No. Honesty was necessary to keep a marriage together. "Something about this orb makes me wonder how it truly works."

"You're the battle mage. Magic is lost on me."

"I understood Elise's incantation," I said. "The orb and nail will seek the thief. But then, how does the orb know who the thief is? Elise mentioned no names. And none of the words to her incantation provided any physical specifications."

Rory frowned. "Don't spoon feed me, Ingefær. You know I don't like it."

"The thief violated a glyph." I avoided a vendor trying to hawk his wares. "Maybe the second ward going off sets up a tracking beacon on the intruder. Or maybe it's because she has a drop of blood from the thief."

Rory's brows furrowed deeper, staying silent for a few heartbeats. Then, "Does it matter?"

It didn't. We'd already discussed the possibility that the thief was a relative. I was giving voice to my questions regarding Elise's magic.

Rory locked his eyes with mine. "Love of my life, I'm going wherever you go. If you want to quit, I'll quit. If you want to find the thief, then I will help. I'm not as concerned at not bringing the miscreant to the Order of Gixus as you are. And a thousand dreki coins will help pay for the larger house you—we—both want."

Not turning in the thief was my burden to bear. I sighed.

*Think of the positives. A larger home, and our first official job.*

I said, "We find the thief and recover the stolen goods."

A few minutes later, I pointed to the right. "This way."

Rory snarled at the indicated direction.

I didn't disagree. The buildings surrounding us had taken on a decrepit look to add to their lackluster appearance. Between the wind, rain, and lack of care, it was a wonder they remained standing. Colors ranged from dingy gray to rotting brown. Windows were boarded up—even windows belonging to merchants who, based on their soiled and worn clothes and the used wares they hawked, might become thieves themselves as soon as the sun went down.

Rory said, "Great. Just great. I love visiting the soiled underside of a city."

I agreed. "Not far now. The nail is swinging leftward more than forward."

We rode for a block and I pointed. We jigged and jogged for a couple minutes more.

As we passed a saloon, *Suds and Spuds*, the nail spun from forward left to rearward left. I halted my gelding, turned around, and rode past it going the other way, keeping my eye on the vacillating nail.

"He's inside," I said.

Finding a place to stop, I dismounted. Rory followed suit.

I scanned the area and scowled. "I don't like the idea of leaving the horses out here. You stay, and I'll go in."

"Not a chance, beloved. I'll go in."

"You'll have to work the orb," I said.

"Is it hard?" Rory narrowed his brows. "You know, it doesn't matter. The thing is, I don't like the idea of splitting up. Not here, not anywhere. Not anytime. Not ever."

"I love it when you talk sweet." After pecking him on the cheek, I said, "We'll both go in."

Rory nodded, his gaze sweeping the area.

The foot traffic was sparse and moved in a single direction: away from the docks. Either heading home or for a meal or a second job.

Rory nudged me and pointed with his chin toward a darkened doorway. A man sat in the depths of the entryway to a shanty with a weathered door that hung askew. He wore a hooded cloak, and his beady black eyes studied us from within the hood's shadow. Or perhaps he was admiring the horses.

I said, "Let me see if I can cast a sigil like Conjuror Elise."

I'd been practicing, but this would be my first attempt in an actual situation. While I clenched my hand three times in slow motion, I threw a pinch of ground bindweed over the reins and evoked a ward spell: "*Beskyttje Thunder og Muffin.*" A soft orange glow settled around the reins, then faded out.

I giggled. "I did it."

"What will it do?" Rory asked, grabbing his crossbow and slinging it over his shoulder.

"Protect our horses from thieves," I replied.

No one could touch the reins without me knowing it.

I held the orb in one hand and undid the cinch to my longsword with the other.

Rory chuckled, undoing the loop over the hilt of his sword. "It's been a while since I visited a saloon two hours after the midday meal. That brings back memories. Few of them good."

I whispered, "You don't see your fylgjæ already, do you?"

Rory shook his head. "No Roskva yet."

I'd never seen his sparkling spirit for myself. Rory described her as a foot tall, as thin as sticks, with a block-shaped head. All of her shaded a creamy orange.

I said, "Let's hope we don't see her today."

Rory grunted and led the way into the saloon.

Once inside, I glanced at the orb. "To your right."

Despite the open windows, the place was dim and stunk of rotted potatoes, apple cider, and urine.

Rory stopped and scanned the saloon. My gaze followed his. A half-dozen men, not counting the barkeep, looked at us. All were dressed in tattered clothes—shirts and pants displaying six or seven patches apiece and, judging by the stench of sweat and toil, none had been washed in a moon. Each man had at least one mug in front of him.

One man, sitting by himself at a table, had his legs up on a chair. No shoes. And the bottoms of his feet were black, like he walked through soot on a regular basis. He stabbed lazily at a potato as large as my hand. With darkened fingers, he pulled a mug to his mouth and drank.

I had yet to see any weapons.

Rory's gaze swung right, and since the silver nail pointed that way, I followed. Two men sat at a round table with a mug beside each of them. The clack of ivory rattled off the wood tabletop. They were rolling dice.

One of the two was our thief. I couldn't believe how fast we'd found him. This could be the easiest thousand silver we'd ever earned.

The one with a dirty blond mop of disheveled hair looked at me. He wore a red kaftan and a blue vest. He had to be young, as I didn't see any facial hair. His jaw muscles tightened, and he squinted. Was he glaring? Was he trying to scare me?

Rory cleared his throat. "Excuse me. I—"

The shrill undulation of a pair of horses whinnying pierced the air.

I rumbled. "Someone's trying to steal our horses." I made a quick decision to stop the horse thief or thieves rather than collect Elise's robber, who had been easy to find. "Come on!"

I spun on my heel and raced outside.

Four men had the horses surrounded. A round man, about as tall as me, was trying to unwrap the reins from around the post. The sigil's whinnying continued to wail.

Rory sped past me, his sword drawn. "They're not yours!"

Thunder sent one crook flying with a hoof kick.

The stout thief raised his hands and backed up. The ward stopped shrieking.

Yet now the air was pierced with a different howl...this one lower pitched and coming from behind me—from inside the saloon.

The foursome of thieves ran off.

Rory looked at me. "Do we chase them?"

I shook my head. "Let's see what's causing that squealing."

We scurried back inside the *Suds and Spuds*. I looked to the right. The blond-haired man was gone. The other dice player sat back and gulped the contents of his mug.

"We can still catch him," I said.

Rory shook his head. "We can, but let's be thorough here." He sidled up to the man sitting with two mugs beside him.

Rory sat opposite the lone drinker while I stood by the table.

The man burped loud and long. "Ye going to buy me a fresh one?"

I looked at the orb. The nail pointed out the back door of the saloon. "He's getting away."

"For now," Rory said.

I fumed at my husband. He was relying on his fast feet to catch Elise's thief. Yet there were other considerations for not giving the man time. I placed my hands on my hips.

Rory ignored me and asked the man sitting down a question. "Who were you playing dreki dice with?"

The man leaned forward, his loose-jowled face grizzled with a week's worth of growth. "Don't know."

My husband can be persuasive when he wants. He shifted over a seat, getting closer to the man. "If you don't tell us, then we'll take you into the Order of Gixus as an accessory."

"I ain't done nothing."

"You know the man who was here." Rory reached out with his left hand and placed it atop the man's right hand, holding it in place. "It would be a shame for us to waste your time by dragging your carcass out into the streets. So, tell me, and let's part as friends."

"Go goblin—yaargh!"

He never got the rest of the insult out. Rory squeezed and rolled the man's knuckles against one another. Their cracking twinged my back.

The barkeep came around with a walking stick adorned with a metal knob. I turned and placed my hand on the hilt of my sword. "Be careful. You may end up behind bars with your customer."

"You ain't the Order of Gixus," the barkeep said.

"I was once," I said. "Retired now, going on a year. I have many friends. A few in quite high places. So, either you tell us what we want to know, or you spend a moon, maybe two, in jail until the Tyrrell Order sends one of their masters around with a truth spell."

I had hoisted a lofty reference for their criminal minds to ponder. Eyes jerked back and forth. The man with the soot-covered feet belched. I glanced at Rory. He was patting the man's sore hand with one of his.

I was about to pull out the decree from Foremost Aerica, giving us the authority as Realm bounty hunters, when the barkeep lowered his weapon.

The man said, "You tell them Burt, or you're cut off." The barkeep turned around and walked to his bar.

I took my hand off the hilt of my sword and surveyed the rest of the saloon; the occupants appeared uninterested or at least sufficiently cowed. Or maybe they didn't much care for Burt.

Burt groused. He drained the last of his mug. After a loud and warbled burp, he said, "Was Manick Mick, who was sitting here. We was playing dreki dice. I ain't stole nothing."

Rory said, "That may be. I ain't accusing you of thievery directly. But you know the man. Where's he gone? What's he do when he's not here?"

Burt tried to pull the departed man's tankard closer, but Rory, quick as lightning, reached over and tugged it toward himself. Burt's lips curled in distaste. "Mick's alright. He works down on the docks like the rest of us."

"How come you two aren't working now?" Rory asked.

"Took the day off."

"Why?" Rory nudged.

"You's a pain in my ass," Burt said.

Rory again covered the man's hand with his.

The man freed it. "Mick said he got silvers from his ma, for helping her some place she works. So, we took the day off to drink and roll dice."

That sounded like a fishy story to me.

"Where's he live?" Rory asked.

"He bunks at the boarding house near the Shrine of Eirene."

Rory pushed Manic Mick's mug toward Burt. "Thank you."

I asked, "Why did he leave screaming like he did?"

Behind me, several men guffawed.

Burt chuckled into his friend's mug. "Ah, you don't know Mick. If you find him, you'll see."

Rory grabbed for the man's hand to get a better answer, but I waved him off. If the other men thought it was funny, it wasn't anything dangerous. "We have the nail. There's no need to break fingers."

Rory didn't like brigands. He liked to take the time to teach them a lesson. I tugged Rory's sleeve. This bandit wasn't worth our time.

Outside, I undid the reins with a quick flick of my hand and stated Thunder's name. As I mounted the chestnut gelding, I said, "We didn't need to question him."

Rory shrugged. "Maybe. But what if this Manic Mick evades us and the spell on the orb lapses? Then the information we've gathered helps us out."

"If he told the truth," I said.

My nose turned up at the fish stink coming from the harbor. “I hope we don’t have to slog around here for three days.” I hefted the orb and looked at the nail. “He’s heading south. Toward the shoreline.”

Toward the stench.

## Chapter Six

# MANIC MICK

## RORY

As we rode for the docks, I asked Ingefær, "Did you get a good look at Manic Mick?"

She nodded. "Blond and thin. He was sitting, but I think he was as tall as you."

"He reminds me of Elise," I said. "But I need to get a look at his face straight on to be sure."

"I had a feeling the thief was related to her." Ingefær checked the floating nail. "Might be a nephew...or a son."

I rumbled under my breath. "Explains the pledge."

I wanted to be mad at Elise for the blood-based incantation upon me and Ingefær, but I knew if it was my kin, I would avoid the Order of Gixus as well. Didn't mean I couldn't bethwack the little turd when we caught up to him.

We trotted the horses, following the shifting silver nail. He had maybe a quarter of an hour head start on us.

I understood why Elise had a hard time bringing her brigand family member to heel. If Mick behaved like his ale-drinking friend had described him, his tantrums would arouse the attention of, well, everyone. And Elise lacked the magical firepower to take him before he squawked and ran.

I hoped we would catch Mick before the nail's spell waned. Without it, finding him in the city would be nigh on impossible...if he played it smart and hid himself. Would he make the mistake of returning to where he made his bed? I sighed. I assumed the drinker at *Suds and Spuds* had told the truth.

After five minutes of riding, the nail pointed to yet another saloon. This one was called *The Brine*.

The area had plenty of people working about, and the sounds of activity from the docks wafted over to us. When the shouts and groaning and boxes and barrels sliding and thumping subsided for a breath, the ocean's waves sloshed against the piers and scaffolding. The wind was constant, ruffling my wife's shortened, yet still gorgeous locks, and cooled me as the almost-summer day heated up.

The area had a weathered appearance, but I didn't feel like I'd take a knife in the back, like the area near the *Suds and Spuds*. At least by day. The smells coming from the tavern included mutton and baked bread but also hops and barley. By the strength of the aroma, I suspected they brewed their own stock. Perhaps a decent spot to keep in mind if we had to eat another meal in the city.

On the other hand, sailors and laborers tended to drink more than they should. And when they did, they would be a handful. Especially after they got a look at my wife. Beautiful women and ale led to coarse words and punches. And drawn steel.

We tethered the horses, and Ingefær cast her ward. "If anyone touches the reins, we'll know."

I smiled. She had set the sigil on the reins. Anyone dumb enough to approach Thunder from the rear would get a swift kick in the face. And Muffin liked to bite those she didn't know.

We entered the tavern. The noise level was as deafening as a dreki's roar. Once my eyes adjusted to the dimness, I counted forty heads. *The Brine* was twice as deep and thrice as wide as the *Suds and Spuds*, so the two score bodies left plenty of space for others to grab a table.

Waitresses bustled about, hoisting mugs and pitchers with grace. An occasional platter of fried fish strolled by and my nose snarled of its own accord.

The clothes folks wore identified them as dock laborers. Gray or brown tunics, and pants made of linen or wool. Most held their leggings up with a strand of rope. Brown or black boots rose past the ankles. Most of the men wore vests of natural colors, and many wore caps to keep the sun out of their eyes when outside. Inside, the hats did a good job of hiding eyes.

I glanced at Ingefær, who studied the orb. She chinned toward the depths of the saloon.

I followed her.

At the end of the tavern, Manic Mick sat at a table with four others. There were five pitchers and mugs, dozens of dice, a pile of silver coins in the center, and lots of laughing and jeering.

Manic Mick stood out from the others with his red kaftan and blue vest and a white linen undershirt. He looked up and made eye contact. "How-how did you find me?"

His actions and query shut the mouths of the men around the table.

"We don't want any trouble, Mick," Ingefær said, tucking the orb into her hip pocket.

Didn't he know how Elise had found him yesterday? "We just want to talk to you," I said.

Mick jumped to his feet, screamed like a banshee, and flailed his arms about as he hopped atop the table. "Robbers! Cutthroats!"

The four men started to rise, but silver sloshed over the edges of the table from Mick's foot stomping. The foursome staggered and bumped into each other, one looking to fight and the others grabbing coins.

Judging by their lack of balance, they'd been here a while, enjoying the establishment's finest...or cheapest.

I held my hands out, palms flat, and facing them. "Don't let him rile you into doing anything stupid."

While I yapped, I studied Mick, who looked left, then right, searching for a way through the bodies and tables. He had the same nose and same color eyes as Elise. But what confirmed it for me was the down-turned mouth.

If I had to wager, I'd put my life savings on the fact Mick was Elise's son. Which Ingefær had already suggested.

It explained how Mick knew about the items Elise had left out in the open on the fourth floor. And it might explain how the orb truly worked. Blood. Mick's blood. Yet another item my wife had gotten right.

I didn't know the details, but I imagined his mom saying, "The Temple needs funds. I will be gone for a couple of days. You need to stop by and take care of the dog."

How he had gotten past the wards was something I wanted to discuss with him. But there was an un-welcoming committee in our way.

Chairs scraped along the floor. The four table companions had sorted themselves out. They stood, fists clenched, most holding silver. One pulled a dagger from his boot. Another found a cudgel. Where he'd hidden it, I didn't want to know.

Ingefær backed up a step, her hand on the hilt of her sword. She said to the men, "Don't go starting things. We just need to...*ugh*...talk to Mick."

I scowled at her apparent distress. What was bothering her?

I took a more direct approach. "Sit your asses down. You won't be happy with the results if you don't."

Talking tough was an art form. My words and tone had to dissuade, sounding like I didn't care how many bones I broke. And it had to entertain. I had to sound like...no way in Hel would I shirk my duty to instruct them in the ways of inflicting bodily harm.

My hand moved to the hilt of my sword, and my feet shifted into an attack stance. I checked my backside, making sure it was clear. "Mick's...*ugh*...we're...*ugh*...authorized bounty hunters."

I had wanted to say something different but found I couldn't. A pain had jabbed me in my lower bowels at the thought of saying, '*Mick's wanted for stealing.*' Now I had a clue what had bothered my wife.

At my announcement of 'bounty hunters,' the din of the saloon dimmed. I glanced about. So far, no one else had gotten to their feet. Perhaps five on two seemed fair to them.

Down by her tush, Ingefær waved a hand at me to *take it easy.* While I agreed hurting innocents in the line of duty was to be avoided, if they pulled a weapon, they were no longer innocent. Two had done so already.

But I couldn't kill more than a dunderhead or two. Deaths of bystanders wouldn't bode well for our relationships with the city's officials, and, by extension, Tyrrby. I took a breath.

*Alright, I'll pound some sense into them.* I smiled. "I haven't broken many fingers in a while."

Mick let out with a howling yowl and went on the move. The young man was quick—his russet pantaloons flopped as he jumped from table to table. Folks screamed at him as his feet landed in their meals, or worse, toppled their mugs.

But instead of heading for the door, which meant passing by me and Ingefær, Mick made for a window five feet off the ground and facing the ocean.

By the time I realized what he was doing, he had slipped through and out.

I turned on my heel and raced to the door.

Behind me, a chair screeched. "Oi, pretty lass, I'll play tie up with you."

Those words slowed my feet. Nobody trades innuendos with my wife. I turned around, forgetting about Mick.

*Smack!*

A broad-shouldered man held his bloodied nose. Ingefær spun on a heel and waved me out.

"I was just flirting," the man said.

Ingefær didn't miss a beat as she spoke over her shoulder. "Me, too."

I shoved through several chairs suddenly blocking my path. I stomped on a few boots as I made my way out. "Sorry." But I wasn't.

Reaching the door, I rushed outside and heard Manic Mick scream from around the backside of the tavern. I gave chase without using my magicked feet.

As I reached the corner of the tavern, I glanced at Ingefær. She mounted Thunder and held my mare's reins in her hand.

I turned the corner of *The Brine* and picked up speed at the next building. Thirty strides ahead, Mick looked over his shoulder and shrieked at the sight of me.

The rat turd was quick. He turned left at the back of another building, making for the piers used by the locals to dock their fishing boats. Ingefær galloped down the street. Perhaps to keep him between her and the shoreline.

I added a burst of speed, invoking my fleet feet, and raced past another stone building. I breathed down Mick's neck as he reached the pier master's hut. Reaching out with my hand, I made to grab Mick by his scrawny neck when he slid to a halt. A stride before him, Ingefær, Thunder, and my mare skidded to a stop, throwing up dirt.

I crashed into Mick and we tumbled to the ground.

Mick screeched, cursing the gods, and yanked at his tawny hair, which hung past his ears and over his collar. "I've been betrayed! Yaggh!"

I got to my feet and drew my blade. Cornered rats were dangerous.

But Mick rolled to his knees and began crying. He took turns howling at the moon that had yet to rise and pleading with the gods for aid.

Sheathing my blade, I yanked him to his feet by the dirty collar of his kaftan. "That was stupid."

He spun about and tried to kick me.

Speed imbued, I avoided his boot and backhanded him across the mouth.

From atop her gelding, Ingefær said, "Don't hurt him. Too much."

Using my gift of speed, I jigged behind him and got him into a bear hug, trapping both his arms. I called for rope. Manic Mick squirmed and cried and cussed us out, but we wrapped him up tight.

Mick growled. "I am placing you into my book of grudges. Right after my ma."

I might have snickered.

A couple of passerby fishermen looked at us.

I wanted to say, "he's a thief." But the words wouldn't come. Instead, a fire flamed in my belly and nausea took hold. Swallowing bile, I said, "He-he's w-wanted for questioning."

They moved off, darting narrowed eyes at us.

With Ingefær looking on, I patted Mick down. I glanced at her. "Nothing on him but silver drekis and dice."

She moved into his field of vision. "Where's the stuff you...ugh...you know?"

"What stuff?" Mick replied.

I raised my hand, ready to slap him silly. "The stuff you...ugh...Fraegah Temple."

"I don't know what you're talking about."

We tied his hands. Then, because he wouldn't stop yelling at the gods and the Realm and accusing us of being cutthroats, Ingefær gagged him.

"We take him to Conjuror Elise," I said. "Maybe she can talk sense into him."

I took a huge breath to settle my innards and turned to Ingefær. "You have a pain in your gut when your words...?"

My wife nodded. "Aye. I had to rethink things a couple of times."

Me? Three or four times. Elise's spell aroused sheer internal agony. I didn't know if I wanted to vomit or shit my pants.

Mick struggled and screamed at us through the rag in his mouth.

Ingefær said, "There's little we can do with her spell on us."

I hoisted the turd thief atop Thunder, behind my wife's saddle.

She mounted and looked over her shoulder at Mick. "If you struggle, you'll fall off. And since your hands are tied, it may not end well for you. Be still."

I mounted my roan mare, Muffin, and we cantered to the Fraegah Temple.

Since we didn't have to talk about thieves or ask about the stolen items, the pain inside me waned. I laughed the entire way. Retrieving Mick was the easiest thousand silver I'd made in my entire life.

## Chapter Seven

# ELISE'S SON

## INGEFÆR

We reached the Fraegah Temple two hours before dinner. Rory helped Mick dismount, and I followed them in after tying off the horses.

Bypassing the paintings and the statue of Fraegah, we found Raemoni sitting at her desk, playing with several spiders, each thrice the size of a dreki coin. The gods they were huge!

I shuddered. "Conjuror Elise, please."

Without securing the arachnids—much to my dismay—Raemoni jumped to her feet and held the burgundy tapestry to the side. "She's been asking about you since you left."

We hadn't been gone that long. Maybe three hours in all. Capturing Mick had been rather easy. He was fast on his feet, just not as fast as Rory, or as Thunder at a gallop.

Mick's foolish behavior brought back memories of my father. When he was alive, he used his leather belt when he had to, but never when it wasn't deserved. I couldn't say the same for my uncle, who I had lived with for five years before joining the Order of Gixus.

Was Mick's father about? If not, it might explain his wayward ways.

Stepping beyond the heavy curtain, we found Elise pacing behind her desk, a finger at her mouth as she chewed on her nail. When she saw us, her arm flopped to her side. "Did you have to gag him?"

I shrugged. "He was being impolite, yelling curses at us, accusing us of murder." I removed his gag and untied his hands.

Rory stomped to her. "You've got some nerve. Mick is your son. Go on, deny it."

Elise's mouth puckered, then turned down at the corners. "No. I won't deny my son." Her eyes softened as she looked at Mick, pulling his gag down. "Why?"

Mick hung his head. "I don't know, Ma. I guess I was tired of being poor. You's all this wealth sitting here and you's can't use any of it."

"Doesn't matter. Stealing is wrong." Elise came around her desk and put her hands on her hips. She looked at me, then at Rory. "Did you get the items?"

We shook our heads. "He only has silver coins on him."

Rory said, "We had...*difficulties*...in questioning him about the, *ugh*, crime."

She peered at her son. "Where are the items you stole?"

Mick paled. "Ah...um...I don't know."

Rory turned and stepped within reach of Mick. He asked Elise, "You want me to loosen his lips?"

Elise glowered at him. "No."

I returned the orb with the silver nail to Elise. "What did you say about failing to retrieve the items yesterday?"

Elise's eyes narrowed at Mick. "I chased him all day. I used the orb, but whenever Mick saw me, he would run. No one would stop him. No one would help me."

Mick jutted his jaw out at her. "That's cause they's my friends."

"You need to find better friends," Rory said. "You should listen to your mother, too."

Mick glanced about, his eyes shifting left and right, but always coming back to the draped doorway.

We had caught Elise's thief but hadn't earned a thousand silver, as we hadn't yet retrieved the stolen items. Only one thing to do: convince Mick to give them up.

I stepped behind him and jabbed a finger into his backside, like my finger was the point of my sword. "Out with it. Where's the stuff you...*ugh*...you know?"

Elise's spell irritated me.

"Stole," his mother said.

Rory inched closer from the other side, stopping within a foot of the young man. "Don't make my wife ask you a second time. I've upheld my pledge of secrecy. But the pledge doesn't stop me from whipping you. How old are you?"

Mick's feet fidgeted. His hands clenched, then relaxed. "Eighteen."

Elise said, "I need the magic items, son. Where are they?"

"All I have is the dagger." Mick looked from face to face. "Honest. I sold everything else."

"To whom?" Elise asked.

Mick shrugged. "I don't know."

Rory was quick. He backhanded Mick across the mouth, drawing blood.

Elise shrieked as she rushed forward. "Don't hurt him."

"I'll not be lied to," Rory said.

"There's no need for violence," I said. It didn't bother me to slap him a time or two, to let him know we were serious. But if anyone was going to apply corporal punishment, it needed to be his mother. "You're going to cooperate, aren't you, Mick? How did you get past the wards on the windows?"

No way a thief bypassed the sigils without help.

Mick wiped the blood from his mouth with the sleeve of his kaftan. His head hung lower.

Standing before her son, Elise tapped a foot. "Yes. An excellent question. How did you bypass the wards? You've shown no talent for magic. Though, much like your miscreant of a father, you have a gift for twitchy fingers."

"Where is his father?" Rory asked.

"Dead. Hung ten years ago. For thieving." The dour mouth came out in full force. "We never married."

Mick's chin rose. "Aye. I has his hand. I's picked locks and lifted purses. And I's yet to be caught."

Elise slapped him.

The thwack surprised Mick, his jaw agape.

"And when you do, you'll be hung like your father." Elise's jaw muscles tightened.

I wondered if she had ever smacked Mick before. The fact that Mick had turned to thieving suggested she hadn't.

Rory sighed. "Mick. Take it from someone who has traveled the dark road. It's nothing but misery."

Rory had spent five years drinking, half of it behind bars, and all of it broke and hungry.

I got us back on track, choosing my words with care. "Who helped you with the spell to defeat the wards?"

Mick hemmed and hawed and worked himself up before he let it out. "Jarl Retzlaff."

Elise gasped.

I recognized the name. "The man you were going to sell the ring to?"

Elise closed her eyes, then nodded.

*Oh dear.* What an unexpected complication. Mick's actions suddenly made a lot more sense. Based on what I'd seen of Mick so far, I doubted he'd devised the crime on his own.

Rory focused on Mick. "Did you sell everything but the dagger to Jarl Retzlaff?"

Mick nodded.

"How much did he give you?"

"Two thousand silver." Mick grinned like he'd eaten all the cookies and didn't share a crumb.

I asked, "You have two thousand silver coins?"

"No." Mick gave me a bemused look. "I has two hundred silver coins. Well, had. I's spent several coins on ale and lost more gambling. The rest is in a letter of credit drawn on a merchant here in town. A Jarl Robertson."

Mick fished inside his blue vest. He unfolded a trimmed piece of parchment and laid it atop the desk. "See."

I looked down. It was made out in the amount of eighteen...*something*...drekis. Leaning close, I eyed the smudges on the parchment. A stain had dried or something had been rubbed off.

Rory said, "It says eighteen, not eighteen hundred."

"What!?" Mick's eyes bulged.

I pointed. "Where the hundred may have been written is now a gray smear."

"That crook!" Mick turned beet red and wailed.

The howl had to have woken the dead. I was sure of it because my ears throbbed and rang with such a pain, they longed to die to escape the onslaught.

"Enough," Elise hollered. "Stop your incessant caterwauling."

Rory grabbed him by the scruff and took a good grip of the lad's neck. "You've done plenty of damage, young man. Where's the dagger?"

Mick's red face lost its color. "Retzlaff is going to the top of my grudge book." He tried to stomp around, but Rory held on.

Rory shook him. "Focus."

"I has a hidden spot in my room."

"Which is where?" I asked.

"Near the Shrine of Eirene."

So, his gambling buddy at the *Suds and Spuds* had told the truth.

I turned to Elise. "We'll go get the dagger and bring it back here. But I think it's time to remove the spell you cast on us."

"Why?" Elise's mouth pinched even more than normal.

"It's no longer necessary." I fiddled with my snowflake. "We brought you your son without revealing his...activities...to anyone."

Rory added, "In order to retrieve the signet ring, we have to get Jarl Retzlaff to admit to his involvement in the...*ugh*...you know. Which means we will have to talk about Mick."

"Which means you can run to the Order of Gixus as soon as the spell is lifted...and implicate my son."

Rory roared. His fists clenched at his sides.

I said, "Your insults and lack of faith make me want to quit the assignment."

We had found Mick rather quickly. True, we hadn't yet recovered the stolen items. But Elise's constant derision of Rory's and my honor frustrated me.

I glanced at Rory. His fists remained taut, but he shrugged, telling me it was my decision.

Elise chuckled.

"What's so funny?" I asked.

"You're compelled to retrieve those items," Elise said.

Rory scowled. "I thought we were compelled to find your son and keep quiet about it."

"Compelled, like a Geas?" I asked.

I had heard the additional words to her spell, but had figured it was all tied to staying quiet. Was the spell even greater than that?

She shrugged. "Not exactly a Geas. There's no punishment phase for failing to complete the assignment. Nor a time limit." Then she flashed a smile that struck me as wicked. "But you won't be able to think about anything else. More and more each day, your thoughts will turn to the stolen items, wondering where they are."

"For how long?" I asked.

"Until you think of nothing else, not even eating." Elise hugged herself. "Might take a year. Maybe two or three. Though I've never heard of the spell being ignored beyond three moons."

Rory stepped forward, almost nose to nose with her. "Does the spell dissipate if the caster is dead?"

Her color drained. But she kept her eyes on him and shook her head.

I replayed the three extra words Elise had uttered when she'd used our blood. They didn't sound like a Geas, but the word *compel* had punch to it, so my stomach said.

I clenched my jaw. If we quit, were we risking our lives?

I put a hand on Rory's arm. "Come on. Let's get the dagger and then talk to Retzlaff."

Rory scoffed. "He's not going to give us the ring without persuasion."

After a deep breath, I said, "It's worse than that. We can't accuse him outright. What if everything Mick said is a lie?"

"Hey!" Mick objected.

I darted a glance at Elise. "If he's anything like his mother, he's deceitful."

The corner of Elise's lip turned up, yet her eyes bristled at me.

Rory glared at her. "I ought to report you to the Order of Gixus."

She wagged her finger. "Ah-ah-ah. You cannot reveal my son's part in all this."

I turned Mick around, gazing into his eyes. "Did you really sell the stuff to Jarl Retzlaff?"

He nodded, picking up the letter of credit and pointing at the signature. "See?"

I waggled my head at Rory. "Let's discuss this."

We moved to a corner. I whispered. "What do you think?"

"Elise is a witch."

"A cunning and untrustworthy woman, for sure."

Rory shrugged. "Magic is your domain. Are we compelled? My stomach says yes."

"Mine too," I said. "Maybe there're ways around it."

Maybe our friend Vidarr Allefar could dispel it. The Tyrrby Order was known for casting Geas spells on their adherents. Maybe they knew how to remove one.

But I wanted to complete our first job successfully. And, if I judged Mick's involvement correctly, the true devisor of the crime would go free without us.

And that irked me more than Elise's bad manners.

I looked at Mick. His eyes were puffy and red. He stood with his head down, hands stuffed into his pockets. I asked my husband, "What do you think of Mick?"

"Lousy parents," Rory replied. "A thief for a father and a lying witch for a mother."

I nodded. "Yeah. I feel sorry for him."

Rory chuckled. "Sounds like before he was just a petty pickpocket. Now he's graduated to grand theft. He got himself involved with a mage, and committed a crime worthy of hanging."

I looked into Rory's dark brown eyes. "Remind you of anyone?"

A smirk blossomed on his face. "Yeah. We either grow out of it...or we die."

"So, we help?"

He nodded.

We moved back to Elise and Mick.

"You put us in a precarious position," I said. "But we'll talk to Jarl Retzlaff. Mind you, just talk. After Mick takes us to the...*ugh*...dagger."

I rolled my eyes. I couldn't even say *stolen.*

"You need to modify the spell," I continued. "Permit us to ask questions of Retzlaff unimpeded by magic. I don't know how else we'll get any answers."

She chewed on her lower lip, then nodded. "I drank a vial of healing earlier, so I'm able."

Her left hand pinched some yellowish powder out of a pouch, then she dusted our heads. Her right hand waved, and she muttered in Varanusian.

Translating, I said, "No silence with Retzlaff."

What a horrible job. No. The job was alright. It was the taskmaster that was the problem.

Rory asked, "Where can we find this...Retzlaff? He doesn't deserve the title of jarl."

Elise held her son's hand. "The Hexerei Mansion is outside the city to the east, just south of where the Mid Dreki Mountains end."

I asked, "What kind of magic does Jarl Retzlaff know?"

Elise put a finger to her chin. "I think he's like me, an Aether specialist. But also, like me, he's not powerful...or so I've heard. The family has fallen on hard times, what with the decline of magic over the centuries. According to the Temple records, his great grandfather was skilled with the fire and air elements."

"A battle mage?" Rory asked me.

I nodded and turned to Elise. "You said Jarl Retzlaff isn't powerful. Is that assessment based on his talents before or after magic returned?"

"Before. I don't know what they're like now." Elise bit her lower lip. "Since magic's return, all I've experienced is that my spells no longer fail. I've no more power or stamina."

My spellcasting had improved as far as stamina went. And, like Elise, failure was no longer an issue. But over the past year, my powers hadn't increased much either. At least nothing I couldn't ascribe to experience and training. Then again, I'd been honeymooning and working through land ownership issues.

Elise said, "Retrieve the ring, or get Retzlaff to pay the agreed three thousand six hundred silver. All coins, no funny letter of credit. And bring the dagger back. The jewel and the potion are your payment."

"But you paid eighteen hundred for the ring," Rory said.

"The price of doing business," Elise replied, a flash of a thin smile on her lips. "It costs time and money to keep valuables safe." She stood straight. "Our bargain remains."

It wasn't much of a bargain. And our job had increased in difficulty. From retrieving the stolen items from a thief—for which we had a magic nail to locate—to being compelled to get them from Jarl Retzlaff. Could we convince the jarl to pay for the ring and return the other items?

Doubtless, not without violence.

I glanced at Rory, who winced as he shook his head.

I, too, had my doubts. Retzlaff was a mage who had dispelled a ward. And then he'd used chicanery with the letter of credit, decreasing the amount from eighteen hundred to eighteen.

A shiver ran down my back.

I didn't think our task was simple at all.

## Chapter Eight

# STEALING FOR GOOD

## RORY

I eyed Elise. "We'll retrieve the dagger, then head to Hexerei Mansion." I cleared my throat. "Do I have your permission to use the weapon if circumstances dictate?"

Mick hiccupped. "Oh-*hic*-dear."

Elise's lips twisted. "I'd rather you bring it back here. For safe keeping."

I scowled. "You don't trust me?"

Elise growled like a bear. "Oh, alright. But I hold you responsible if you don't return it."

I tried to pierce her with my eyes, but she was as hard as iron. "If we fail to bring it back, it means my wife and I are dead. Thank you."

Mick's chin lifted. "After I give you's the dagger, I want to come with you...to Hexerei Mansion."

Elise gasped, a hand flying to her mouth. "No."

"I don't think so," I said, eyeing his mother. I'd almost wanted to say yes, just to disagree with the woman.

*You want to compel me, witch? I'll take your son with me to face off against a mage.* I cleared my throat to prevent myself from laughing maniacally at the mental image.

Mick pulled at his tawny locks. "Gagh! I's a grown man. I makes my own decisions."

*Not wise ones,* I thought. *And grown men don't behave as you are right now.*

He strutted back and forth between the desk and a pile of clothes, then started a combination of crowing and clucking—not quite like a rooster, but with the half-step stomping and his head bobbing forward with each exclamation, a rooster was the image popping up inside my mind. It was like he was incapable of expressing himself like most adults.

The lad was like a willow in the wind, easily swayed. I half raised my hand, ready to smack him. Instead, I stopped myself and studied him.

I suspected he'd grown up with the wrong friends. And in the robbery, he'd been Retzlaff's stooge. Was all this a result of his father being hung when he was young? Or had his mother been as conniving with him and his father as she was with my wife and me? That would make any boy want to escape, leading him to wander down dangerous paths. Mick desperately needed a stern, but fair, hand.

He stopped strutting and straightened himself. Had he convinced himself to stand up to a conniving mage? Was he trying to be brave, but landing on foolish?

I sighed and flipped over an open hand. "Why do you want to come?"

He blinked his brown eyes to refocus. "He robbed me of a lot of silver."

I chuckled. That was the wrong answer. None of the silver had ever been his. "No."

Ingefær whispered. "I think he should join us."

I shot my wife a puzzled look. Though I felt sorry for Mick, I didn't see how his presence would aid us with Retzlaff. There were approaches to take, and if Retzlaff spotted Mick, it would waylay all of them straight off. Not that we would lie to the man, but we had to question him without getting his hackles up. And maybe everything Mick had told us was a load of troll shit.

But what if Mick had told us the truth? Might he know something about the mage, something he didn't realize was relevant? We hadn't gotten the chance to ask him any proper questions yet. A few I wanted to ask without his mother around. Boys, even men, keep secrets from their mothers.

Before I could reply, Elise grabbed her son's hand and pulled him to her. "You don't need him."

"We might," I said, taking my wife's cue on faith and indulging my contrariness. Throw me into a dreki's den—I didn't like the woman.

Ingefær added, "If he doesn't come with us, then Rory and I will ride to the Tyrrby Order. We'll seek their aid with your compulsion spell."

We'd already discussed the Order's help...and rejected it. So, my wife bluffed—something she rarely did. But Elise's behavior had crossed a line with Ingefær.

Mick jerked his hand free. "I's coming with you. I has a score to settle with Retzlaff."

Shaking my head, I said, "If you're coming, it's to seek justice, not vengeance."

There were times I needed to take my own advice.

We'd backed ourselves into a standoff. Glances were exchanged. Time seemed to stand still.

Mick's jaw thrust forward, staring at his mother.

Finally, Elise's lips twitched. She closed her eyes, then opened them. She pointed a finger at me. "Get the items back. Keep my son safe."

I nodded and pointed my finger at Mick. "Everything we recover that was...*ugh*...that belonged to the Fraegah Temple will be returned to your mother."

Mick stood tall and seemed to consider his words. "Fine. I just want to smack Jarl Retzlaff upside his head for his dirty trick."

Was it anger, bravado, or a genuine desire to right wrongs? He'd spoken like a man with a mission; his speech ticks all but gone. I eyed the wisp of a man trying to move out from his mother's shadow. He stared back at me. His face was a little flushed, but his eyes were clear and his chin raised.

I suppressed my initial retort to belittle him. It took guts to face off against a mage. And me, as he knew enough of my skills to not get crosswise with me or my wife.

I was sure Retzlaff had more talent than Elise was letting on. The disappearing *hundred* on the letter of credit was something I had never heard of or seen before. With magic like that, folks would have to learn how to deal with less than honorable mages.

My gaze swept over to Elise. "It won't be easy."

Ingefær said, "My husband is right. This will be dangerous." She stepped closer to Mick. "What are your skills? And don't puff yourself up."

Ingefær was the strategic thinker. I wondered if she saw something in him I didn't. Pinching things without getting caught might be a useful skill. Though I didn't see how it applied here.

I asked, "Have you really lifted purses and bypassed locked doors?"

He had admitted to it before. But it had sounded like bragging.

Mick licked his lips. His eyes swung to his mother, then to me. "Aye. Maybe a dozen times altogether."

"Son!" Elise swooned. Again.

This time, I let her hit the floor. She had it coming.

Ingefær found a half full glass of water and flung it in Elise's face. The conjuror righted herself to her feet, drawing a sleeve across her eyes.

Ingefær shifted her focus back to Mick. Her blue eyes scrutinized the young man. "Taking things...that aren't yours...is wrong." She heaved a sigh and closed her eyes for a moment. "But deft fingers can be used for good."

Mick frowned in puzzlement.

I followed my wife's lead, being careful with my words. "To capture...someone who's guilty of something...sometimes you have to be as sneaky as they are, and as violent. But means and ends always fight each other for dominance. Righteousness can lose out in the process."

Ingefær nodded. "Before your mother, vow to not do evil, to not seek personal gain. To use your gift for apprehending those who are wicked." She asked, "Can you make such a pledge?"

Mick thought about it. A fresh spark came to life in his eyes. "Aye. That sounds...interesting."

Elise's lips twitched, and she suddenly looked frail, almost...human like. "Please don't go, son. You're all I have."

She had realized the dangers we could encounter. Retzlaff wouldn't admit to the crime just because we asked him to. Good chance magic would fly before our engagement was over.

Mick took a deep huff of air. "I have to, Ma. I have to help fix what I broke."

A boy had turned into a man, right before my eyes.

Elise closed hers and sighed. "Do be careful. All of you."

We said goodbye. Elise hugged Mick until he squirmed free.

Outside the Fraegah Temple, with Elise out of sight, I stepped before Mick. "Now's the time to fess up. Did you sell the stuff to Jarl Retzlaff? Was he your accomplice?"

Mick's chin dipped. "Aye. But Jarl Retzlaff trolled me."

Mick's mind was full of mush. But at least he had hung his head when he confessed. Which meant Mick had a conscience. Maybe we could work with him after all.

I pointed toward the Shrine of Eirene. "Take us to the dagger."

As we hiked, with me holding the reins of my mare and Ingefær guiding Thunder, my thoughts wandered to Retzlaff.

How quickly would words turn into blows? And since he was a mage, to flashes of magical energy?

My worries multiplied. Ingefær liked to talk things through, but there were times a firm hand was needed instead. A hand wielding a sword. More times than not, the first one to act lived to tell the tale. Suddenly, I had second thoughts about confronting the mage.

I stopped the procession and faced my wife. "Are you sure you want to do this? A thousand dreki isn't worth your life, or mine."

Her jaw muscles twitched, but she thought over the question. "We agreed long ago, before we married, to help those in need against those who are evil. Especially if they are also powerful. And while I despise Elise's...approach, it sounds like Retzlaff is both."

I agreed with a grunt. While I enjoyed helping others, for my wife, it was a passion. But now we were under a compulsion spell...and that irked me something fierce.

But the danger had escalated. Our misadventure in Vanaby last year had taught me that the situation was always more complex than it appeared. Were there more twists to be had before this mission came to an end? Were Retzlaff's sorcerous talents more powerful than Ingefær's?

Ingefær leveled her gaze at me. "We cannot quit. Her invocation aside, our reputation is important. And I do not want to see the guilty party get away with it."

Reputation meant nothing to the dead. Sometimes letting the criminal go was the smartest play. We couldn't right every wrong in the Realm.

Yet *Injustices Righted* was our love child.

"While I agree with everything you said, what I want to know is...if we wanted to, *could* we quit?"

We'd talked about it before. But now we'd suffered physical ailments under the spell.

Ingefær chewed on her lower lip. Then she gave a slight shake of her head. "Probably not. Not without chancing a trip to Tyrrby to see if they can dispel the compulsion. It's beyond my ken."

A week's ride, one way. I put the thought away. For now.

Ingefær twirled the snowflake on her choker necklace. "Retzlaff not only robbed Elise, he enticed a young man into a dangerous misadventure and had him betray his own flesh and blood."

Ingefær made Mick sound quite naïve, if not innocent. I figured the lad had made his own choices. At least, I didn't think Retzlaff had ensnared the young man with a spell. Not like Elise had. Mick had boasted about his pick-pocketing misdeeds.

But with Ingefær, violating family lines caused her sense of justice to flare hot. Her parents' murder at the hands of a now-dead mayor—covered up by the now-deceased head of the Order of Gixus in Himmel Drakken—had built a pyre of vengeance inside of her. She and I held a similar dislike of authority. Jarls in particular.

I grunted. We were about to interview a jarl. But not just a jarl—a mage, too.

*Great. Just great.*

With Mick's brown eyes watching me, I cleared my throat and spoke aloud. "Alright. Move on."

A dozen minutes later, at a boarding house down the street from the Shrine of Eirene, we retrieved the magicked dagger, still in its bejeweled sheath, from under a floorboard in Mick's room.

I inspected the foot-long scabbard. It had a dozen jewels—three each of blue topaz, red rubies, white pearls, and green emeralds.

Gripping the handle, I pulled the dagger from the sheath and ran a finger crosswise against the blade. "Lokke's spawn!"

I glanced at my thumb. "I just lost a layer of skin."

The dagger's metallic tip glinted in the sunlight. *Oh yeah, this is a beauty of a blade.*

After I'd sheathed the weapon and put the dagger into my rucksack, we went outside. "We have coins to earn," I said. "And a spell to get out of our guts."

Ingefær looked at the sky. "It's getting late in the day, and we haven't eaten since breakfast."

I nodded. "Aye. We'll head out to the mansion on the morrow. There're a few things I need to do first."

"We're not going today?" Mick asked.

"It's almost dinnertime, and it's a five- or six-hour hike to the place your mother described. I prefer not to show up on a mage's doorstep in the dark of night...especially when I'm hungry." Clearing my throat, I added, "I'm not personable when I've missed a meal."

Mick guffawed. "You's must be starving."

I mock-cuffed him, mounted my mare, and rode toward the docks with him taking extra-long strides to keep up. Thunder clopped alongside, Ingefær sitting tall in the saddle.

Knowing the retrieval of the remaining stolen items would take longer than expected, I made for the merchant's warehouse. There was work to be done on the farm, and I needed some motivation. Putting the supplies and tradesfolk into motion would be the perfect boost.

At the warehouse, I bought canvas tenting, a pair of tillers, a dozen shovels and hoes, and food supplies, paying an extra twenty silver to have everything delivered to my parents' old home in a week's time.

Business finished, we made for an inn, where I paid for a room on the second floor with one bed. I wasn't too happy with Mick sleeping on the floor, but I didn't trust him in his own room. I wanted to keep him where I could see him. Tonight, I would place a chair underneath the door handle and pile my leathers and Ingefær's chainmail on the seat. If he wanted to make a run for it, he'd have to risk waking us with the racket at the door, or climb out the window. I didn't think he'd try to take off, but I needed to see more of him in action before I could take him at his word.

In the adjacent tavern—an eating establishment built for twenty—we found the last open table and sat down. The cacophony of plates, utensils, and general conversation soothed me. The scent of seasoned meats made my mouth water. While we waited for our food, we got to know Mick.

When he wasn't yelling and pulling his hair out, the young man was quite the chatterbox.

"And there was the time I's slipped my fingers into a winter coat, snipped the strands of a purse with my rondel dagger, and came away with fifteen silver coins. The old lady didn't know what happened."

Ingefær frowned. "You know that's wrong, right?"

Mick's eyes shone brighter. There was no evidence of the shame he'd shown before. "Aye. Sure. But the sense of daring and adventure...oh, that's living, that is."

He'd said he hated being poor, but now it sounded like he hated boredom. Maybe Ingefær had him figured right. Maybe he didn't steal so much for an item's value as he did for the excitement of the act itself. I decided to test his mettle. "You ever fight a troll?"

"What? No, of course not. Trolls hide in the mountains. Few folks see one and live to tell the tale."

"I've seen two," I said.

"Killed both with fire," Ingefær said. "Well, *we* didn't do it—our friends did."

"Your ball of fire helped," I said, though it had fizzled. That was before the return of magic.

"You's having me on." Mick dabbed butter on his second slab of bread.

"Oh no," I said. "But trolls weren't our toughest challenge."

We had his attention, so I regaled him with our exploits of defeating the trolls and, later on, a pair of Draugars.

My purpose in telling the tales was to instill in him that we could be dangerous, and we pursued danger when needed rather than running away. He needed to know what he was in for by coming along with us. If I gave him any second thoughts, he didn't admit to them.

After our meal, as we headed to our room, Ingefær told him, "It's one thing to want an adventure. It's another to be enmeshed in one not of your choosing."

Memories of Vanaby flashed with Ingefær locked in a jail cell. Definitely not of our choosing.

"Wise words." I winked at Mick and chuckled as the color drained from his face.

Maybe Mick stealing for a good cause would help the lad find his balance. Even after our stories, he appeared excited about the mission. Or maybe it was agitation. I hoped it was a balance between the two, and that he realized our tasks would not be easy.

Unlike him, Ingefær and I were magically compelled into whatever lay ahead. The thought took away some of the good flavor of my meal. The lone ale I'd had got raucous in my belly.

## Chapter Nine

# RETHINKING THINGS

## INGEFÆR

As we ate a dry breakfast in our room, I thought about Elise's spell. Something about it kept bothering me. It wasn't about the compulsion—the job interested me for other reasons. It was the deceitful way Elise had maneuvered us into helping. I tried to understand the depths of her desperation. Thefts occurred all too often, so I couldn't see why she'd so vehemently refused to accept the loss. Was there something more between her and Retzlaff?

I twirled my snowflake pendant at the thought of confronting the jarl. We knew nothing for certain about Retzlaff. And facing off against a mage hadn't been in the job description when we'd first signed on.

With a full night's sleep behind us, I sounded Rory out with Mick listening in. "We still going?"

My husband wanted to go, to get rid of the compel incantation. I agreed. Retrieving the stolen items served three purposes: we earned coins, our reputation would be enhanced, and it was the simplest, most direct way of removing the incantation.

I double checked my mage belt contents and then tucked the belt under my leather jerkin, which lay beneath my chainmail hauberk. Concealing it would slow my casting by a breath, but I didn't want to reveal my talents to Retzlaff unless I had to. And I hoped it wouldn't come to an exchange of fireball blasts.

Rory frowned at Mick, who was dawdling. "It's a half-day hike from the city, and the sun's already up. Time to saddle the horses."

Mick scowled. "I's don't have a horse, and I ain't never ridden before."

I shook my head. It was all I'd done as a kid, so I couldn't imagine any other life. And Rory had a decade of experience in the saddle. "It's easy. We'll get you a donkey. They don't buck or scare easily."

A docile mount was the best way for a new rider to learn. And it wasn't as far to fall. Donkeys also wouldn't go faster than a walk—unless a svartkatt, the predatory giant black cat, was on the prowl.

At a nearby stable, Rory bought a donkey for a dozen silver, and we spread a blanket on its back.

Mick sniffed at the beast, and his nose curled. "It stinks."

"Come on," Rory said. "Let's get going."

I helped Mick to get up and over. "Just roll with its stride." I handed him the reins. "Don't pull on them."

"If I can't pull, why you's giving them to me?"

"It gives the donkey confidence that you know how to ride, and you know where you're going. If the reins just hung there, the donkey wouldn't move at all."

We mounted and set off at a walk, letting Mick get used to the undulations. I glanced over at the young man now and then to make sure he was still riding upright.

Along the way to Hexerei Mansion, we debated our approach.

Rory said, "You know me. I like to be direct. I say we knock on his front door and ask what he's been up to."

Mick snorted. "Like he'd tell you the truth."

While I didn't think the direct approach would work, all the other methods presumed Jarl Retzlaff guilty, which we were a long dreki flight from proving. All we had was Mick's word.

To further complicate things, the compel spell might redirect our questions, even though Elise had changed it. We would soon know if her adjustment proved sufficient.

Per Mick, Jarl Retzlaff had been the one to dispel the ward while Mick climbed down from the roof via a rope and swung himself through the open window.

"How'd you get up there?" I asked.

"Retzlaff levitated me," Mick said. "Was cool. Kind of like flying, but really, just straight up in a herk-and-jerk kind of way. Then over. Took all of a dozen seconds."

That's a spell I didn't know. But it was related to one I did. A wall of air can be used as a floor and lift and lower a person.

Mick went on. "I's didn't know about the second ward—the one ma had placed on the items she'd left out on the table."

There were surrounding bits of information to support Mick's story, like the goofy-looking letter of credit. Though it appeared to have been signed by Retzlaff, we had no definitive proof the man had provided it, or that the numbers had, in fact, been altered. While Mick's reactions had reinforced his contentions, it was never a good idea to rely on the word of an admitted thief.

In the end, I agreed with Rory. "Aye. We knock and ask questions first. With tact."

"For all the good it will do," Mick said. "He might turn you into a toad."

"Weren't you listening last night?" Rory asked. "We've been up against mages before."

Mick frowned.

We had survived several arcane energy battles. But in those cases, we knew we were up against evil and were prepared—ready to fire first, then ask questions. Here, we would do things backwards.

As we rode east along the main road toward Vanaby, the road hugged the end of the Dreki Mountains. Off to our right, maybe a half-hour ride, was the Mid Dreki Ocean. We were too far away to hear waves, but the leaves fluttered in the breeze and the birds cawed in the salty air.

I asked Mick to tell us everything he knew about the jarl.

Mick shrugged. "Don't know much. He, uh, found me pinching a coin purse. Said he had a job, if I was interested."

"What can you tell us about his magical prowess?" I asked.

Mick scratched at his tawny hair. "Uh, well, not much besides what I's already told you. We always met in a public place, similar to the tavern we ate at last night."

"So, what else does he know besides how to dispel magic and levitate?" Rory asked.

Mick shrugged. "Not sure."

Was Mick being forthright? Was he not very observant?

I swallowed my frustration. "Did he talk about the other planes of magic, like fire or air?"

Mick shook his head. "No. He seemed like a guy who wanted to have fun. Said we weren't hurting anyone. That was after we'd shared an ale a few times."

By which time Mick had probably let on he did what he did because he was bored and liked the excitement.

I needed information about the jarl that pointed to his moral turpitude—to his respect or disrespect for the law. Was the robbery a one-time affair, or was he in the habit of pilfering magical items? "Anything about his life? Is he married? Does he have kids?"

"Well, now that you's ask, I think he's single. Never mentioned a wife, nor any kids. He gushed at the mouth about the return of magic." Mick tugged at his collar. "He said he was working on something important, and the night before we's robbed the Temple, he said he needed a magical ring."

So...the robbery wasn't just a chance opportunity. But why steal the ring if it was already going to be his? Why not pay for it? "Did he seem he was on hard times to you, Mick?"

Mick shook his head. "No. Bought me supper a couple of times. Ale, too."

*Yeah, to loosen your lips.*

Mick's brows narrowed as he raised a clenched fist. "When I see him—"

I interrupted. "How about his clothes?"

Mick's shoulders scrunched. "Looked like a jarl to me. Fancy silver piping on his burgundy tunic and a silk purple cloak with a hood." After a pause, he added, "I's never seen a horse or carriage. But I's figured he had himself a room at an inn."

Rory asked, "It didn't bother you to steal from your mother?"

Mick shrugged. "Ain't hers. The ring's been gathering dust ever since I'd been born. Longer."

Everything Mick said jived with my earlier thoughts—the heist was planned by Retzlaff. And the ring was the target of his obsessions.

*How did he find Mick? Was it all serendipity?*

I didn't think so. What did that portend regarding our coming confrontation? Retzlaff wouldn't admit to being involved in a robbery, let alone working with Mick. Did Retzlaff have the ring now? Or was Mick spinning stories, maybe covering for some other accomplice?

After a midday meal on horseback, with Mick leaning against a tree next to a signpost labeled *Hexerei Mansion*, we left the road and wound our way up a trail. We switched back and forth around and over the rolling hills, but ever higher. Not another person in sight, but squirrels and robins were prevalent. Retzlaff lived in a beautiful area.

Mick lagged. Several times, Rory had to chide him to get a move on.

"Donkey's being an ass. He don't want to go." Mick pouted, kicking the beast in its ribs.

"No." I pointed at my heels. "Don't kick. Just nudge. And lift your legs higher, so you make contact with the flank, not the gut."

After we got moving again, a stream joined the road, and the two twisted and turned in unison. The pines crowded out the oaks and maples, and bushes filled in the gaps amongst the strewn rocks.

We took a brief break.

Mick heaved several deep breaths and massaged his butt. When he stopped grumbling over his posterior, he looked out over the vista. "It sure is beautiful out here."

I eyed him. One moment, he looked ready to screech and run off. The next, he seemed determined to confront Retzlaff. And then a third, he was a kid enjoying his surroundings.

His inconsistency worried me. But I wasn't his mother, so I let it go and did what he did. I took a moment to enjoy our surroundings.

The sun was warm, but not hot. A breeze came from the ocean, now maybe an hour's ride south, and cooled me. The scent of grass, wildflowers, brush, and pine trees mingled. I agreed with the lad's sentiment. The view was splendiferous.

Rory distracted both of us and pointed at the ground. "See there, Mick. There's a set of horse hoof prints and wagon wheels. Two days old."

Mick snorted. "How can you tell how old it is?"

"Deduction," Rory said. "It rained two days ago. A day later, the ground would have been drier, leaving shallower prints. So, judging by the depth of these tracks, the horse had to have arrived right after the rainstorm."

We set off once more. The last mile grew steep. We stopped often to wait for Mick, who wasn't having much luck with the donkey.

"Get off and walk up," I said.

Mick dismounted and rubbed his butt. "Ah, that's better."

"Get a move on," Rory said.

Ten minutes later, an overgrown track forked north, and the stream left the main trail and followed the offshoot. The dirt path we were on headed east, and it soon turned to paver stones. The effort of paving would have cost quite a lot of silver no matter when it had been constructed. It made the footing surer...though it would be treacherous in rain. The flat, wet stones would turn as slick as squished wyrms. Horses wouldn't like it at all.

Rory said, "See the grass and weeds growing where the flagstones have broken apart?"

"Yeah?" Mick said.

"Tells you the owner hasn't done proper maintenance in quite a while. Lacking for coin, or for staff, or both."

"Or maybe he doesn't care," Mick said. "You know, he's lazy."

"He's a jarl. He should have staff," my husband replied.

Mick's eyebrows furrowed for a moment, then he nodded.

I eyed the horizon. "A couple more turns and we should arrive." I pointed. "See the red tiles? That's a rooftop—a spire, I think."

Mick squeaked, then hiccupped several times in quick succession.

"What now?" Rory demanded, spinning Muffin about.

I looked at the lad. "Are you all right?"

Mick, holding the reins in one hand, held a finger up with the other and took a deep breath of air. We waited. After almost a full minute, his face turning redder, he let a gush of air out. Then he panted. "See? Gone."

Sure, his hiccups were gone. But what had caused them to come on so suddenly?

"You're not afraid, are you?" I asked. Perhaps not a fair question. I wasn't confident either. Courage isn't about not feeling fear. It's about acting anyway—overcoming, despite being scared.

"Is it the nearness of Retzlaff?" Rory asked. "I won't blame you if it was."

Mick squawked, his chin jerking. Then he clenched his teeth and swallowed. A moment later, he said, "I needs to go on. I needs to gut him."

My eyes widened. That was not why we were here. At least I hoped it wouldn't come to blows. Should Mick even be here?

I did a quick recalculation. I had wanted Mick to join us. His coming to retrieve the stolen items—after stealing them—was chivalrous in a way. And having Mick close would help us check Retzlaff's answers without having to ride all the way back to town for confirmation.

Still, I had cause to worry. Mick was rash—the kind of person who acts without thinking. And when he wasn't hiccupping or squawking, his words more than hinted at a violent streak. Mick hadn't come to right wrongs; he was sore over the false letter of credit and wanted revenge. That I couldn't abide. Justice, not vengeance.

Worse still, I now realized, once the jarl saw Mick, he'd know why we were here. There would be no element of surprise...no question we could raise where he wouldn't understand the implication.

I came to a conclusion. It was a bad idea for several reasons to have Mick stand with us at the front door. Mick might lash out in panic or anger. And if the jarl was guilty, he would shut up at the first sight of his accomplice's face. He might ask his valet to bar the doors. Or he would cast a spell.

And we weren't the law. We couldn't bust down a door. We couldn't strike first—not unless we were certain. And I wasn't.

"Mick," I said, "Retzlaff can't see you."

The lad licked his lips. His eyes darted toward the mansion's spire, then back to me. "You think Retzlaff will try to kill me?"

Rory chuckled. "Not while there are witnesses."

Mick screeched.

I held up a hand, asking him to calm down. "No. He's not going to do anything."

I gave Rory the stink eye. *Don't frighten Mick. He might lash out first.*

I continued. "As soon as Retzlaff sees you, he'll know why we came. We weren't going to hide the fact. But it will give him a slight advantage to prepare for our questions...and to shade his answers."

Mick's nose twitched. "He owes me coins."

I shook my head. "He does not. Those coins belong to your mother."

Mick snarled. "It's a dirty trick he pulled on me."

No worse than what Mick had done to Elise, but I had to manage him, so I played along. I scratched my neck. "True. But you need to stay here. Rory and I will talk with him."

Mick's head lurched on his feet. "No. I's coming with you."

Rory looked at me, his brows raised in question. I had been the one who'd wanted Mick to come. Now I didn't.

Rory dismounted and walked up to Mick. "Listen, lad. Ingefær has experience. If she thinks it's to our disadvantage to have Retzlaff see you, then I'm inclined to agree with her." He looked back at me. "I'd just as soon have Retzlaff attack us. Give us a reason to defend ourselves. We'll be done a lot faster that way."

"You's ain't worried about a fireball?" Mick asked.

"Always," Rory replied. Then he sighed and put a hand on Mick's shoulder. "But there's magic about me. I'm mighty fast on my feet."

Mick's mouth pinched for a moment. "You's caught me. So, yeah."

"I wasn't even trying." Rory shushed Mick, who'd started to object. "I'm not disrespecting you. I have a fylgjæ. She speeds me up—"

"What's a fylgjæ?" Mick asked, looking into Rory's eyes.

"A spirit from the planes. She stands about a foot tall and is thinner than you. I can run twice as fast as any man without her. With her, I'm four times as quick and I never tire. Retzlaff can shoot lightning at me if he wants. He won't get me. But—and I think this is Ingefær's point—you don't have the same quickness. You're fast. Don't get me wrong. But you're not magically fast."

I hadn't even considered Rory's point. Now I was doubly sure Mick shouldn't show his face.

Mick chewed on his tongue for a moment. "You's having me on."

Rory shook his head.

"No," I said. "That's just one part of it. You'll have to trust my instincts. Retzlaff shouldn't see you, not until after we've questioned him."

Mick stomped to his left, then turned around on the narrow path and stomped back. "Ain't right. You's said I could come."

Rory said, "How about this? You and I will race back to the fork—where the river turned off. If you win, you can come with us. If I win, you stay right there."

Mick's mouth pulsed. "A rigged race? We both know you's faster than me. How about a roll of the dreki dice?"

Rory chuckled. "No. We don't leave life to chance. How about this: you stay behind, or I'll pound your face and tie you up?"

Mick crowed liked a rooster. He stepped left, his chin jerking forward and back. All that was missing was the rhythmic strutting. At the side of the hill, he turned back. "You's mean, mister." He sniffed and grabbed the donkey's reins. "Fine."

"Thank you." I winked at Rory. "And this way, we can continue with Rory's idea of a friendly approach."

Rory stuck his tongue out at me. "I know it's better to ask first before bashing heads. Well, most of the time."

"Sorry, Mick," I said. "I should have thought of the issues earlier." I hadn't considered Mick's volatility. And Rory's point about evading magical spells. "I'm sure you don't know, but we can't just ride up and accuse the man of stealing."

Mick shrugged. "Why not?"

"It's against the law to besmirch a person's character," I replied. "Jarl's are a persnickety lot."

As I sat atop Thunder, doubt over Retzlaff's guilt swirled in my head. Was there anything that gave the jarl plausible deniability…like he'd been at the mayor's gala on the night in question? What if another individual had impersonated the jarl and Mick had the wrong man? Or what if Mick had lied about the whole thing from the start?

The realization of such possibilities made me rethink my line of questioning. We needed to play nice…pretend we didn't know things. Which wasn't too far from the truth. I would give Mick the benefit of the doubt and assume he had told us what he believed to be the truth…as he saw it.

Mick yanked at his tawny hair. "What am I supposed to do while I wait?"

I pointed. "Go down the road past the hill's crest. Stay out of sight. We'll compare notes soon enough."

Rory jerked his chin. "Better still, go where the stream turns off. It's where I spotted those tracks. The overgrown path has been used recently. Go check it out for us—make yourself useful. We'll meet back at the junction and compare notes. Wait until sundown, and if we haven't returned, you can roust the Order of Gixus. Mention Foremost Aerica."

Mick turned green.

I shook my head. "My husband is being melodramatic. Don't worry. We'll be fine and will catch up soon." I added, "You be careful. Keep a sharp eye out. Holler and run if you have to."

Mick giggled. "It's what I do best. Don't worry, pretty lady. You's the one's got to face Retzlaff."

He walked off, pulling the donkey behind him.

I blew a sigh of relief. He had listened to Rory's reasoning…or maybe the threat of getting pounded had done the trick.

Either way, it meant he had a little sense in him after all.

Rory took a deep breath as he settled back into his saddle. "Good. I know we said we wanted him around, but I worried over his safety in case things turned ugly. I'd hate to see him hurt, or worse, and then have to tell his mother about it."

And without Mick, we could adapt our approach, depending on Retzlaff's responses.

We rode the rest of the way up the trail. Before us stood a five-story-tall mansion. Well, one spire was that tall. The main building was but three levels. A second spire to our left rose to four stories. It had a grand view of anyone coming up the path. Or it would have, if the windows hadn't been shuttered.

The lawn before the manor was large and flat and was overgrown with long, green grass. The rose bushes under the shuttered windows needed pruning and more water. Aside from the wilted rose bushes—despite the recent rain—purple flowers dotted the landscape on either side of the house. In the center of the house, right in front of us, stood an arched double set of doors. Big enough for a troll to walk through.

I shook my head to clear it of the hideous green beasts. We tied off our horses at a railing, designed for the purpose. I left the leads long so the horses could graze.

I un-cinched my longsword and dipped my fingers under my chain-mail shirt and into the pouch containing sawdust. Just in case Retzlaff was a troll of the human variety, and deadly darts of fire became necessary.

I tugged on Rory's arm. "Be gentle. Retzlaff may have a plausible explanation, or Mick may be a liar. We need to go at it like we're investigating a crime and haven't fingered Retzlaff as a suspect."

Rory eyed me. He heaved his shoulders. "Aye. Mick may have spoken false."

"Intentionally or not," I said.

Rory frowned. "There are times you overthink things." Then he grinned. "And yeah, I know—it saves lives."

## Chapter Ten

# JARL RETZLAFF THE FIFTH

### RORY

Outside of Retzlaff's manor, I readied my blade but kept it sheathed. We were going indoors, so I left my crossbow tied to the pommel of the horse's saddle. Besides, I didn't want to appear like we had come to fight. I considered taking the magicked dagger out of the rucksack to keep it safe. But out here, there wasn't anyone around for miles. Hel, it had taken the better part of an hour to climb the trail.

Questioning a jarl was one of my least favorite things to do. Most were uppity and walked around like their very presence blessed everyone around them. And Ingefær wanted me to be nice. Well, we had little choice, as all we had was Mick's word for just about everything. Though some circumstances bolstered his story.

Besides, an angry jarl could make trouble; he could file a complaint and threaten us with arrest. Or he might loosen magic. It didn't help that we were meeting him at his own home...where he had more rights.

Hiding my worry, I glanced at Ingefær with raised brows. She nodded.

Approaching the door, I pounded with a fist. Can't appear timid.

I looked left, then right. Because of a lack of paint on the shutters, door, and wood trim and years of weather, the exterior seemed old and weary. But it was made of stone, so it wasn't about to fall down. The closed shutters were odd. Maybe he was a private person. Or he harbored secret desires of being a dvaerg, the stout bearded miners who, at best, tolerated the sun.

My friend Rikk Mluvnal, a skald, once said, "It required a voyage of countless seasons to grow accustomed to the glaring golden globe's fierce brilliance upon me tender eyes."

Or after he'd had a few, he'd say, "Damn bright ball still stings me eyes."

After a minute of waiting, I pounded again.

With the tracks I'd spotted, I knew the place wasn't deserted. Yet the closed shutters implied the occupants were on an extended vacation. A mansion this size should have a dozen servants running about the place, keeping it clean. How many folks were inside?

As I was about to pound a third time, I heard metal scraping on the other side of the door.

One half of the large wooden door swung inward, revealing a man about my height, but as white as a ghost. He had stringy black hair reaching for his shoulders. It matched his overlong and straggly beard and mustache.

His dull charcoal eyes added to his lifeless appearance, yet I couldn't shake the feeling those orbs could suck the life out of me if given the chance.

His voice croaked like he'd woken moments ago—after being dead. "What do you want?"

He wore a dark red tunic with silver stitching underneath a purple robe. Mick had at least seen this man, having gotten the description right. The tunic was tied at the waist with a leather belt, from which hung four colored pouches: red, green, blue, and white.

Married to a mage, I knew each color corresponded to one of the material magical planes. Gold—or yellow—was missing, which corresponded to the Aether plane. But hadn't Elise said he was an Aether specialist?

With the wardrobe Mick had described, coupled with the mage belt, it had to be Retzlaff standing before me. Where were his servants?

"Greetings," I said, trying to sound cheerful. "Are you Jarl Retzlaff by chance?"

The man's lips twitched at the corners. He groaned out. "Who wants to know?"

*Great. Answering a question with a question.*

I stuck to our plan of being nice. "I am Rory Belkin, and this is Ingefær vod Renku. Once more, are you Jarl Retzlaff?"

The man's eyes shifted from me to my bride. He seemed to regain a bit of color, and his words were less haggard. "You are at my home. I presume you know where you are. So, yes, I am Jarl Retzlaff the fifth."

"Good fortune," I said, faking more cheerfulness. "There was a robbery..." I surprised myself at uttering the word without a stomach cramp. But that wasn't why I'd paused. I had started to say, *at the Fraegah Temple*, but didn't want to give everything away. Though I suspected the man—the mage—would soon figure out why we were here.

Retzlaff blinked an extra time, then said, "There's been no robbery here."

Ingefær cleared her throat. "Mistress Elise said she'd conversed with you several times about selling a family ring back to you."

"Yes," Jarl Retzlaff said. His curt tone softened. For the first time, his mouth formed a hint of a smile. "But she hasn't let me know how much. We've yet to agree to terms."

I narrowed my eyes at him. Elise had mentioned a specific price, and said she was planning to visit the jarl. "You don't have the ring with the letter *R* etched on it?"

"Are you saying my family heirloom has been stolen?"

Another non-answer. Though the surprise in his voice sounded sincere. Was the jarl being honest?

I imagined Manic Mick, at this very moment, walking beside the stream. Had the lad lied to us? Was he laughing his ass off? Had Ingefær and I been duped?

No. Defeating the ward spell required mage skills. And the disappearing hundred on the merchant's letter spoke of chicanery beyond the lad's capabilities. Another mage could have pretended to be this jarl.

Ingefær filled the space as my thoughts rushed around. "Yes, I'm afraid so, and our investigation into its loss has led us here. In addition to the ring, a jewel and a magical brew have been taken."

"Oh dear," Jarl Retzlaff said. He held out his hands for inspection. "I'm sorry you've wasted your time. I have no ring. And I'm even sorrier to hear my family heirloom is lost."

Except he didn't sound distraught at all.

Then he spoke with a jarl-like snark that caused my fists to clench. "It seems Mistress Elise needs to increase the protection around her precious Temple. When word gets out..." He trailed off as he shook his head.

I ground my teeth. The conversation had gone as I had feared, leaving us with little leverage and no genuine progress. Time to shift our approach. Time to drop hints and names and see how he reacted.

"I apologize, Jarl Retzlaff," I said. "Our information comes from a lad named Mick. We'll have to have another *chat* with him."

"You can't trust the word of a thief," Retzlaff said.

I avoided flashing my eyes to Ingefær and wondered if she'd caught the slip. I'd said *lad*, not *thief*. He knew the kid. Now I was certain Retzlaff was a grimy goblin who had been involved with the ring's theft. Yet, outside of Mick's testimony, I had no proof.

Ingefær played with the choker at her neck. "Excuse me, Jarl Retzlaff. But what makes you think Mick is a thief?"

Retzlaff's eyes darted between us. He sniffed at the air. "The name is familiar to me. He tried to pick my pocket two moons ago. I assume we are talking about the same young man. Blondish hair?"

I narrowed my eyes. "It's a mighty strange coincidence."

Retzlaff jutted his jaw at me. "What do you mean?"

"I mean, our source is someone you know. The stolen ruby ring was about to be sold to you. And the manner of theft required knowledge of magic."

Ingefær said, "Mick does not have the skills required to dispel wards."

"And it seems you didn't report him to the Order of Gixus for his attempted pick-pocketing," I said, "or he'd be locked up right now." That was the most damning part. A jarl wouldn't hesitate to set the law on folks of Mick's caste.

Retzlaff stretched himself tall. His words were gruff. "Are you accusing me of having a hand in this theft?"

We'd arrived at the trouble spot.

Though differences cropped up at times, laws within the Realm were mostly consistent. Depending on the severity—which came down to value—theft was punishable by hanging, as were the more nefarious crimes like murder and rape. Accusing a man of theft without proof had penalties as well, like a fine of a year's wages or two years' hard labor in the swamps. Accusing a jarl could receive a mighty harsh sentence—up to ten years in the swamp after a dozen lashes. With open, bloody wounds, mucking filth in the swamps meant certain death before fulfilling a third of the sentence.

Some folks said justice was a harsh mistress. Others scoffed and said justice existed for those with coins. The latter had more of a ring of truth to it to me.

"We are not accusing you of anything," Ingefær said, her cheeks reddening. "We are making inquiries."

"Our apologies, Jarl Retzlaff." I turned toward my bride so the mage wouldn't see my wink—alerting Ingefær of my impending tactical shift.

I needed the man to not be alarmed, to not overreact, to not ride to the Order of Gixus and file a complaint. We had a letter from Foremost

Aerica giving us rights to inquire, but not to accuse...to sully a man's reputation. We hadn't crossed the line. Yet.

I watched his hands. So far, they'd stayed away from his mage pouches.

I smiled at Retzlaff, my skin crawling with the effort. I hoped to put him off. "It's obvious Mick lied to us."

Ingefær nodded and stepped closer to the man, clutching her hands to her bosom. "I wonder if we'll be able to catch him again."

I cursed Mick loud enough for the jarl to hear and made a show of reassuring my bride. "If he's still in Slangeh Buktah, we'll get him."

Her head waggled side to side, her shortened hair swaying back and forth. "If not, we'll have flubbed our first assignment."

She was angling for sympathy, though it was couched in the truth.

"If we're done here," Retzlaff said, backing out of the doorway.

Ingefær took another half step and pawed at his robed arm. "I wonder, would it be possible for some fresh water?"

The jarl scoffed. "Really?"

I smiled and put warmth into my words. "Our apologies, Jarl Retzlaff. Every investigation must deal with unpleasant subjects, and in order to be effective, they require direct questions." I swallowed rising bile. "I assure you, we meant no disrespect."

Did Ingefær know how much I detested uttering such pleasant words to this scum of a man? I had half-turned to leave when she'd shifted directions by asking for water. We had water on our horses' backsides, so I deduced she was trying to get inside the mansion. The *why* I didn't know, but I trusted her instincts.

Jarl Retzlaff's lips twitched.

Ingefær said, "We had to follow up on the one lead provided. We're sorry to have bothered you. Truly sorry."

She flashed a smile and placed a hand on his robed arm, this time leaving it there. "It's a long ride from Slangeh Buktah. And the way up the hill is so steep. We used up all our water to give to the horses."

"There's a stream half a mile down the hill," Retzlaff said.

"I know." She squirmed while standing. A neat trick four-year-olds pulled off often. "But I also have to use your privy. Please?"

Retzlaff laughed. "Ah."

We crossed the threshold, and he guided us to the left. And then to the right of the stairs going up, which, presumably, led to the spire on the far left of the mansion. He waved at a door and Ingefær went inside.

I stayed outside with Retzlaff, forcing a thin-lipped smile onto my face.

After a long minute, Ingefær came out, pulling her mail shirt down. She flashed a smile and appeared embarrassed. "Would you mind sharing some fresh water? The stream has bugs and animals doing...you know...what I just did."

With a fresh twinkle in his eyes, Retzlaff moved to our right and beckoned. "Please, follow me. I, too, worry about the nasty things floating in open waters."

Ingefær blushed anew and tittered like a girl with a crush. "Oh, you are so sweet. Thank you so much."

I didn't like her flirting with the cretin. No, I didn't like it at all.

"So, this Mick of yours said I stole my family ring?" Retzlaff laughed, turning to lead the way. "Now, why would I steal a trinket I can buy?"

"He told us several fairy tales," I said. "I'm sorry I only slapped him once."

Thoughts flew around in my head. Retzlaff had opened his own front door. Where was the servant for the task? I looked at the floor, where tracked mud lay before us. That meant no one had swept the floor in at least two days. No house servants around at all?

"His mother begged us to not drag him to the Order of Gixus." Ingefær flashed another smile as Retzlaff turned his head at us and pointed down the hall, away from the spire stairs.

How she could twist the truth into a lie was impressive.

She went on. “We told her since a theft had been reported, it was our job to either turn the thief in or to recover the stolen items.”

I said, “We’ll have another talk with the lad...after we catch him and he’s in jail. The threat of the noose loosens lips.” When dealing with miscreants, it didn’t bother me to lie straight out. Not one bit.

And I had to catch up to Ingefær’s play...and hope things didn’t go goblin on us.

## Chapter Eleven

# A TRAP

## INGEFÆR

Rory and I followed the jarl down the hallway. A light coating of dust lay everywhere, including on the lone painting hanging opposite the double door we had entered through. I saw no potted plants or vases of flowers. This time of year, most mansions of this size would have quite the assortment on display. Maybe it was a personal taste...or he had a physical ailment stemming from flowers and plants. Either way, it gave the home a cold feel.

Past the main hallway, the windows had the drapes closed to keep the sun out, which I thought unnecessary as they were already shuttered. The man must have a strong need to keep peering eyes out.

Other than its size, the mansion was like any home. But because of its size, much of the walls were barren, and the floor rugs thrown here and there did little to unify the space. Our boots echoed off the walls as we headed for the far wall.

With Retzlaff leading, we went through a parlor room with seating for a dozen on divans and chairs, their cushions displaying large black orchids. Obnoxious luxury stared back at me in the form of tan leather cushions and garnet-hued silk throw pillows. It appeared tidy, undisturbed, and un-lived-in. So far, I hadn't seen a single servant. Where were they?

Elise had said the family had fallen on hard times. Maybe Retzlaff couldn't afford much help. But not even one servant? She had also said Jarl Retzlaff had wanted to purchase the signet ring for close to four thousand silvers. So, which was it? Rich or poor?

At the end of the room, we turned left through an open archway. The kitchen was vast, taking up a quarter of the ground floor. It contained its own fireplace, which had dying embers in its bed. The dining table was made of mahogany and ran sixteen feet, with six chairs on either side but none at the ends. A giant, unlit candle chandelier hung from the ceiling. The table itself was bereft of plates, utensils, and even place settings. And didn't contain a centerpiece.

There were breadcrumbs and bits of eggs at the far end. How long had they been there? There were dirty dishes stacked along the walnut countertop.

Retzlaff grabbed two stone mugs off a shelf in the pantry, which looked in need of restocking from the brief view I had. He moved to the side and worked the pump handle until water dribbled out. "Freshest water in all the Realm. Strained through a coal box before it arrives here."

Wow. Most homes didn't have a personal well inside the home. Let alone one with a straining system.

"Does it come from the creek we passed?" Rory asked.

Retzlaff smiled, handing us the mugs. "Yes. My ancestors diverted a part of its flow. It fills a cistern built long ago. The excess runs back to the source. An ingenious design."

It was, and spoke of long-ago wealth.

I turned my thoughts to our next steps. My water and privy request had been a means to lower the man's guard and get a peek inside the mansion. Having gotten in, I needed to gain the man's confidence further. I had thought to strike up a conversation with a maid or a chef. But as none were around, it proved impossible.

I sipped and gushed over the water. "It's delicious. I wonder, Jarl Retzlaff, if you'd be so kind as to show us the rest of your marvelous home."

"It's beautiful," Rory said, nodding in agreement and following my lead. He pointed. "My favorite wood. I'm sure you don't care, but we're having a home built. And from what I've seen, I can tell you I'm ready to change the design."

I nodded with vigor. "Oh, this is so lovely. It's given me ideas." I turned to Retzlaff, grinning hard. "Please?"

His eyes narrowed at me, then darted to Rory. A corner of his lip turned up. "Of course. Since you're building a home." Retzlaff pointed the way.

We made our way through the back side of the mansion with Jarl Retzlaff pointing and describing and us *oohing* and *aahing* at the sights. A study and a library were next to the kitchen on the backside of the house. They looked a little more lived in. Meaning that they were more disheveled.

Beyond those two rooms were servant quarters: small spaces with quaint, shuttered windows. While the bedrooms appeared tidy, they also looked unoccupied: no slippers under the beds, and no evening robes hanging on hooks.

Asking to see inside the closet broached etiquette...and would raise suspicions. I was sorely tempted to dilly dally and fall behind for a chance at a peek. But Retzlaff waited for me to exit.

"Does this give you ideas?" Retzlaff asked.

I nodded. Wanting to see the upper floors, I asked, "Can we see the views from the tall spire?"

Retzlaff smirked before chuckling outright. "There's a hidden passageway."

Why was that funny?

He led us back to the kitchen and opened a cupboard inside the pantry. Behind a stack of plates was a lever. He lifted it. A trap door appeared in the floor, right in front of the kitchen fireplace. He said, "You go down and over, then up."

He smiled. "Alas, I have a bad knee and don't like to climb stairs. You can go up, though it is dark until you reach the top."

I looked at Rory.

He peered into the darkness.

Retzlaff said, "There's nothing scary down there. Or up at the top. It's just narrow and has lots of steps. I assure you, the view is spectacular."

Retzlaff waved an arm toward the opening. I was surprised he had revealed his family's secrets. Was he being polite, or did he have ulterior motives? I glanced at Rory, my brows arching high.

*Do we go up?*

My husband tapped his sword and looked at his feet.

*Yeah, easy for you to run.* But I knew he wouldn't leave me behind. We were pretending to be interested in Retzlaff's manor, and the man had maneuvered us in such a way, the sole way to keep up the pretense was to go into the tower.

I led the way into the tight stairwell, my hand reaching for my hidden mage pouches. I trekked down and over, my other hand sliding along the wall to guide me as it turned. The light grew dimmer the deeper I went. And the moldier the stink in the air became.

Rory shuffled down the steps behind me.

Before me was a steep and narrow staircase, and it was as dark as a moonless night. I stopped. Even if I wanted to reveal my sorcerous abilities, I didn't have a light spell. "I can't see."

Retzlaff's chuckles echoed through the passage. The trap door slammed shut. It was like a hood had been draped over my eyes. I couldn't see my hands before my face.

"That troll," Rory said. "I'm going to gut him when I get out of here."

Rory moved. It sounded like he stumbled. His curse confirmed it.

"Ingefær, help me push."

I felt my way back to the first steps and fumbled my way up. Moving around Rory's feet, I stood next to him.

"On three." Rory counted down, and we heaved.

It didn't budge, not even a cat's whisker. He climbed a step higher to get more leverage. I joined him, and we pushed and pushed.

"It seems our ruse didn't work," I said. What had given us away?

"Obviously." Rory sat down on the step. "Now what?"

I sat beside him. "I have read that these types of doors can have two control mechanisms." Unable to see Rory's expression, I continued. "So, we go up and see if there's a lever in the walls or on the top landing."

"Maybe it's what he wants us to do," Rory said.

"I'm open to suggestions." I twirled the pearl-white snowflake. "A fireball in these confined quarters will kill us—if not from the flame, then the smoke. Ditto for a bolt of lightning."

Rory grumbled. "Gutting is too kind. I'm filleting him first."

"I can detect magic."

"Do so."

I got him to stand behind me, and I cast a find magic spell on the trapdoor. Nothing glowed.

"I guess that's good. Means physical force will work."

Rory grunted. "A sword blade will snap. We need pry bars and sledgehammers."

"So, let's go up and see."

By touch, we hiked up the spire steps. By touch, I searched for protrusions and obvious levers. But the walls felt smooth to me.

As we climbed, the light returned. At first, it was as dim as a moon waxing its first day, but it brightened with each turn of the steps. When we reached the top, light filtered through the gaps of the closed shutters. It wasn't much, but it allowed us to examine our surroundings.

The top floor had a set of blood-red divans with a dozen purple silk throw pillows. The place smelled of dust and mold. It hadn't been swept out in a moon.

I scanned the walls, searching for anything odd. Anything resembling a release lever.

I sneezed. "The furniture is beautiful."

Rory raised his brows. "You're evaluating the fixtures?"

He moved to a window and undid the latch keeping the shutters closed. When he swung them open, I blinked, adjusting to the sudden infusion of light.

Stepping to the window, I looked out. Despite our predicament, my eyes feasted. "What a magnificent vista!"

The sun's position told me we were looking north. Rolling hills climbed and morphed into giant mountains...maybe a day's hike away.

Rory peered down. "The ground is about forty feet below."

I joined him and looked down. "You can't jump."

"Remember the wall of air you used at the Furæyar Shrine?" Rory pointed at my waist. "You have any goblin bone dust?"

I nodded. It could act as a levitate incantation. "Aye. Great idea. But my range is twenty feet."

He winked at me. "I'll roll with it."

I kissed him. Good and hard. "And then what?"

"I'll race around the front and force my way in. Once inside, I'll find the lever and open the trapdoor. Be there. Be ready to flame the troll...if I haven't killed him already."

I nodded. Rory liked action as part of his plans. "The door is huge. How are—"

"Not the door. A window." Rory winked at me. "The shutters are much easier than the beast of an oak door."

"Try not to kill him. He should be arrested. He needs to explain himself."

His mouth twisted. "I like my way better." He flashed a grin. "Let's let fate decide."

Which meant that if Retzlaff was in Rory's line of sight, he would die. I wanted to argue, but I also wanted to escape the spire. Besides, if Retzlaff spotted Rory, I had a feeling he would cast a spell, which meant Rory's life was in danger. And with me not there, I had no right to demand he not fight back.

I pinched goblin bone dust and waved my arm in a rectangular shape, while I summoned magical forces from the plane of air. Uttering the Varanusian words, I formed a wall of air—the goblin bone dust allowed me to shape it—outside the window. I nodded at Rory.

He climbed to the windowsill and dangled his legs till he found a firm footing on my incantation.

"I remember saying something about a diet." Grunting at his weight—which I had to hold aloft—I lowered the wall of air, feeling the range of my power to control the shape and size.

"That's as far as I can go." I groaned with the effort of holding the shape at such a distance. Not to mention his mass.

Rory looked up at me, then down at the ground.

The secret to jumping was all in the landing. Rory used his magic feet to generate speed. When he hit the ground, he rolled forward once, then slammed to a stop, face down.

"Rory!" I let the spell go.

It took several seconds before Rory moved an arm, then his legs. He climbed to all fours and shook his head.

After he stood, he looked up at me. "Nothing is broken. But I have a headache."

"Go. I'll meet you at the trapdoor."

## Chapter Twelve

# RETZLAFF'S MANSION

## INGEFÆR

Rory flashed right and disappeared. No doubt he would beat me to the trap door if Retzlaff wasn't around. I took my time going down the spire's staircase, letting my eyes adjust to the darkness as I descended to the ground floor.

When I reached the crossover part, it wasn't dark at all. I looked up and saw Rory's smiling face.

"What took you so long?" he asked.

"Steep stairs in darkness are fodder for cautionary tales." I climbed up and out. "Have you taken care of Jarl Retzlaff?"

Rory shook his head. "Haven't seen him."

I patted Rory's shoulder. "Thank you for freeing me, good sir. This damsel will be forever grateful. And now, let's find Retzlaff and arrest him."

Retzlaff's aggressive action of locking us up gave us sufficient cause to take him into custody. We could sort out his business with Mick with the Order of Gixus supervising.

Rory cleared his throat. "I doubt he'll come peaceably."

I winked at him as I pinched sawdust from my pouch. "If he resists, then he deserves his fate."

We moved through the first floor, this time checking the closets. I paused to search nightstands and dresser drawers, but not with a huge time investment. Finding the jarl would lead us to the stolen goods faster.

We hiked up to the second floor, where Rory and I traipsed through four bedrooms. These were quite large, but equally devoid of life. We came to a second parlor room, this one a massive gathering area, thrice as big as the inn's room we had stayed in last night. Like the seating in the first-floor salon, this one was adorned with teal silk pillows to accent the leather.

There was a set of instruments assembled on a stand designed to house them. I counted three lyres, six sets of cymbals, a dozen trumpets, and a giant harp. Between them, the wood plank floor was inlaid with a shuffleboard design. I didn't see any of the equipment to go with it, like a push stick or the sliding wooden stones. There was a fireplace against the far wall that seemed to line up with the one downstairs. The entire room had a thick, undisturbed layer of dust.

Rory said, "He hasn't been up here in at least a week."

"So, where did he go?" I spun around. "He wasn't downstairs."

"Let's be thorough," Rory said. "If there's one secret passage, there's bound to be more."

"I like the way you think. He might be above us after all."

The third floor was a sequence of bedrooms turned into storage rooms. Lots of wood crates filled them. One room was an armory of sorts. A series of swords lined one wall. A pair of crossbows hung from hooks on another. I didn't see any armor, but there was a stack of shields in the corner. Were they for the guards when the Retzlaff clan could afford them?

Having reached the top floor with no signs of Retzlaff, we stomped down the stairs.

"There's the other spire," Rory said.

Back downstairs, a smidge to the right of the main door, I stopped. "Hold on. Maybe he left. What if he stole our horses?"

For a moment, I felt stupid. That should have been the first thing I checked. But then I remembered Rory had run around the front entrance to set me free. He would have noticed if our horses were gone.

To double check, I opened the enormous door, which swung with ease. Thunder and Rory's roan mare, Muffin, remained tied. I took a moment to go out and place a feed sack on each. "We won't be much longer," I assured them.

As it was, we'd been here well over an hour; much longer than I thought we would.

Back inside, Rory led the way up the second, shorter spire. Natural light filtered down the stairs from above.

"Be careful," I whispered at his back.

When we reached the top, the view from the windows was grand. None of them were shuttered, as it had appeared from outside. Had Retzlaff opened them after trapping us in the other spire?

The top landing contained a pair of emerald divans with fuchsia silk throw pillows. A short bookcase stood against a wall, but it contained only dust.

Rory moved to the window and reached out, waving his hand in the sunlight. "Huh? From the outside, I could have sworn the shutters had been closed."

He stood there for a long while, so I moved beside him. "Oh!"

"Aye." Rory grinned at me. "It's beautiful. You can see all the way to the ocean."

The sun was getting on as it cast glittering rays on the far distant waters. In between the ocean and the spire was a long, tree-covered slope. Pines at the start, but way off, after a series of rolling hills, ever lower and ever smaller, oaks and maples dominated the skyline.

We went back down the stairs to the giant door, which I had intentionally left open.

A tingle ran down my spine. I looked left, then right. Something felt off.

Rory's words about more secret passages filtered through my foggy thoughts. I turned and stared at the wall with the lone painting. Pointing, I said, "There's a hidden door there."

Rory cocked his head as he looked. "Are you sure?"

"Step it off to the far wall and I'll go to the shorter spire staircase."

We measured the house width in steps. Climbing back upstairs, we confirmed the distance and width.

Moving to the ground floor, we searched through the kitchen and the servant rooms and library, taking measurements along the way.

I nodded. "Positive. There's missing space. By our feet, it's at least five strides by six."

Rory scowled. "Alright. I agree with you. Retzlaff must be hiding inside. You ready to cast magic?"

I chewed on my cheek. The fight went out of me. I wasn't scared. But, like steep unlit staircases, I'd learned a life lesson about storming a defended castle. "I've cast two spells already. He has cast none that I know of, and I don't know his capabilities."

Rory nodded. "And we've been gone for a long time. Two hours now. Mick is probably worried."

"And the horses need watering." I scrunched my nose and shrugged. "We know where he lives."

Rory paced, growling under his breath. After a few turns, he stopped and nodded. "He's got nowhere else to go. Let's find Mick and have another conversation. I want to know more before barging into Retzlaff's hidden sanctuary."

We went outside, closing the door behind us. Danger lurked everywhere, but no place more than a man's hideout—where he expected trouble and was prepared to deal with it.

Poor fortune, we no longer had surprise on our side.

As we mounted our horses, I said, "We know Retzlaff is guilty of stealing. High certainty he has the items. We also know he's a mage, but we don't know his powers. I would have liked to know how well he commands the plane of air—the levitation spell is proof of that. No doubt he can summon the Aether."

"Because he dispelled the wards," Rory said.

"Right." I nudged Thunder forward. "We also know his servants are missing. I think he had a couple as recently as a week ago."

Rory nodded. "Aye. Those were the signs I saw in the bedrooms. I would say the dried mud on the first floor was no more than two days old. Upstairs, longer. A week."

"So, where are they? Do you think he just had to let them go? He's struggling with coins, is my guess."

"Right you are again," Rory said. "Come on. The sun will set in an hour, and we told Mick to run to the Order of Gixus if we didn't show by then."

He heeled his roan away from the mansion.

I followed Rory on Thunder, pondering our failures. Failure to identify Retzlaff as a culprit before he imprisoned us; and failure to apprehend him.

## Chapter Thirteen

# THE WATERFALL

## Rory

While trotting down the trail, I looked over my shoulder, up at the four-story spire—the one which had the shutters open with a magnificent view of the surroundings. Tall pines, rolling hills, and maples and oaks in their full greenery. The view down the hill towards the ocean had been breathtaking.

Except from the outside, the shutters were closed.

I pointed. "Is that an illusion?"

Ingefær craned her head. "Aye. He's either quite strong with the Aether, or it's a Hel of a family heirloom spell."

My stomach churned. I didn't like the idea of facing off against a powerful mage. I could outrun fireballs and even dodge a lightning bolt. Well...if I saw them coming. But speed didn't help with surviving illusion spells. I would need to be clearheaded in order to have a chance to see what I was facing. And in that, I had doubts about my abilities.

I glanced at Ingefær. Her hand fumbled with the snowflake around her throat. She was worried too.

Still, it irked me to leave empty-handed. That wasn't our way. I hated failing more than waiting. And while I could think of it as a learning experience, I preferred gaining my knowledge through victory.

A dozen minutes later, we met Mick where the trail and the river joined. He was as wet as if it had rained hard for an hour. Yet he had a wide grin on his face. I expected him to be mad at us for taking so long.

I asked, "What's got you so happy?"

"Come look." A mad giggle escaped Mick's lips. He hopped and skipped, jerking the reins to his donkey as he led us around the hillock. We followed on our horses.

The stream we had traipsed next to for most of our journey up the trail followed this offshoot of a path. Green grasses, a field of daffodils, and a ridge of pines brought to mind tranquil thoughts, like cuddling with my beautiful wife. So, maybe not so tranquil. But very pleasant.

"Wow." Ingefær's jaw dropped.

I nodded. "It's so hidden." I glanced toward the mansion. The hillock obscured the spire.

Mick batted a hand at the air. "Bah. That's not it. Come on."

We followed him farther. The trail and the stream wound its way ever higher and deeper beyond the hill the mansion fronted.

From the higher vantage point, I looked behind me, and there stood Retzlaff's spire looking down on us, maybe four hundred strides off.

I frowned. I didn't remember seeing the stream and this gorgeous gorge from the top of either tower.

*What the Hel is going on?*

Ingefær had been searching over her shoulder as well. "It's an illusion spell. I'm certain of it. Yet I wonder if the illusion is for those *inside* the spire."

For what purpose? And I had poked my hand through the window, so the shutters couldn't be real. Could they? I was flummoxed. "Why would he do that?"

"What are you two talking about?" Mick asked. "And what took you so long?"

"Sorry." I dismounted and cleared my throat to clear my mind. I told him what we'd found inside the second spire.

Ingefær jumped off Thunder and started to explain our delay, but I shook my head just a smidge. Then I shifted my eyes toward Mick. We needed to question him first. He'd been cooperative on our way up, but had he told us the entire truth?

She got my hint and trailed off.

Shifting Mick's attention, I asked Ingefær, "You think Retzlaff is looking down at us now?"

"It's a possibility," she replied, eyeing me with a sideways cast to her head.

Manic Mick hiccupped; his face whitened. "He's looking at us?"

"Nah," I replied. "I doubt he went up the spire steps. Said he had bad knees." The liar. "Don't worry."

Questions circled in my head. When it came to Retzlaff, how gullible had Mick been? His fear seemed real, and I hated to believe he had me hoodwinked with an act. Was there something the young man knew, but maybe didn't know he knew? The trick was to get the information without upsetting him more.

Mick had dabbled with pick-pocketing. But by breaking and entering, and stealing such valuables, he had elevated his thieving to a new level. And Jarl Retzlaff had coaxed him into it. Of that, there was no doubt. Retzlaff's slip of the tongue, calling Mick a thief, confirmed his association with the young lad. And his attempt at locking us away in his prison-of-sorts confirmed his evil nature. A normal person, if he thought we were being nosy, would have asked us to leave. And if we'd crossed a line, would have asked us to leave and reported us to the Order of Gixus.

I said, "Retzlaff said you tried to steal from him."

Mick scowled. "Aye. I's tried to pick his pockets. He caught me."

"What did he do about it?"

Mick guffawed. "There's the funny part. Instead of hollering for the militia, he near whispered, 'There's better trinkets elsewhere.' We became a team."

Confirmation—Retzlaff wasn't an honest jarl. Well, there were few of those, though they preferred to rob vast riches rather than a one-off trinket. "You didn't think to tell your ma when the *better trinkets* turned out to be in her place of employment?"

"Ah, I's already told you, the baubles were just lying there. Many for centuries. It wasn't doing anyone any good. Just gathering dust or rusting. I figured there was no harm in it."

Mick shrugged, then blinked. A confused look fluttered on his face before clearing. "It sounds wrong now that I say it. But we's done a few jobs together by then. Seemed bad to leave a...a friend hanging." His blue eyes turned ice cold. "But then he ripped me off."

He had chosen a fake friend over family. That showed a lack of judgment.

I studied the lad, who mumbled and kicked at the dirt with a leather boot. He was naïve about certain things. I had no doubts he was immature, but a new idea formed. Maybe I had Mick all wrong.

What if the jarl had befuddled the kid's mind? Was it possible for Retzlaff to invoke a beguile or friendship spell? Or, like Mick's ma, a compel incantation?

It might explain a lot. Mick's current attitude toward the jarl told me, if a spell had been in place, the invocation was no longer active.

I mentioned the possibility to Ingefær, with Mick listening in.

Mick growled, his hand going to his dagger. "That troll turd. Why, gutting's too good for him."

Ingefær frowned. "I've no way of knowing. But if you're right, I think it's waned now."

It didn't excuse Mick, as he'd tried to pilfer Retzlaff's pocket. But it could explain why the young man wasn't torn up over stealing from his family. Time to find out what Mick was made of.

"You said you'd done about a dozen jobs before meeting Retzlaff?" I asked.

Mick nodded.

"Don't puff yourself up. Stealing doesn't impress me. And your mother isn't here."

Ingefær frowned at me. I suspected she wasn't following me.

Mick looked down at his feet. "Not a dozen. I thought about it at least that many times, though. It's hard, you know. What if I got caught? And a couple of times I knew I'd get a beating and then get turned into the Order. I had to pick on older folk, or pudgy ones."

Ingefær crossed her arms. "So how many attempts before stealing from Retzlaff?"

"Three." Mick chewed on his lower lip. "I failed the first time. Apologized for bumping into this old lady. The second time I told you about—the hunched-over woman I's took fourteen silvers from. The third time, I's got caught with my arm up in an old man's coat. He looked an easy mark, shuffling along with a limp, but his hands were fast. But I's run off with him hollering like his hair was on fire."

"So, you're not a very good thief." Ingefær peered down her nose at him. "Retzlaff caught you, too. I count four attempts with one success."

Mick shrugged. "I's good. After Retzlaff, I practiced a lot in my room, and I's got better. Me and that skunk Retzlaff pulled three jobs."

"What did he do, be specific?" Ingefær asked.

"Well, the first job he had me go in, said the leatherworker was asleep. I worried about waking the man, but Retzlaff assured me he wouldn't. We's got two dozen silver then."

Two dozen silver wasn't much. Room and board for a moon. But had Retzlaff caused the leatherworker to sleep through Mick's thieving? "And the other two?"

"I's lifted a coin purse of this lady merchant after she closed her fruit stand."

That didn't sound lucrative, either.

"What did Retzlaff do there?" Ingefær asked.

"I don't know." Mick looked at us with furrowed brows. "He waved his hands and mumbled, the woman stared at him the whole time while I's did the deed. Why's you asking all these questions?"

Ingefær said, "Because we're trying to gauge how good of a mage he is. And how good of a thief you are."

I told him about our escapades with Jarl Retzlaff, including our imprisonment and escape.

Ingefær finished up. "We searched the mansion and couldn't find him. We think there's another hidden passage."

Mick's lips turned white around the edges as he pressed them together. A hand went to his hair, and he yanked and pulled. "I's told you he was a troll."

"Calm down," I said. "Whatever you do, don't yell. Retzlaff can't hear you, but you need to learn to control your emotions before it causes a problem for all of us."

After a few moments, Mick's hands released his hair. He worked his mouth. "I'm alright now."

I sighed and chinned up the path. "How much farther till we get to your surprise?"

Mick's color had drained, so the smile he flashed was sick-looking. "Oh yeah, the reason I's wet. It's not far now."

We hiked around two curves when the sound of water burbling became louder. Two more bends and the bubbling turned into gushing. "That sounds like we're near the Rohd River."

The Rohd River ran west from Rohd Mina, where I used to work guiding a caravan every third moon. The river was wide, at least thirty feet across. But what made it roar was the steepness of the hillside as it plummeted down.

A twist later, the rumble of the water filled the tight gorge. Conversation was difficult. We arrived at a waterfall—a drop of forty feet from the source above us.

Ingefær yelled. “Wow!”

Spray from the waterfall dampened my hair and clothes.

Mick turned around with glee on his face. “It’s beautiful.”

And it was.

I scanned the landing area around the pool of water and pointed.

“What?” Ingefær asked.

I shouted. “There are tracks on the trail all the way to here.” Pointing at the rippling pond’s shore, I bellowed my question at Mick. “How far did you go when you were here before?”

Mick cupped his hands around his mouth. “Right to the edge of the pool!”

We tied off the horses, and I pointed at the tracks of a horse, wagon wheel ruts, and two pairs of boots that didn’t match the sole of Mick’s shoes. What did the tracks portend? Where did they go? The boots and horseshoes ended right at the water’s edge, with no return tracks. Where were the horse and the wagon?

We looked around for a few minutes but found no other tracks. None of Retzlaff or a servant leaving, nor any horses going back down the trail.

The sun hung low in the western sky as I pondered aloud. “Retzlaff knows illusion spells. He may know a beguiling or friend incantation. What else?”

Ingefær said, “There’s a secret door inside the manor. And we don’t know his stamina or his power.”

My wife had referred to two of three prongs mages were classed by. Stamina referred to spell capacity—how many a mage could cast before passing out or needing a healer? Power referred to the number or size of spells. She could cast three fiery darts per spell. Other mages but one or two. I hadn't seen a mage do more than three—well, except for a now-dead witch.

The third prong was creativity or knowledge. A few folks split it into two categories. Our scaled mage friend Hombir, a d'oglemann from Kobber Unter Smuss, loved devising new spells by combining the powers of the planes with unique phrasings and odd material. He'd converted a heal spell into a warmth spell. Damn useful when living on the Ice Plains.

We didn't know enough about Retzlaff. I said, "We need to go back to the city."

Mick grumbled. "You's not going to arrest him?"

"Don't know where he's at," I said. "Perhaps he's hiding out behind a secret wall, ready to blast us. I think we need more information before we go barging in."

Mick grunted.

Ingefær put a hand on his shoulder. "He may have cast a befriend spell on you."

Mick's hand went to his hair and tugged. "When you's was talking to him, did you's ask him if he stole from me?"

"No," I said. "Without proof, we couldn't accuse him of a crime."

Ingefær agreed. "It's the law. One thief's word against another doesn't sway anyone. And he's a jarl."

I ground my molars. "We need to know what his capabilities are...and see if we can find anything about the construction of his mansion."

"Improbable," Ingefær said. "It's an old structure."

I figured as much, but to give up without trying was an admission of failure. Would we need more help? And if so, how would we ask for it without revealing Mick's role, compelled or not?

Once more, Elise's spell bound our efforts. We needed to talk with her about the possibility of Retzlaff's undue influence over Mick and his attempt at holding us hostage.

With a plan—not a great one—in mind, we descended the path, returning to the main trail.

It pleased me to see Mick take such delight in nature's sights. I couldn't help but think he was alright. Just misguided, influenced—maybe charmed—by the jarl into a life of thievery.

Hours after the dinner bell tolled, we entered the city and made for the Shrine of Eirene. Mick wanted to retrieve more of his gear at his humble abode down the street.

On the way, Ingefær and I discussed our next move, all within Mick's hearing.

She said, "I'm certain Retzlaff has the three stolen items. He's moved them to his sanctuary."

"He may even have them in his pockets," I said. "We need to have a chat with Elise about Retzlaff and her spell. We need to research the family and the mansion."

Ingefær nodded. "Agreed."

## Chapter Fourteen

# RETZLAFF HISTORY

## RORY

At the shack Mick called home, a stone's throw from the Shrine of Eirene, the young lad changed clothes into ones more suitable for adventuring. He replaced his red kaftan and russet pantaloons with a padded, tan leather gambeson and matching linen breeches. He elected to keep his sky-blue vest on over his leather jerkin.

After replacing his baggy articles of clothing with more form-fitting ones, his beanpole stature could no longer hide, even with the added bulk of the leather on his chest and the padded shirt underneath. After the sky-blue vest, his most noticeable feature was his bulbous knees.

I turned to Ingefær. "How can he run so fast with those legs?"

She chuckled. "I don't know, but he sure can sprint."

"I caught up." But I had the aid of my magicked feet. I turned to Mick. "Why did we come back here?"

"I done told you's," he replied.

I looked down my nose. "Do I have to hogtie you to get a straight answer?"

"Fine," Mick said. "I got a dagger in each boot, a blade in the back of my breeches, and a slingshot and stones in my jerkin."

I had seen him slide a very short sword down his right butt cheek into a hidden leather sheath. He wouldn't sit in comfort. But the other items I hadn't seen him palm at all. Maybe he had a little skill.

I asked, "You got...more stuff?"

Mick grinned. "Does a horse have flies?"

It was an answer, but I still wanted to slap him silly.

"Let's go see your mom." Ingefær nudged the young man out of his tiny bedroom.

I was sure it had once served as a pantry to the small decrepit home it was a part of.

At the Temple of Fraegah, we checked with Elise about using the orb to find the ring.

She shook her head. "No. It's not good for objects. Just people. And I have to have a drop of blood to find them."

That confirmed my prior suspicions. I asked, "What can you tell us about Jarl Retzlaff?"

"Well, he's Jarl Johan Retzlaff the fifth." Elise put a finger to her chin. "He's single, never married, and there are no heirs. No uncles or aunts. There may be a distant cousin, but if so, they don't live in the city. The family fell on hard times quite a while ago. Hence the sale of the ruby ring several decades back."

"He showed us his hands, which didn't have the ring," Ingefær said. "But it could have been in his pocket." She shifted the subject. "There were oddities to his home. What can you tell us about his manor?"

"Not much. But if you check with the city library, there is a section on local jarls and historical buildings."

I hadn't expected that. A possible boon.

I sighed. We had concerns to discuss. "Based on what we've seen at Hexerei Mansion, we're disturbed by the possibility Retzlaff is more powerful than you know...or you've let on."

Elise darkened. "No. He's a simpleton. Can do two spells, maybe. Nothing beyond lighting a room. Nothing dangerous."

Ingefær said, "But you're basing that on information more than a year old, right?"

Elise nodded. "But not much has changed. Not for me, anyway. Yes, spells don't fail anymore, but my power, my stamina, they're the same as before."

Based on what I knew of my wife's sorcery, it sounded true. Since magic's return, Ingefær had increased her stamina a tad and her fiery darts now had three instead of two blasts. But Ingefær didn't sit in a building all day. She worked her magic almost every day.

I explained the illusions we had run into and the chance Mick had been enthralled.

Elise's eyes widened. "He's playing with the forces of necromancy."

I looked down at her. "Enthralling is necromancy, but compelling others isn't?"

"You agreed to the spell," she said through a clenched jaw.

"To help, yes. To keep quiet, too. But not the part about not being able to quit. This job has gone troll shit on us. It's not just your son we're chasing, is it? Death is a real possibility."

Mick hiccupped.

Elise glared at me. "You agreed to retrieve the items."

Ingefær put a hand on my arm. "We did. And we still will. But we shouldn't be compelled to do it. We know so little about our adversary. Your description of his capabilities doesn't match what we've seen."

Elise crossed her arms. "No. You'll just quit."

I shook my head. "No. You aren't listening. My wife said we'll find your precious stolen items. We just don't want a spell on us."

Elise smirked. "Well, too bad. I need the ring back."

My hands clenched.

Mick growled. "Ma!"

Elise's hands flew up, and her right hand gyrated while her left went into a pouch.

I drew my sword.

Ingefær tugged at me. "At ease. She's casting a find magic incantation."

"Yes," Elise said. "To see if Mick is still charmed."

I sheathed my weapon and glared at Elise. The conjurer had deflected the issue.

When Elise finished waving her hands, Mick didn't glow orange.

Elise sighed. "I guess that's good." She peered at her son. "Are you sure you were beguiled?"

Mick shrugged. "Don't know."

I stepped close and jabbed my finger at her chest. "Now remove your spell on us. We've made progress. We may need help. Like another mage or another trained swordsman."

Elise shook her head. "No. Not possible. No one else can know the items were stolen. My demands haven't changed. Nor can I let you quit." Her eyes dropped to the floor. "If you don't bring back the ring, I'll lose my job."

"A small price to pay, relative to losing a life or limb," I said.

We glowered at each other for a minute.

Mick pawed at his ma. "They are trying to help."

But Elise stood resolute and shook her head.

Ingefær gnawed on her lip. "You need to work on your trust of others. I'm not for quitting. Not when I know who the miscreant is and what they've done. Hel. Even when I don't. After I escaped prison in Vanaby last year, Rory and I searched for the true culprit. We didn't run away. We risked our lives to get to the truth."

Elise's pressed lips formed a thin line. Her nose pinched. "Nice story. If we're done here..."

I looked at Mick.

He shook his head. "Come on. I've seen that look before. You's ain't moving her."

If I had a grudge book, Elise would be in it. Not getting what we wanted from her, we moved on to the library.

Along the way, I said, "I don't like your mother, Mick."

Mick yanked at his tawny hair. "Aye. I get it. We's gone round and round several times, too."

Ingefær asked, "Is it true she'll lose her job if we cannot retrieve the ring?"

I scoffed. "Oh, who cares?"

My wife gave me one of her frosty glares.

Mick said, "Yeah. Good chance. After the mage conclave last summer, ma told me Maerek had asked to be put in charge of the Temple. He said he was the better mage." The lad shrugged. "I don't know if it's true."

Ingefær sighed, her breath whistling. "There's but one Fraegah Temple in the city, if memory serves. Who decides who is in charge?"

Mick scratched at his head. "Um. So, there was this big shindig last Summer Solstice, right after things got crazy about the return of magic. There's a ranking system based on ability and years of experience. I'm not sure, but I think there's a vote amongst the Temple leaders."

He went off on a tangent. "When magic returned, I've never seen ma so excited and happy. Of course, her enthusiasm waned in short order. Her skills didn't shift one bit. And I didn't develop any, either."

"Get back to Maerek," I said, trying to understand the dynamics.

"Ma and Maerek went to Steine Havn. They was gone for a moon. Before they left, her and Maerek got along alright. When they came back, they hissed at each other all summer long. That's when ma told me what had happened. Maerek's powers were growing. Hers weren't."

That sounded like a job demotion, not firing. Elise remained a turd pile in my book. I glanced at Ingefær.

She curled her nose in such a cute way. "We don't have a good employer. But the job remains."

If not for the compel spell, I would have argued. What did I care if Elise was no longer in charge of the Temple?

At the library, we asked for help and were shown to a small room. Books on local families were stored in alphabetical order.

Ingefær, being more learned than me, took charge. She pulled out three books and handed one to me and one to Mick.

Mick said, "I don't read."

"Your mother is a mage," I said. "How is that possible?"

"I guess it's more right to say I don't like to read. It gives me a terrible headache."

"Skim it," Ingefær said. "We're looking for anything about the Hexerei Mansion or the family, Retzlaff."

Taking the book she gave me, I thumbed through pages, reading the first paragraph, then moving on. About midway through, I came to Jarl Johan Retzlaff, the first. He had risen to the rank of sorcerer within the Fraegah hierarchy. Which meant he had broad knowledge of the magical planes. Well, three of them. But with spell failures so common a hundred twenty years ago, it wouldn't have meant much relative to other enchanters and conjurors.

I read further. The book said the elder Retzlaff had been accused of practicing necromancy, for which he'd been expelled from the order. Back in those days, locking up a mage with actual talent, intermittent or not, required a willingness to chance the lives of others. Few wanted to test their strength against a mage with 'true' power. Later, the book said he'd squandered the family riches in pursuit of extending his life.

I told Ingefær and Mick of the necromancy accusation and the quest to live forever.

She jabbed her book with a finger. "Says here the mansion was built nine hundred years ago. There's no floor plan, but it's rumored to have a massive cave complex beneath it." She added, "There's a reference to secret passages and hidden entry and exit points. And of a dungeon."

Confirming things we suspected—well, not the dungeon—I scratched my jaw and recalled the rolling hills and the way they surrounded the backside of the mansion. What was odd was the stream. Most of the water east of the city rolled west, toward the Slangeh River. But the stream had run south. Come to think of it, it didn't run down the entire path. It just...disappeared. I had paid no mind as we had weaved our way down the hillock, but now I wondered where the stream began and ended. And then I puzzled whether any of it mattered before pondering the strange disappearance of the wagon and horse near the pool's edge.

Mick said it first. "You think there's a secret entrance near the waterfall?"

The prints on the path to the waterfall said yes. Why not come and go through the front door? What had been delivered? And where the Hel were the servants and the horse and wagon?

My guts roiled and rumbled. Did we want to find out? "Is it reckless to invade a mage's home?" I asked. "Is it right?"

"We know he's the thief and a possible beguiler," Ingefær said. "We're justified."

"If not for Elise's compel spell, I'd get more help," I said. Hel, I'd call in the Order of Gixus.

The job in Vanaby had challenged us, but there had been more at stake than magical trinkets—like our freedom and lives. All this job offered was a reward of a thousand silver. Funds we could use. But the sensation in my gut told me our lives were at risk.

"I don't want you's to quit," Mick said. He must have read my face.

I turned to the young lad and put a hand on his shoulder. "Listen, Retzlaff's done most of the planning for sure, and maybe cast a spell on you. Not just to get you to steal the ruby ring, but also in setting your mother up so she would take it out of the cupboard. He's been at this since before Spring Equinox is my guess."

"He's smart," Ingefær said. "Yet your mother said he was of meager talent."

I hated when things didn't line up all nice and neat.

"You know, with him having the ring, his power and stamina are now augmented. He is more powerful than Elise described."

Great. Just great. Ingefær's words soured my guts all the more.

Mick hiccupped. Covering his mouth, he looked from me to Ingefær and back. "I say—*hic*—we should make for—*hic*—the waterfall and see what there is. *Hic.*"

The young man had convinced himself to go...no matter the odds, no matter how much he got scared. I liked him all the more.

I said, "We'll go back." Pointing at the books, I asked, "Anything else in there? Anything about the current jarl?"

She scanned the front pages. "It's an older book. Fifty years since its printing." Looking up, she flashed her pretty blue eyes at me. "We know more about the mansion than we did."

"Yeah. It's got tunnels and maybe a dungeon, and in all likelihood, lots of secret doors." I closed my eyes and wished there was a god to pray to.

Ingefær said, "We go back."

"Alright," I said. "The front door, or the waterfall?"

Mick hiccupped. "The waterfall. Something's strange there."

I nodded, but looked at my wife. If we found a secret passage, we would be trespassing.

She curled her cute button nose. "I don't enjoy sneaking about. We're officers of the law. Well—appointed bounty hunters, at least."

I said, "We go look at the waterfall. If there's a secret passage there, we come in the way he doesn't expect us."

"You hope," Ingefær said. But she had a twinkle in her eyes.

Aye. I hoped. I wished to be done with this job, so I could take my wife home so we could do husbandly and wifely things together.

I stood. "Does it make sense to buy a vial of healing before heading out?"

She nodded. "Yes. And the Shrine of Eirene is near at hand."

Mick lunged to his feet. "Your time's up, Retzlaff. *Hic.*"

Despite my misgivings, and Ingefær's too, we had little choice with the compel invocation—we would soldier on.

Time to break the law in pursuit of a miscreant. I cheered up at the thought.

## Chapter Fifteen

# WATERFALL SECRETS

## INGEFÆR

We exited the library a little wiser, but with no better plan than to seek a hidden entrance. I looked up at the cloud-covered sky. It was late and we hadn't eaten in quite a while.

"I think we should spend the night and head out in the morning." I pointed at the darkest of the clouds. "It's going to rain soon."

Mick grumbled. "Rain don't do nothing."

Rory said, "Aye. We could tough it out and arrive at Retzlaff's manor around the mid of night. But that leaves us with nothing but moonlight. And further assumes the clouds clear off. We'll need light to find clues. Ingefær is right—we go with the sun. We'll sleep on it and head out at first light."

After a quick jaunt to the Temple, where we acquired a vial of healing for the princely sum of a hundred silver, we secured two rooms at an inn near the east gates of the city. Rory bought bread, a bag of Anna apples—one of the few to ripen early in the season—and a smoked leg of lamb for our evening meal and for our journey. I bought grain for the horses and the donkey and fed them in the inn's adjoining stables.

After eating our meal with little conversation, we turned in for the night, securing two rooms.

While snuggling in our bed—the first privacy Rory and I'd had in two days—I asked, "What do you think of Mick?"

"I'm beginning to like the squirt. Retzlaff took advantage of him."

"Hmm. I agree. But his personality isn't well suited for confrontation." Especially when the need for stealth was at a premium.

Rory cupped my head in the crook of his arms. "He spoke up against Elise. Maybe not with force. But the intent was there."

"I'm scared."

"What? My wife doesn't get scared. She worries...a lot." Rory looked deep into my eyes. "Do we saddle up in the morning and ride for Tyrrby?"

"No. You're right. I'm worried. We've never dealt with an illusionist before." Illusionists were so rare, they weren't mentioned in any of the books I'd read over the past eighteen moons.

Rory grunted. "We'll have to question everything."

I chewed on my lower lip. *If we have time to think.*

Rory smiled and leaned in close. "Let me do that for you." He nibbled at my lip, then pressed his mouth against mine.

We put aside our thoughts about the job and focused on each other.

By morning, refreshed in every way, we saddled up after loading our fresh supplies.

Mick said, "I'll walk. Can't ride with the sword down my hip."

The donkey wouldn't go faster with him on it, so I didn't mind. I scrutinized the young lad's rear. "Huh. Can't see a thing."

"You admiring his butt?" Rory asked, a twinkle in his eyes.

"No. Trying to spot the short sword outline."

"Hey!" Mick turned around. "You's can go first."

I laughed. "No. Rory will lead; you're in the middle—"

"And my wife can appreciate the view," Rory finished.

"Cad!" But it was all I had time to say as Rory heeled Muffin to set us off.

We took rest breaks along the way, but our conversation was sparse. We knew where we were going, but not what to expect when we got there.

When we reached the split in the path, the sun neared noon. From this far down the hill, I didn't see any part of the mansion. Either way, we were now trespassing, and Retzlaff could claim self defense in case things turned violent.

We turned left, following the stream as it meandered. I glanced over my right shoulder often, trying to spot the four-story spire. In one spot, the hills parted in the right place to provide a view. The windows still appeared shuttered. It had to be an illusion spell. But I also suspected it to be an heirloom spell, not cast by Retzlaff. Most spells waned in minutes, or at most, an hour.

"Let's speed up," I said. "In case the old buzzard is watching."

The stream burbled beside us as we half-trotted and Mick jogged.

Arriving in the narrow gorge of the waterfall, Rory stopped a dozen strides from the pool. He cupped his hands around his mouth so we could hear him above the cacophony. "Let me see if anything has changed."

He traipsed from one end to the other. "Last night's rain washed everything away. At least, there are no new tracks since then."

I jumped off Thunder. "We search the area, grid by grid." This was a process I had learned while training to be an Ære Warrior, or Honor Warrior. Over five years ago, I'd entered the school, sponsored by the Order of Gixus for fifteen- and sixteen-year-olds. I had emerged as the first female to graduate.

My size and strength had helped. But what got me through was my ability to think quick on my feet and my persistence—I was too stubborn to quit. Back then, I hadn't yet felt the pull of the arcane powers of the planes.

"We searched already," Mick whined.

"Not with care," I said.

"We do it again." Rory moved off, leaving his roan mare by the pool. She lapped at the water.

Mick caught himself screeching and changed it to a curse. He clawed the air with his hands and moved in the opposite direction from me.

What had him so upset? Was it all tough talk while in town, but now that Retzlaff loomed over us, his fears had resurfaced?

I affixed a long lead line and looped the reins of the two horses and the donkey. I scooped out a handful of grain and placed it before each of them. "Be good. But give a warning if you get spooked."

Thunder was a battle-trained mount. He would whinny and stomp his hooves. But he wouldn't bolt and run. Not at first. At the sight of a svartkatt, he'd line up his rear to launch kicks. If he got the scent of a kjottspiser, though, he'd be ripping at the lead line.

Looking up, I couldn't see Rory or Mick. Where had they gone?

I hollered, cupping my hands around my mouth. "Where are you?"

Rory didn't reply, but Mick did, his voice barely audible above the roar of the water. "I's over here."

I moved in the sound's direction, though the gorge's reverberations had me off kilter. Thirty paces later, now level with the gushing water to my left, I called again. "Where?"

"Here."

I about jumped out of my skin. Mick sounded so close and so...hollow. I scanned around, but didn't see him.

Narrowing my eyes, I peered at the enormous boulder to my right and meandered toward it.

A form jumped out of the rock. "Ha!"

My brain revolted and, on instinct, I half-pulled my blade before I stopped myself.

*Mick jumped out of a rock!*

"What in the Realm?"

"A neat trick, yeah?" Mick said.

If *neat* meant being invisible one moment and not the next, I guess so. I studied the rock—another illusion incantation.

"How did you find this?"

Mick laughed. "Well, it wasn't smarts. I's walking one way and looking another and next thing I know, I tripped. Instead of bashing my skull against the rock, I fell into it."

"It's another illusion spell," I said. A damn good one, what with the sun bearing down on us.

I scanned, looking for Rory. I didn't see him anywhere. The path ended, so maybe he had climbed up to see what he could see. "Rory! Come back!"

Not sure if he could hear me over the din of the waterfall, I moved through the boulder illusion. The other side was dim, like a thick set of clouds covering the sun at dusk. Before me stood a cart, big enough to be towed behind a horse. But not one I'd want to take on a long trip. It measured a stride wide by a stride and a half long and didn't make it to my waist, height-wise.

"No horse," I said aloud.

Mick said, "There's a hidden entrance around here."

I cocked my head at him. "And you know this how?"

"Has to be. Master Belkin found the hoofprints. None went back down. So where are they?"

Alright. Good logic.

"Where are you?" Rory's shout breached the roar of the falling water.

Together, Mick and I jumped out of the boulder illusion.

"The gods!" Rory stumbled backward and almost fell into the pool.

We shared Mick's discovery once my husband caught his breath. Back inside the massive illusion, we checked over everything.

After consultation, where I agreed the cart was unlikely magicked, Rory pulled it out to inspect it under direct sunlight.

Moving the cart revealed a lever—a metallic pole, about eighteen inches tall, sticking out of the ground. It had been obscured by the spokes and shadows of the cart's wheels.

"That's a funny-looking thing to see out here," I said.

Rory pointed. "It's pointing toward the manor. What would happen if we pulled on it?"

"We're not doing anything until we check for magic." I waved Rory and Mick to one side and cast a find magic invocation. The lever didn't glow, but the illusionary boulder lit up like it was the sun itself. Instead of yellow, it was a vivid orange. The presence of magic always left a calling card. As did sigils, though their color was stark white.

Before I could stop him, Rory pulled the lever northward. Behind us, the waterfall slowed in increments until it stopped. The sudden silence hung over us, and a creepy-crawly sensation shimmied up my spine.

The water level dropped in the oblong basin. When the water had drained to mere inches, a deep rumbling noise filled the gorge as a series of stone pillars rose, creating a path to a now-revealed cavern behind the waterfall. The staircase that led to the opening of the cavern was wide enough for two hefty men to walk side-by-side, and the steps were a foot in height and a stride deep. A very easy climb.

"Well, I'll be," I said.

We'd come looking for secret passages...and we found one. I should have been thrilled, but angst tore at my gut.

Rory said, "I'm in the lead."

He stepped into the now-empty pool and walked up the pillars serving as steps. Arriving at the cavern ledge, he hopped up the last step and turned about.

Mick said, "Easy enough." He jumped into the pool and raced up the steps to join Rory.

I called out to Thunder to ease my mind. "Stay safe. Run if you have to."

Then I followed with care, stopping at the last step. Behind the waterfall, inside the cave, it was darn near pitch black after the first dozen feet.

The cavern was deep: three strides tall and maybe four wide. In the dimness, two steps in and to my right, I could make out the outlines of boxes and chests. Across from these, a massive stalagmite took up space. Surprisingly, the floor was rubble free.

Rory moved through the cave. Returning, he made an exaggerated motion and pointed with his sword at the far wall with the stalagmite. "There's a lever behind it. It's not disguised. It must turn the water off and on from in here."

Mick jumped to his feet and ran to investigate.

He was about to touch it, but I stopped him. "Don't! It might be magicked."

"But one way to find out," Rory said.

I shook my head. "No. There are two ways. One is messing with it, and the other is using magic."

Rory put a hand on my arm as I moved to the stalagmite. "I think it's safe. If the outer lever wasn't warded, then this one isn't either."

"But the one outside was disguised, hidden by an illusion," I said.

"This one was hidden, too," Rory replied. "By the waterfall."

The entire conversation wasn't about the waterfall, but about the use of magic. All mages had limits. I could cast a max of six without resting, and I'd used one just minutes ago. How many more would be needed to gain entry, to find the jarl and the ring?

Rory gave the young lad permission to touch the lever, and Mick pushed the iron rod toward the wall. The stone pillars receded in a rocky rumble before the water flowed once more. The roar was a welcome sound to my ears, though the little light we had in the cavern faded to pitch black.

We were well hidden, though our horses outside gave away the fact someone was around. The deeper I went into the cavern, the darker it got.

Rory said, "I didn't think to bring any torches."

Mick laughed.

Rory growled. "What's so funny?"

I heard Mick fumbling inside his vest. He said, "*Lis na*!"

I turned my head and squinted to avoid the sudden light. After my eyes adjusted to the illumination, about as bright as ten candles put together, I peered at the stick in his hand. The twig had a small glass globe attached to it.

My jaw dropped. "You know magic."

"Nah," Mick said. "It's a magical item. All I need to know is the command word."

Rory asked, "How did you come by it?"

Mick chewed on his tongue for a moment. "Conjurer Maerek left it lying about several moons ago."

I put my hands on my hips. He'd stolen it; I was certain. "How did you learn the command words?"

Mick smirked. "Eh. I tricked Raemoni into revealing it."

Ah, the wonder of magical items. Most required elemental power from one plane to activate; many needed representation—like wood for fire—along with gestures. Some required all the above, and a few items needed only a command word.

Rory asked, "What else you got in that pretty blue vest of yours?"

Mick smiled. "A tool or two to open a resistant door." He patted his pants pocket. "And a dash of powder to help me disappear."

"Say that again," I said.

"Well, not so much that I disappear, but a powder to blind and dumb anyone caught in it. Helps me to get away."

"Handy," Rory said.

"The light stick is stolen property." I eyed Mick. "Which you'll return when we're done here." I held out a hand. "May I?"

I borrowed the magical implement and examined it. "How long does the light last?"

Mick shrugged. "Never needed it more than an hour."

"How do you turn it off?" Rory asked.

"*Stopplys*," Mick said.

The light stayed on.

Mick said, "You's have to be holding it for the light stick to respond."

Using the magic light, I searched the area. The crates were stacked eye-high in two piles, leaving an eight-foot-wide open section between them. I jabbed with my longsword. "What do you think? A secret door?"

"One way to find out," Rory said.

I passed the light stick to Rory and cast a detect magic spell. Finished, I studied the rock wall. Before us glowed a rectangular glimmer of orange, about eight feet in height and six feet wide. An obvious outline of an exit and entry point.

"What a huge door," Mick said.

"Don't touch it. I want to check for wards." But the stone façade was clear of any white marks. I cast a dispel magic on the door, just in case.

Nothing happened. Well, nothing bad. The orange light disappeared, leaving a ragged crack in the rock wall which revealed the outline of a door. But there was no handle.

Rory came up behind me. "Stand back."

"I need to check for magic again." Sometimes wards themselves were hidden by magic. Rare, but I'd seen it done.

"No. With no ward visible, there's no reason to waste your energy to check." He turned and smiled at me. "This isn't a devious operation, with decades of planning to resist an unplanned assault. I got this."

Without a handle, all he could do was push one side, then the other. The other did it. The stone slab slapped against the inside of a tunnel.

Rock on rock. It must have been hinged and cantilevered into place, because the weight of the door had to be as much as four grown men. Yet Rory had shoved it aside like he'd swatted a fly.

With Rory holding the light stick high above his head, I peered into a shaft as dark as charcoal. The artifact allowed me to see about twenty feet before things got murky again. But if there was any metal in the light's path, it would reflect.

I sniffed the air. A smell of horse dung reached my nostrils. Followed by the stink of urine-moldy straw.

Mick crept forward to stand beside me. "Yuck. I'm no fan of dark, underground places." Then, "Eww. What's that smell?"

Which earned him a chuckle from Rory. "You have no idea the places we've crawled through." He beckoned. "I have point."

With slow steps, we hiked down a slope. As we neared a landing with a long staircase, an opening revealed itself to our left.

I peered around the corner. Two Shire horses stood in their stalls. One of the huge draft horses was black and the other grey. The grey one chewed on his railing, a sign of boredom or agitation.

When they saw us, they whinnied and stamped.

"This is atrocious," I said. "Look at this place. When's the last time they've been fed and watered?"

"Easy," Rory said. "We'll take care of them. But there's work to do."

"Hmph." I pointed at Mick. "Find a shovel and pitchfork." To Rory, "Look for fresh straw and hay or alfalfa. I'm mucking stalls."

It took a half hour to right the wrongs of the makeshift stables. I was furious with Retzlaff. Such neglect of animals...I ground my molars.

"Don't explode," Rory said.

I picked up a bristle brush. My husband sighed, but got one for himself.

"Shouldn't we be going?" Mick asked.

"Hush," I said. "I cannot let cruelty to animals pass."

Mick looked at Rory. My husband smiled. "Retzlaff's in the soup now."

I spent a quarter of an hour brushing the giant draft horses, then slipped them each an apple. They nipped my fingers as they devoured the mottled red and green fruit. "When I find your owner, I'm going to whip him good."

"Now you's talking," Mick said.

As we got back on course, I looked over my shoulder. "We'll be back for you...one way or the other."

We hiked down the stairs with Mick in the rear. I kept count: two hundred thirty-one steps. If their height was standard—which felt right to my achy knees—it was the equivalent of twenty-one stories.

Rory said, "I'm not sure, but we may be level with the mansion now." He patted the wall. "The light's not the best, but these walls are smooth. Rikk would love them."

"Who's Rikk?" Mick asked.

"A dvaerg friend of ours," I replied. I stepped to the other side of Rory. "It's a wide shaft. I could lie down on a step."

Mick looked up. "And tall, too. How far up? Twelve feet?"

"The gods!" Rory exclaimed.

I shivered. What was the purpose of making the tunnel so wide and tall?

What was Hexerei Mansion hiding?

# Chapter Sixteen

# TUNNELS

## RORY

At the bottom of the stairs, the tunnel shot forward. I suspected we were headed east, for I didn't think the stairs had turned one way or the other, and that was the last direction I had certainty about. After a hundred strides, I sensed the tunnel swept to the right, pushing us southward. I needed to check.

Stopping, I turned to Mick and handed him the light stick. I pointed with my sword, which I had drawn upon entering the staircase above. "Run up the shaft back to the stairs. Hold the light by your head."

He groused but complied, hiccupping at intervals.

Ingefær asked what I was up to.

"You'll see." When the light disappeared, I hollered. "Stop. Come back ten paces." My words echoed around me.

When Mick returned and halted, all I could see was a tiny ball of light. But the odd thing was, to look at his head, I had to lift my chin. I was looking up. The light was at the edge of the wall, too, confirming the shaft had turned.

"Oh," Ingefær said. "He's about six feet above us."

After asking him to come back, I counted his steps.

I said, "That's six feet of rise over sixty-five strides, or a three percent grade. I felt like I was leaning backward to keep from racing down the shaft, so I wanted to check. The tunnel turning is more obvious."

Ingefær pointed her sword into the depths ahead. "I heard something."

I hadn't.

Mick scurried behind me. His jaw worked like he wanted to scream. But he got a hold of himself. "Are you sure?"

"No," she replied. "Nothing is certain when you can't see. And even then, it's not certain what you're seeing is real. Remember the boulder?"

Mick hiccupped louder and more than once.

I put a finger to my lips, then turned and peered down the shaft and saw...nothing.

Taking the light stick from Mick, I took the lead. In my other hand, I gripped my sword.

Step by step, we walked down the tunnel. It wasn't straight, but it didn't turn sharply either. Just drifted rightward.

After maybe ten minutes of hiking, making it a half-mile long tunnel at our cautious pace, we stopped twenty paces short of a giant double set of doors. The doors weren't the problem, but the huge purple spider was. It had to be four feet long and two feet wide, with legs as long as mine. And as hairy as a dvaerg's chin.

*The gods! I have never seen a spider that big before.*

Mick shrieked.

The spider's protruding hair made it look bigger than it was. I lied to myself. The damn thing would be huge even if I'd shaved it.

It must have heard Mick caterwauling and raced up the side of the tunnel wall, head high. Scurrying, it advanced toward us.

Mick screamed in one long, loud note.

I cursed, for I'd left my crossbow with my horse.

With my blade at the ready, I raced forward to meet it halfway. Spiders were quick. But if anyone could sidestep its mandibles, it was me. I hoped the purple arachnid wasn't poisonous.

With my aggressive move toward it, its hairy legs slowed. It stopped advancing and climbed higher up the wall. Out of reach of my sword, unless I jumped.

Behind me, Ingefær told Mick to shush. "Get a grip."

I lunged and stabbed, but the enormous spider reared back. How it stayed up there was beyond me. The walls were smooth. Yet there it perched; its mandibles opened wider than my head. Goop dripped from them.

*Poison!*

At the visible confirmation of my prior thought, Roskva, my pinkish-orange foot-tall fylgjæ, sparked into being. She gave me speed without tiring. But what I needed was height or an ability to jump five feet into the air.

Ingefær fired a blast of her fiery darts, lancing the arachnid three times. The shortened, magical arrows struck its head and abdomen with a squelch.

The spider lunged at me!

With magically-sped feet, I moved rearward and hoisted my blade into its path.

The scrunch of pierced skeletal mass brought bile up my throat. Its sudden weight caused my sword arm to dip. With a rush of frantic energy, I flung the blade tip toward the double doors, but held on to the hilt of my sword. The arachnid flew off and slammed against the doors, leaving a trail of ooze as it slid to the floor.

Hairy legs spasmed in the air. I blew air out I'd been holding. "It's dead."

Roskva winked out of sight.

Behind me, Mick shut up, but his hiccups returned.

"You sure?" Ingefær asked.

I shrugged. To be certain, I would have to advance and stab it a couple of more times. Peering down the tunnel, I spotted an intricate, silvery web.

Ingefær joined me. "Wait a minute. It's purple. No such spider exists."

I looked at her, then pointed with my blade. "That disagrees with you."

Mick hiccupped but had crept forward to stand behind us. "I's never seen one so monstrous."

"Buck up. You'll see worse someday." I blew more air out. "I hope not today."

"No," Ingefær said. "Purple spiders four feet long don't exist. Anywhere."

"You shot it with your fiery darts!"

It was her turn to point. "See."

I looked at the dead spider. "Yeah. I see it." Hefting my blade before her eyes, I said, "I got its guts all over my sword."

Ingefær grabbed my blade and ran her hand up it. She showed me her hand.

I thought about barfing at the sight of the yellowish mucus on her fingers.

She licked her hand. "There are no guts. There're no spiders."

"What—?" Mick said, then hiccupped, then burped like he'd gulped a tankard of ale.

"It's an illusion," Ingefær hiked to the door and walked around. She walked to the spider and kicked at it.

The hairy thing flopped...but it didn't move quite right. I blinked twice, thinking. No way would Ingefær lick the guts of a spider off her hand.

In an eye blink, the huge purple spider, all gooey guts splayed out on its belly, popped out of sight. It was my turn. "What?!"

"An illusion. It's not there."

I blinked once more. The webbing was gone. "That's not a magic I like."

She grumbled. "No. I know nothing of illusion spells."

Mick walked forward. He kicked at air. "What are you's talking about? It's here."

Ingefær moved to Mick and put her hands around his face. He tried to jerk free, but she held tight. "It's not. You have to disbelieve it exists."

She waved at me to come. "See his blade. What do you see?" She licked her hands again. "See?"

Mick scowled. Then scrunched his eyes shut for a moment. Opening them, his head swung to the spot he'd kicked. "Oh. He's wicked mean."

I closed my eyes. A prayer to the gods would be in order...except they sucked worse than spiders. Oh, the gods existed, I knew—locked away on their plane. But they were all mean and selfish and happy to see us all dead. Which left me with no one worthy to pray to. And I longed to do exactly that.

I cocked my head, recalling the sequence of events of our little imaginary skirmish. "Roskva didn't show until I thought I saw poison on its mandibles."

Ingefær smiled. It creeped me out. Purple hairy spiders are not to be smiled about.

"Roskva didn't show until you felt your life was in danger. She's your clue if what you're seeing is real or not."

I scratched my head, puzzling over how my fylgjæ's presence would make a difference. There were times Roskva showed before I knew I was in trouble. "That's a very thin line." With the purple spider, I believed my eyes.

"I's confused," Mick said. "Who's Roskva?"

I re-explained my talent. "It's how I could catch you. Well, I can catch you without her, but she makes me all the faster."

Mick grinned. "You big cheater."

I forced a smile. "Listen, Mick. You have to control your screaming. Down here, it could be life and death."

Mick stared at his feet. "I know."

Ingefær put hands to hips. "Loud noises attract beasts and brigands. Almost always in numbers. Alright?"

Mick nodded. "Sorry."

After we caught our breath, we examined the door without touching it. It was made of wood...based on its color and apparent texture. It had three faded yellow, overlapping triangles etched into it at eye height, each one as tall as my head. It was an old door, and cracks and crevices lined the joined planks. At the bottom, the gap was wide enough for a rat to crawl through. But not a huge purple spider.

I didn't think the door was an illusion, but now I doubted everything I set my eyes on.

Mick said, "This tunnel creeps me out."

I put an arm around his shoulders. "Aye. Me, too."

Ingefær said, "What's a mansion like this need tunnels for? Why a secret entrance through a waterfall?" She shook her head. "Why did Jarl Retzlaff want the signet ring so much he had to devise such an intricate plan to steal it?"

All good questions. But I had no answers.

She pulled a skin of water from her backpack and took a drink. "Anyone else?"

We each took a swig. I eyed the door. "Now what?"

Ingefær waved us behind her and pinched green powder from one of her belt pouches. She waved her hands and muttered in Varanusian. She shook her head. "Nothing."

Then her legs wobbled.

In an eye blink, I was at my wife's side, holding her up. "Maybe we should rest?"

She growled, but kissed me on my cheek. "I know you hate waiting."

"True, fair lady. But I know you've but one spell left in you before you go horizontal."

"You's talking funny," Mick said.

"Excuse our banter," I said. "We're discussing tactics in a circular way."

Mick rolled his eyes at me.

I kept track of Ingefær's spells, just like she did. Except she liked to be chivalrous about it and push herself. She'd hit five, and the sixth one would put her on the ground. The last thing we needed was for her to pass out during battle and smack her noggin.

"Time to use the vial," I said. "It's why we bought it."

Ingefær shook her head. "It's too soon. We've barely explored anything."

"True enough. But like you said, I hate waiting, and we're hours away from the dinner bell. So, drink up, my love."

She objected. "What if one of you gets hurt? We should save it."

I leveled my eyes at her. "We should have bought more. But neither you nor I expected to find...this. Remember the book at the library? All the caverns?" Seeing her pout, I upped the stakes for her. "It's like you said...we've scarcely explored anything. And the horses are waiting."

She snarled her nose at me, then puckered her lips and blew me a kiss. She dug through her rucksack, pulled out the vial of healing, and quaffed it.

Since she wasn't injured, just exhausted with her magical stamina nearing depletion, her healing process had no physical manifestation—no itching, no burning, no discomfort at all. So she'd told me several times before.

Ingefær cleared her throat. "I'm ready to go."

Grunting, I switched my attention to the waist-high pewter handle set in the wooden door. "Get ready," I said. "I'm going to open it."

Ingefær hefted her sword waist high.

I turned to Mick. “Ready?”

He put a hand into his blue vest, pulled out a sling, and set a stone in it. “Yep.”

I smiled, recalling his boasts about his weapon assortment—but I hadn’t seen him sneak it into the vest. “By the way, your slingshot could have been useful against the spider.” If it had been a real one.

“Oh, yeah.”

I tugged and pushed while yanking the door handle up and down. Nothing. Neither the handle nor the door would budge. “It’s either locked or it’s stuck.”

“Move aside, you barbarian.” Mick elbowed past me and tucked his weapon into a hip pocket.

I clenched my jaw rather than retort in a manner appropriate for the cocky scoundrel.

Mick’s hand flashed inside his blue vest once more, this time coming out with a shiny, flat, thin piece of metal. “Hold the light up.”

I did so. Mick scraped with the implement, swearing often. After a few minutes, there was a snap.

“Oy. That did it.” Mick stepped back and swept his arm in a bow. “After you, Master Belkin.”

I gave him an eye roll and swung the handle down while pulling. The door opened with a modest squeal and a rush of stale air. The shaft we stood in was met with a crossing tunnel, lit in an eerie blue.

“Odd taste in lighting,” Ingefær said.

An understatement. *Gloomy* didn’t quite cut it. Mick hiccupped. *Scary* was more accurate.

I peeked through the opening and scanned the walls. High up, sconces dotted the walls every twenty feet. No flicker of flame. The light had to be magic.

The tunnel before us ran left to right. Its width was about the same as the shaft we were in. The floor looked to be level, with no ascent or descent.

I said, "I don't like the looks of this. Underground tunnels cris-crossing is an easy way to get lost. We should mark the tunnel we came down."

"Uh oh," my wife said.

"What now?" I asked without turning around, keeping my eyes on the shadowed walls.

"I need to pee."

Mick guffawed. I turned to glare at him.

"What?" he asked, looking peevish. "I do, too."

Of all the complications to arise when facing a blue-hazed tunnel. Then, I got an idea. "I know a way to mark the tunnel. One at a time, we go do our business on the other side of the door. Yeah?"

I handed the glow stick to Ingefær, and Mick and I stepped into the tunnel to give her privacy. Then she traded spots with Mick to give him a go. And to ensure my bodily needs didn't surface at the wrong time, I went last. The urine would dry, but it would darken the stone for days.

Closing the door on our piddles, I surveyed our new tunnel. "Counting our time since arriving at the waterfall, we've been at this for a good two hours."

Mick shrugged.

Ingefær said, "The horses have feed, and water is nearby."

"But they have no protection," I said. Neither did we. Which is why my wife had agreed to drink the potion—to have enough firepower to deal with whatever we came up against.

By day in the gorge, the horses should be alright. By night, we were risking their lives. Thunder would scare off a lone wulv, but not a pack. A svartkatt would be hard to convince to leave them alone. And Muffin wasn't as beast-proof as Thunder. One whiff of any predator and she'd be jerking at the lead to get away. We needed to get back to them as soon as we could.

Mick took the light stick from me and doused it. "Don't need it here. Saving it, in case there is a limit to its magic."

I eyed him in the blue cast and nodded. He's suggested a very sensible thing.

With the white light gone, the blueness of the tunnel reminded me of swimming under water. I could see, but everything before me moved in waves, and all of it tinted cerulean.

Ingefær sidled up beside me. "What are these tunnels for?"

"Well, one leads outside to a secret entrance," I said.

"Be serious." She slapped my arm.

"No idea," I replied.

The light in the tunnel caused shadows to flicker, revealing a general outline but no concrete details. Off to the right, thirty strides down the shaft, there seemed to be a darkened outline in the wall, about the size of a door. Presumably the south wall, if I hadn't gotten turned around.

I said, "Follow me." I edged my way down the new tunnel until I could better identify the dark shape.

When I stopped, Mick bumped into me.

"Watch what you're doing."

"Sorry, Master Belkin, I's looking at the ceiling, making sure it's spider free."

The gods! I had forgotten and scanned quick.

Ingefær said, "Remember, the spider was an illusion."

"Don't mean there couldn't be real ones," Mick retorted.

"He's right," I said. "But I see nothing."

Returning my focus to the dark outline, I groaned. It wasn't a door, but an opening. "It's another tunnel."

The gap in the tunnel wall ate the blue light like night eats day. Stepping closer, I peered around the wall's edge. Everything before me was cast in a green hue, even eerier than the blue light.

I grumbled. "Stairs. Going down."

Ingefær jabbed with her sword, pointing back in the direction we'd come. "What if we'd turned left? What's the other way?"

I followed her blade and scanned the tunnel, then chuckled. "You must be tired, 'cause you think I know."

She shook her head. "Not tired, but hungry."

We hadn't eaten since breakfast. My stomach was in knots, but not from hunger.

Mick waved a hand for us to follow and returned to the door we'd entered through. Before we passed, he double-checked the handle, seeing if it still swung open. "Good. It didn't relock."

He led us in the direction Ingefær had asked about. Forty strides later, we reached a sharp turn of the tunnel to our right. An unpleasant odor reached my nostrils.

"What's that smell?" I asked.

Two shakes of heads. Mick shuffled forward and we came upon a jail. Iron bars set in the rock for six strides. To one side was an iron-barred door.

Mick reached a hand out.

"Don't touch it." Ingefær sidled beside him. "It could be magicked."

"Why would anyone ward a jail door?" Mick asked.

I said, "She speaks from experience. Light your glow stick."

Mick did so, and we examined the jail cell. It was but four strides deep. "Maybe twenty bodies could be crammed in there."

And I knew where the stench came from. "That's troll shit."

A score of piles littered the floor.

Ingefær snarled. "Gross. But where's the troll?"

It was Mick's and my turn to shake our heads.

But the troll crap wasn't the gruesome part. The cell contained shackles along the back wall and a pillory on the right side. Along the left wall were iron bars about a stride long laying next to a makeshift firepit. Gray ash spilled out of it.

"What's that for?" Mick asked.

"Torture," Ingefær replied.

"You heat one end and poke it into people's guts, eyes, arms," I said. "Whatever you want., depending on how patient or cruel you wanted to be."

Mick hiccupped.

Ingefær said, "Not a bench or a blanket or...anything. Just scat all over."

"I doubt the torture devices have been used recently." I motioned with a hand. "I suggest we keep moving. And keep a sharp eye out for trolls."

Mick hiccupped. "More than one?"

"Don't know," I replied.

There were nods of agreement, and Mick doused the white light.

We meandered down the hall for a minute and came upon a set of stairs going up.

I scowled. "Not sure we should go up just yet."

"We're here to arrest Retzlaff," Ingefær said. "Odds are, he's above us in the manor."

"Aye." I chewed on my lower lip. "But we searched upstairs yesterday and didn't find him. Perhaps by now he knows we escaped. Maybe he's down here...somewhere. Like you asked earlier, what's it all for? What's he hiding? It might give us a clue as to his abilities, and maybe, just maybe, we'll find him."

Her nose twitched, and she twirled a lock of her short hair. "Perhaps before going up the stairs, we should go past the green-lit tunnel and see what's beyond it."

We were grasping at dreki scales. A dangerous game. Truth was, we didn't know which way to go, which way would lead to success. What we needed was a sound strategy. But so far, Retzlaff's tunnels proved to be a cypher.

We went back again, this time past the green-lit tunnel with the stairs going down.

A hundred feet later, we found a door on the left side of the tunnel, though the tunnel continued on.

I reached for the door handle and got my hand slapped.

Ingefær said, "We check things first before touching."

I stifled a tart reply. "Well, we're past the illusion protection spell, so I figured we'd be safe."

She motioned me behind her and cast a find magic incantation. Nothing glowed.

"See?" I said, maybe a little too cavalierly.

"See if I drag your butt out of the fire."

"I deserved that," I said. "Sorry."

I tried the handle. Locked. I looked at Mick. "Care to amaze us with your skills?"

He chuckled. "Barbarian."

It didn't take long to hear the snap. I think he was getting a hang of things.

"Thanks," I said as I turned and pushed. The door swung in. It was quite dark. The blue cast of the main tunnel did little to reveal the room's size and contents.

Mick flicked his glow stick to life with his magic words.

I scanned the floor, then the walls and ceilings, arachnids on my mind. But the room contained nothing but crates.

Stepping in, the apparent storage room stank of mold and...rodent droppings. My nose curled of its own accord.

Ingefær's lips twisted. "Yuck."

Mick and I lifted the lid of a crate. Rats scurried out from under the box, evoking a soft shriek from Ingefær.

"Really?" I said. "I know you've faced tougher beasts. Hel, even Mick didn't scream."

She stuck her tongue out at me.

I spun around. "It's a good place to rest if needed. We could close the door and barricade it against entry." I found my wife's blue eyes filled with horror. "But I'd rather be done exploring before we need to rest."

We poked around a few more crates, chasing rats off to find a new place to scurry to. One storage box had blankets. Another, jars of honey. And a third, sacks of Lodi apples.

But the yellow apples had been chewed on and shat upon. Rats didn't care what they munched on. I stirred the pile with the tip of my sword. "They're wrinkled and soft. Have to be at least a week old."

Mick made a croaking-gagging sound.

I turned to check on him. He got down on all fours and puked his guts out. It was all bile, as we hadn't eaten since dawn.

Why foodstuff here? Why forget about it and let the rats spoil it? I had too many questions in need of answering. But these were low priority. I grabbed a jar of honey, dusted it, and put it in my backpack.

Ingefær scowled at me. "I should have checked it for magic."

I shrugged. "Door wasn't. Besides, the rats would have set it off."

She shook her head. "What if they're an illusion?"

I chuckled. "That's a Hel of a spell, if it can fake the stench of rat turds."

"Let's move on," I said, and moved to the door. "Which way? Further west, or back east and up the stairs?"

Ingefær pouted. "Seeing this storage room, I think he's farther down the green-lit tunnel or upstairs."

"Mick?" I asked.

"I get a say?" Mick looked at me with bright brown eyes. He wiped a sleeve across his mouth. "Uh. I think up. I don't like it down here. At least, we should make sure he isn't up there before going further."

"A sound plan. Shouldn't take but an hour to check the mansion. At least I'm pretty sure we're underneath it."

Ingefær said, "And there's the secret passage to check out."

The one she thought lay behind the lone painting. If she thought there was one there, I didn't doubt her.

Plan made, we headed back out into the blue-lit tunnel, closing the door on the rats. Good riddance—rodents were said to cause maladies, especially amongst the young.

Since we'd come through the secret waterfall entrance, other than killing an illusory spider, we had made very little progress in our pursuit of arresting Retzlaff.

I hoped the mage was upstairs, because searching for him down here creeped me out.

## Chapter Seventeen

# DEADLY DUNGEON

## INGEFÆR

As we walked east, again, through the blue-lit tunnel, I asked, "Do we try to arrest him or go straight into battle mode?"

Rory chuckled. "You know my thoughts."

Mick guffawed. "I like your approach, mister."

"I think we should *try* to arrest him first," I said.

Rory shook his head. "I'm not saying we kill him on sight. But we shouldn't give him a chance to wag a hand and befuddle our minds with an invocation."

I curled my nose. "You have a point."

Rory said, "After he's subdued, I'll inform him of his mistakes, proving he was involved in a theft. Item one: his knowledge Mick is a thief. Two: his locking us up. I'll tell him all we were trying to do is to retrieve the ruby ring, and if possible, the topaz jewel and vial of healing."

I fingered my snowflake with its pearl center. "If it comes to it, we'll mention Elise's spell, which protects him from being taken to the Order of Gixus."

Mick growled. He started soft, but his voice grew in volume as he went. "That goblin turd burns me up. Now that I's think about it, he must have done something to my mind. And he thinks he can get away with it?"

Rory shushed Mick, who tugged at his hair, a prelude to one of his tirades.

We stopped walking, and I hugged the lad. "Don't worry, we'll find him." I looked him in the eye. "You have my word. Come on, let's head upstairs."

And I meant it. Mick was alright. He didn't have an evil mind...he just needed to have the line between right and wrong, good and evil, painted clearer.

I decided Rory was right—we would go with the direct approach. The secret waterfall entrance had been intriguing but taxing. I had hoped it would lead us inside the mansion, where we could have investigated, but it wound up being a diversion.

We bypassed the green-lit tunnel going down deeper into the morass. The sight of it disturbed my inner sense of calm. The book I'd read at the library mentioned giant caverns—which we had yet to see—but never said what was in them.

Who, in his or her right mind, created a half-mile long tunnel with a secret waterfall entrance? What illegalities had been performed in those caves for the past eon?

As we approached the turn in the tunnel and the jail we'd seen earlier, Rory asked Mick to light his stick. Taking it from the lad, Rory led the way, holding it high in the air so we could all see in the flickering, shadowy blue light.

We passed by the jail and its torture equipment and continued on our way to the stairs.

Rory stepped onto the bottom tread.

*Zat. Zzit. Zzip.*

A dozen darts of magical energy jolted out of the walls, stabbing him in his arms, sides, and legs. He crumpled to the floor.

"Rory!" I shrieked.

Mick grabbed me. "Careful, now. There may be more traps."

"Who traps their own stairs?" I yelled at him. But he hung on, pulling me back.

Rory groaned and rolled off the bottom step and onto his backside. Lying on the tunnel floor, his eyes glazed over. He croaked. "Ow."

Seeing he wasn't dead, I cast a find magic incantation on the staircase. The bottom and top steps both lit up in bright shades of orange. And both bore a triangular glyph painted white. A ward.

"Holy Tordenvaer," I mumbled, though I no longer followed the god.

"I don't feel so good." Rory rolled to his hands and knees.

"Careful, Master Belkin," Mick said. "Don't touch the step."

"The bottom and top steps are magicked and warded." I helped Rory to his wobbly feet. I was mumbling the obvious. "But you know that."

"I-I-I need a healer." Rory's eyes had clouded over. His jawbone clenched tight.

His legs quivered, and the arm he used to hold on to me jittered. I've seen him take eight fiery darts before, but not all at once. Twelve had damn near killed him.

Mad at Retzlaff, I spat at the ground. "I'm going to kill him." Taking a breath, I asked, "Can you walk?"

I had always sympathized when Rory complained about losing loved ones. Not since losing my sister—and my parents ten years before—had I felt the stab of an ephemeral dagger twisting in my heart.

My guts jumbled. *Please don't die on me.*

Rory wobbled. "With your-*ugh*-help, and Mick's, too."

I'd been blasted with fiery darts before, too. It had roiled my insides, burned and itched, caused convulsions, and created an overwhelming urge to hurl. But that had been four darts, two at a time. I cursed myself for using our only vial of healing on me.

Mick and I each got under an arm, and we walked back to the first tunnel.

As we shuffled our way out, bypassing a drying stain in the shaft with the illusory purple spider, I thanked the tunnel builders for making them so wide.

By the time we'd climbed the long, steep staircase, my knees trembled and ached. The score of minute-long respites had helped little. Rory was bathed in sweat, and his head hung on his chest. I hoped we hadn't taken too much time to climb.

We passed by the Shire mounts, and for a moment I considered taking them with us. A look at Rory told me he didn't have the time.

"I'll be back for you," I told them.

Inside the cave behind the waterfall, we sat down. I checked on my husband, who was hot to the touch. He was awake, but white as a bedsheet, glistening like he'd run ten leagues, and he groaned constantly. His eyes refused to focus.

"Can you keep going?" I asked.

He grunted. "No-*ugh*-choice."

I swung my gaze to the stalagmite and the lever behind it. I asked Mick to switch it, which he did.

The roar of the waterfall subsided. I joined Mick on the cave's ledge, and we watched the flow of water slow to a trickle. The sun hung low in the western skies. The dinner bell would toll in about an hour. We had been down there longer than I had thought.

Manic Mick giggled. "I like to watch the water receding."

His humor was out of place, but he didn't mean any harm. Waiting for the water to drain and Rory to catch his breath, curiosity got a hold of me, and I watched the stone pillars rise as the water receded.

I cast a find magic spell and pointed. "They're magicked."

But when I'd cast a find magic incantation on the levers, they hadn't shone orange at all. "Why didn't the levers glow?"

"Beats me lady, I don't understand magic. Much to my mother's chagrin."

We gathered Rory to his feet, fortunate the stone pillar pathway was wide enough for three bodies hugging each other. With Mick on the left and me holding Rory up on the right, we ambled our way down the stone staircase and across the bottom of the pool to the path's edge.

We half dragged Rory to the tethered horses.

Muffin whinnied, but all Thunder did was snort.

I set Rory down on the ground and kissed my horse, soothing away his annoyance with me. I picked up the empty feed sack and readied the mounts to ride.

"You figure we should turn the waterfall back on?" Mick asked.

I nodded.

Mick stepped through the giant boulder. Seconds later, he came out. The stone pillars ground like marbles on marbles as they descended. The gush of water soon covered the crunching gravel noise with its own roar.

I smiled at Mick. "At least we know the way is safe if we ever come back."

"*If*? Don't be getting cold feet, lady. There's my loot to recover."

I eyed him.

"And a deal to honor, one you's made with my ma."

He was too young to be so manipulative. "We're compelled," I reminded him.

Mick looked at the ground. "Aye. That ain't right."

With the horses ready to ride, Mick and I got Rory into the saddle, and I led us through the narrow gorge.

By the time we reached the bottom of the trail, Rory had leaned into his roan mare's neck and stayed there. He responded about a third of the time I yelled at him—he was in a bad way.

Something was odd about those darts. Fiery and sparking darts do their damage. If they don't kill outright, then that's that. Over time, you recover. Might take hours if not days. But Rory was faring worse than expected.

I turned to Mick. "We have to ride ahead. You keep going with the donkey, alright?"

"You's leaving me alone?"

"I have to hurry. I don't know how much time Rory has."

Switching my grip, I took the reins to Rory's mare. With a heel kick and a *hiya*, I took off at a canter—an easier gait for Rory to stay put in the saddle. Though without Rory posting, it was hard on the mare's back.

I cursed the gods for the long ride back ahead of us. Then I begged them for mercy. Yeah, I was a mess. If they could have, they would have sent a lightning bolt to ensure our demise.

## Chapter Eighteen

# HEALING

## RORY

At a shout from Ingefær, I pried my eyes open. Shadows shifted. Were the clouds rolling over the moon? When had we gone outside?

My muscles spasmed willy-nilly; my guts cramped. I wanted to let my bowels go…so bad.

I had a hard time focusing enough to make out any shapes, Ingefær included. "Where are-*ugh*-we?"

Was I having a nightmare? Why couldn't I see straight?

"We're outside the Shrine of Eirene. I need to get you down off Muffin and inside. But unless you help me, I'm going to drop you."

The smell of a sweaty horse pushed through my haze. Why were we at the Shrine?

I think I waved my hand at my wife. "Who-*ugh*-needs-*ugh*…"

Pain lanced through the fog in my mind. The gods, I was hot. And my guts roiled, ready to explode into a ball of fiery shit.

"*Ugh*. Let them, let them-*ugh*-come out."

*Smack.*

My cheek kind of stung. "Huh. What?"

"Wake up. You have to move."

I think I waved my hand at her. "S'alright. I'm just-just resting-*ugh*-my eyes."

*Smack.*

A dull ache reverberated from my cheek to my spine.

"What, woman? Jeez."

I threw up. Well, that's what it felt like. My body heaved, my throat clenched, and a bit of spittle foamed at my mouth.

Nasty taste. Bitter. I cleansed my tongue by scraping it over my teeth.

I lifted myself in the saddle. Squinting, I peered at a stone wall before me. The clouds parted, and the moonlight illuminated the ground and a wide doorway. "Where...where-*ugh*-are we?"

Ingefær jerked me out of the saddle. A sort of controlled fall took place. I hit the ground hard, jarring my head and bludgeoning my body.

The blow helped me to focus. I knew what I wanted: to curl up and die. "Leave me-*ugh*-be."

"Since leaving the mansion, those are the first words you've uttered that I understood," she said.

Her hands gripped mine. "Get up."

She pulled and pulled until I stumbled up and forward, right into her arms. My nose cracked against her forehead. "Ow."

I tried to jerk free but failed. She gripped me by my belt and dragged me toward the open door. Crossing the threshold, I crumbled to the ground; my legs felt like butter left in the sun.

My eyes closed, and I had no will to keep them open....

...I found myself lying flat on my back with four pairs of eyes looking down at me. All belonging to women based on the length of their hair. One set of eyes was green and almond-shaped. An alvae? Where was I?

"Hi, ladies." My tongue was dry and felt thick. "It's nice to see you. What, may I ask, is the purpose of your visit?"

Ingefær's blue eyes came into focus right above my head. "Oh, Rory. I'm so happy you're alright. You almost died."

"No." I shook my head, but stopped. The piercing pain convinced me of the error of my ways. "I took a nap, is all."

The light-green-skinned female with her emerald eyes said, "He's dehydrated. Even after our spells. He should drink a lot of water...and get some rest."

Ingefær said, "Thank you for your aid. How much do we owe you?"

I didn't hear the number, as memories of me riding my mare flashed. *Riding* being a generous term. Was Muffin's mane what I tasted on my tongue?

And before that, we'd been in a tunnel. I had wanted to walk up the stairs.

The ladies in the healer tunics walked off, leaving Ingefær to tower over me.

She studied my eyes. "Are you alright? You seem drunk."

"Drunk with your beauty."

She scowled. "The healers said there might be a side effect."

To what? Whatever did she mean?

"Forgive me, my bride, but why are we here?"

"You got stung with magical darts of energy. Well, most of them were of that variety. One wasn't."

She held up a two-inch long needle. "This one had poison on it."

Out of the corner of my eye, I spotted Mick waving a hand at me.

"Oh. Retzlaff. The rat bastard." But I couldn't put much punch into it. Under normal conditions, I could shout and curse with the best of them. But at the moment, the well seemed dry. "What kind of healing spell did they use?"

"They used a regular heal spell the first time. But while that took the imminent danger of you dying away—cut your fever—you still wouldn't wake up. We waited for an hour. You remained unconscious, and they used another. Right about then, Mick showed up. Based on his suggestion, we, uh, undressed you. It's how we found this." She grinned. "Buried in your right butt cheek."

"Hmm. It's unfortunate that I don't remember any of it."

"I pulled it out with my teeth."

My mouth flung open. She was having me on. "Ha, ha."

"Good. You're coming around."

And in an eye blink, I remembered what had happened. The magical trap on Retzlaff's staircase. "Troll magic."

I cursed through grinding teeth. I'd been whacked with a mace before. Sliced and stabbed with daggers and blades. And punched in the face more times than I had fingers and toes. They all hurt, but in ways I understood.

Magic darts of fire and energy hurt altogether in a different manner. It's like scalding your skin on an open flame, yet it was my innards that had felt that way. And, well, I'd never been poisoned before.

"The poison almost killed me?"

She nodded. "It's a good thing we raced back. Another hour..." She shook her head, tears welling in her eyes.

Rising to a sitting position, hammers pounding inside my head, I cupped her chin in my hand. "Oh, dear. I'm so sorry. I was just going up the stairs."

We hugged, which turned into a kiss. A rather long and luscious one. "Hmm."

A throat cleared. I disengaged and looked at the young thief.

Mick's wide brown eyes were locked on us. "Retzlaff is a gobbling turd. Warding his own steps."

Ingefær's words bounced around my head. "When did you get here?" I asked him.

"He arrived about an hour after the first heal spell didn't cure you," Ingefær said.

Mick raised his hands in mock surrender. "I didn't search you's though."

"Thank goodness," I said.

"I's didn't know you's two were so wealthy," Mick said.

I frowned. What was he talking about? I looked at him, then at Ingefær, my brows furrowing.

Ingefær said, "He saw me pay for the services. Three hundred silver."

"Ouch."

"All in gold coins," Mick said, his voice rising. "I's don't see gold coins very often. And you's has a pouch full."

"We don't advertise," I said. Plus, most of it was going for goods and services to build a home and start a farming operation.

I slid off the bench and stretched my back. "I'm hungry."

Ingefær licked her lips. "We need to talk."

I lifted my chin. "About?"

"Finishing this job." She looked at Mick, then at me. "Do we go on? Or do we quit?"

Mick said, "Aw, don't quit. I hasn't got my loot back." He grinned. "I mean, you's haven't finished the job."

Ingefær's lips firmed, and her hands went to her hips. Uh oh.

"My husband almost died. And for what? A thousand silver for us and the return of the ring? None of it is worth his life."

The room stayed silent; despite the approaching Summer Solstice, frost chilled the air.

I asked the obvious. "And the compel spell?"

Ingefær's lips pursed for a moment. "We'll have to convince Elise to remove it."

Mick half-shouted. "Ha. Good luck. She's stubborn when she wants something. And she wants the ring. And her job."

I scratched my neck. "Well, we screwed up by going through the waterfall. We should have gone in through the front door. Hashed it out, face to face."

Having almost been killed by his traps, I lumped Retzlaff in the same category as a brigand. And I hated brigands. Retzlaff would not get away with his pilfering and his deadly dungeon. If we didn't come out smelling like justice, I didn't mind. Vengeance suited me.

I knew how to get to Ingefær—I used an idea that bothered her almost as much as the risk of me dying. "If we don't go, a thief will get away with the crime. I say we arrest him and bring him to justice."

"Hear, hear," Mick said, nodding.

Ingefær wagged a finger at me. "It's not worth any of our lives."

"It's not," I said. "But justice demands sacrifice. We are officers of the law."

Mick said, "You's can't let that goblin turd get away with it. You can't."

I piled on, using Ingefær's own logic. "It's our first job. Our reputation is critical if our business is to succeed."

Her hands crossed under her bosom. "Hmph. I thought you wanted to play at farming?"

I smiled. "Well, I do. But after being poisoned, I think I want a little vengeance, too."

Her blue eyes twinkled. "Aye. Vengeance for nearly killing my love."

I stepped to her and wrapped her in my arms. "My love."

We kissed, tender. Then deep.

"Oh, geez," Mick said. "Enough of that...stuff."

I disengaged and tousled his hair. "You'll understand one day."

I looked at my wife. "So, we go on? The front door?"

She nodded. "But we prepare ourselves. We need more vials of healing. And maybe a potion for poison, too."

Mick said, "Now you's talking."

We agreed to go on. I hated seeing bravado in others and hoped I wasn't failing in a similar fashion.

"But first, we eat," I said.

"And get a good night's rest," Ingefær added. "We ride back at dawn."

My stomach rumbled. "But first, I need a privy."

# Chapter Nineteen

# SERAFINA

## RORY

After visiting the outhouse, I returned to Ingefær and Mick inside the Shrine of Eirene and called out for an aide.

A half-alvae with glistening blonde hair down to her hips came out. She adjusted her citrine dress that flowed to an inch off the floor. She spoke in a halting style. "Feeling...better?"

I nodded.

"How...may I be of service?"

Ingefær introduced her as Serafina and told her what we needed. "We need several vials of healing. And another to cure or slow poison."

"We have the former in abundance," Serafina said, blinking her green eyes. Her tone was so soft, it sounded like she didn't believe her own words. "But the latter is uncommon. We might have one or two. They're expensive."

I asked, "A vial of healing is what, a hundred silver?"

Serafina nodded. "The potion to slow poison is three hundred."

I exchanged glances with Ingefær. If we didn't use the vials on our current quest, they could be useful in later jobs. She dipped her chin, and I said, "We'll take four healing and all the anti-poison you have."

Serafina smiled, not revealing any teeth. Her grayish-green skin was an odd color for her race. Most mixed race alvaes were lighter green in tone.

Another human feature was her oversized nose...oversized for an alvae. It might have been as big as mine.

She spoke in a monotone. "The Goddess Eirene thanks you for your patronage." She turned and ambled towards the back of the Temple.

Ingefær got out the pouch with the gold coins. She was counting when Serafina returned with a cloth sack.

The half-alvae handed it to me. Her words were soft and mushy. "There're four vials of healing and one of the slow poison. The latter is not difficult to make. There's just not much call for it."

"So why does it cost three hundred?" I asked. I raised a hand. "Never mind. I'm not here to argue. We'll take it."

Ingefær handed over the gold coins. Eyeballing our stash, it looked to have dropped by half. And what we would earn from this job wouldn't refill it.

This job had turned to troll shit.

I hadn't expected the darts, and my fleet feet had failed me. The damage from the magic trap would have killed Mick. His scrawny size compared to mine was a major factor. And his leather jerkin and padded shirt combination wasn't as thick as my studded leather.

Serafina pocketed the coins. Her eyes narrowed, putting a finger to her dimpled chin. "What sort of assignment are you on?"

Keeping Elise's spell in mind, I replied, "It's delicate."

Ingefær pulled out the decree from Foremost Aerica. "We're bounty hunters. We've been, *ugh*, hired to retrieve...." She trailed off, grimacing.

Mick came to our rescue. "We're going to recover stolen goods. My ma is the Conjurer Elise at the Temple of Fraegah."

I smiled. He wasn't compelled.

My wife added, "We've run into a spot of trouble."

Serafina glanced over her shoulder. Her next words came out in a whispered rush, like she got caught kicking the family dog. "I'm sorry, but I don't suppose you want to hire on a fourth?"

"You can leave the Shrine whenever you want?" I asked.

Serafina's gaze darted to the back of the Shrine. She straightened her citrine cloak. "I'm...visiting from Vanaby and plan to return home next week." She smiled, but her green eyes remained cloudy, her countenance almost sad. "Keep it to yourself. My employer doesn't know it yet." The hint of a smile faded. "An adventure before I head back interests me."

Not with her tone. She sounded like we were headed to muck stalls where a hundred steeds with the 'flux' were stabled.

She asked about the expected length and nodded approval at my hope for a one-day round trip—maybe two if things didn't go as planned.

"What are your skills?" Ingefær asked.

"Besides healing?" Serafina clarified.

"Yes," my wife replied.

"I can handle a blade or just about any one-handed weapon, like a cudgel or a mace."

Her tone lacked confidence. But she didn't look like she had lied.

"You have armor?" I asked.

Serafina's chin bobbed. "Leather."

I looked at Ingefær. "Let's talk."

We put our heads together, Mick leaning in as well. "With a healer with us, we can get more aggressive with Retzlaff. I see no negatives."

Ingefær's brows narrowed. "Hmm. Possibly. But how much does she want as compensation?"

We were no longer in it for the coins, as we'd spent plenty getting me healed up and preparing for the next round. We were in it to get the damned compel spell off of us, and to earn a reputation as reliable problem solvers.

"Equal shares?" I said.

"Hey!" Mick half shouted. "What am I being paid?"

I turned to face him. "Your payment is, *ugh*, well, you know." Freedom from a rope is what I wanted to say, but Elise's incantation thought otherwise. "If your mother deigns to pay you anything, *ugh*, when we're done, count yourself lucky."

Mick grumbled. "Don't seem right."

Ingefær said, "Yeah, it seems harsh. The job has turned ugly, and he has been helpful. How about this? A tenth of any recovery?"

Mick yanked at his hair, and he shouted curse words at the walls and ceiling, though I was sure they were meant for us.

I placed myself before him, my nose almost touching his. "Don't push it. Take the tenth and be happy."

Mick's odd behavior subsided. "Alright. Fine."

Ingefær said, "That's the easy discussion."

My thoughts swirled. "Meaning?"

"Doesn't it seem odd that she wants to come with us?" Ingefær's blue eyes flashed at the waiting Serafina. "She doesn't know us. Yes, I showed her the decree from Foremost Aerica, so she knows we're legitimate bounty hunters."

Mick said, "Ah. But is she what she says she is?"

I turned. "No offense, Serafina, but we don't know you. We'd like to talk to your superiors."

The half-alvae chewed on her lower lip. "If you must. I guess the lifya, the chief healer, will learn of my departure sooner rather than later."

I went into the back, where a pair of ladies in yellow robes sat around a fireplace. The Shrine extended beyond this room. Based on other healer Shrines I'd visited, there were bedrooms, a kitchen, and at least a workroom where the healers played with their herbs. A Shrine this size had at least a score of healers. But at this time of night, all but these two were in bed.

I got a woman's attention, and we moved to a corner. "Healer Serafina wants to join us for a one- or two-day quest."

Her nose pinched. "Let me get the lifya." She moved down the hall with a quick step and disappeared into a side room.

When she returned, she was followed by a middle-aged woman, her sandy brown hair streaked with gray. The chief healer closed a robe around herself. The younger healer introduced the older one as Miranda.

Miranda's lips were thin. "Serafina is here of her own accord. Pitches in and doesn't complain. She is not one of ours, so she is free to leave if she wishes."

"Not one of yours?" I puzzled over it. "How long has she been here?"

"About three moons." The chief healer flashed a grim smile. "Poor dear was thin, and her clothes were worn out. Serafina professed a knowledge of healing. She's since proven her word. Despite her color not returning, she is a diligent worker and a decent healer."

I nodded. "Where did she come from?"

"That took a while to get out of her." Miranda crossed her arms. "Just last week we learned for certain that she came by boat from Vanaby. I mean, we suspected Vanaby all this time—her being a half-alvae—but I didn't know which Shrine. She keeps to herself. And the oddest of things, she's always looking out the windows and hides in the back whenever anyone comes in to be healed. Oh, she helps in the end, but I guess there's a shyness about her."

Running out of useful questions, I thanked Miranda and returned to the others waiting in the main foyer.

I nodded at Ingefær's raised brows. "She's been a healer here for three moons. Came from Vanaby." Turning to Serafina, I said, "I'm told you're shy."

Serafina looked away. "So, I can join you?"

I nodded.

"Terms of the engagement?" Serafina asked, her gaze now at her feet.

"You mean compensation?" Ingefær asked.

"Aye." Serafina looked over her shoulder. "And any special tasks you may have for me beyond healing the party."

"I can offer equal shares of the spoils," I said.

Mick harrumphed.

Serafina smiled, though she sounded disappointed. "I guess that's fine."

Ingefær explained the math to all of us. "After expenses, and a tenth off the top for Mick, the rest of us share a third each."

Serafina said, "Give me half an hour to get ready."

"Take your time," I said. "I need to eat."

"And sleep," my wife said. "And there're the horses to take care of."

Serafina said, "It's past midnight. There's no place open. Well, maybe a tavern by the docks."

Her green eyes danced between me and Ingefær.

I knew where I wanted to go. Near here, maybe ten minutes away, was *The Brine.* I told Serafina where we were going and where we planned to stay, which was back this way.

She nodded. "I know of the inn. I will meet you there at sunrise."

At *The Brine*, we ate a grand meal of eggs in a white cream sauce, ham still on the bone, and cheesy potatoes. I enjoyed myself, even if my wife refused to let me drink their ale.

Mick gawked at me. "Geez, mister. I's only seen a pig eat faster."

I grinned. "Well, I've been poisoned today, so I'm a little off my game."

Ingefær sighed and shook her head.

When we had finished eating, we made for the inn, stabled the horses, and secured two rooms.

I wanted to woo my wife, to thank her as a husband should for saving my life, but she wasn't having it. I even serenaded her, singing of her beauty.

"Sorry. I'm exhausted. There're the horses to brush down. And you stink worse than hogs in heat."

After I cleaned up, I thought of resuming my romantic endeavors, but she hadn't returned from the stables yet. I lay down, and my eyes said goodnight.

In the morning, as we chewed on buttered bread provided by the scullery maid, Serafina came down the stairs dressed in studded leather from head to waist and padded leather pants. She held a mace in one hand and a shield about half her height in the other. The alvae symbol of a gold oak tree was emblazoned on the shield's face. Her leather cap covered much of her yellow hair, which she had rolled up and pinned underneath. Moving her hair away from her face made her gray-green skin stand out. She didn't look healthy.

"You have a horse?" Ingefær asked.

Serafina shook her head. Miranda said she'd arrived by boat from Vanaby.

After saddling up at the adjacent stables, I bought bread and Anna apples from a street merchant, and we left the city. Ingefær and I rode while Mick and Serafina walked, taking turns leading the donkey.

On the way to Retzlaff's mansion, we debated alternatives to door knocking...like door bashing or using a wall of air to enter through a spire window.

"My wall of air spell has a range limit. I knew I could lower you down still twenty feet above the ground. We'd done it before. But I can't lift anyone forty feet above my head."

I remembered jumping, but not twenty feet. "You got me lower than that."

"I tilted the wall. You did the rest."

"We could always go down the third tunnel. The green-hued one," Mick said. Then he shivered. "Yeah, alright. It's a lousy idea."

Serafina's lips curled like she'd swallowed a rotting fish. "You didn't tell me you were up against Jarl Retzlaff."

"What do you know of him?" I asked.

"Cheap and mean," Serafina said. She spoke softly, her eyes clouding over. "And I've only been in the city for three moons. His reputation is soiled. No one wants to work with him because he stiffs payment or argues about the fee after services have been rendered."

"What will our direct approach get us?" Ingefær asked.

"Well, if you're facing him, maybe spittle as he hollers at you. If your back is turned, maybe the point of fine metal." She shrugged. "I don't know. I can only tell you what I've heard."

"How strong is his magic?" Ingefær asked.

Serafina smirked. "*Strong* isn't the word I've heard. Meager. But he is petty. Holds a grudge, or so I've been told."

Ingefær needled Mick. "He's got a book like you."

I scowled. "Yet the mansion is beset with traps and illusion spells."

"Illusion?" the half-alvae asked.

We informed her of our findings.

She scowled. "Ugh. I've not heard of this kind of sorcery before."

We moved on down the road, breaking for a late morning snack before turning up the path to Retzlaff's mansion.

As we munched on dry bread, I turned to Serafina. "What's your real story?"

"What do you mean?"

"I know what the chief healer said about you. Arrived by boat. But you seemed nervous back at the Shrine. And, no offense, you look like you've been sick, and you sound gloomy all the time."

"I'm not sick," Serafina said. "I was. But now I'm better."

I looked into her green eyes. "Go on."

"I don't want to say just yet." Serafina shoved bread into her mouth and talked through it. "I want to get to know you better."

It was an odd reply for someone willing to travel and work with us. After healing me, she had to know she risked her life in our company.

We resumed our walk and I let Serafina and Mick get ahead. Leaning over, I whispered to my wife. "She talks...funny. Sad, dejected. All the time. And her skin color is off." I jabbed my thumb eastward. "Alvae are emerald or kale hued. She's like a day from death with her gray sheen. It doesn't look to me like an extra dose of humanness."

Yet it suited her entire persona, in a wyrm drowning in a puddle kind of way.

"Her hair is beautiful. Reminds me of Safraan," Ingefær said.

I grunted. "Aye. It is lustrous. But Safraan's was wavy and curled. Hers is flatter, but shinier." Like gold.

Ingefær waggled her head at the path to the mansion. "We need to catch up."

Serafina was a healer, and we needed one, so I set my niggling doubts aside. But something was squirrely about her. No one just up and leaves the comforts of a home to travel with three strangers into a maw of danger. Serafina had seen me near death...yet here she was.

# CHAPTER TWENTY

# THE DIRECT METHOD

## INGEF□R

It approached high noon by the time we reached the top of the knoll and the mansion's front door. Warily, we tied off the horses and the donkey in front of the shuttered windows and set them to graze on the overgrown grass.

With blades drawn, Rory got into position and I moved to his left, four strides away. At my urging, Serafina took the right flank, and Mick stood a dozen strides behind Rory.

I had proffered a plan, and, after some haggling, we'd agreed to talk to the man first. But if he came out blasting, we would return fire. My plan assumed an illusion spell didn't take us all in.

I pinched sawdust as Rory advanced on the troll-sized door. He knocked and knocked again. We waited for quite a while, pounding on the oak door at intervals.

Nothing.

Rory made to grab the handle, but I stopped him. "Let me detect magic."

"Really?" he said. "Seems a waste of your talent."

"You want to get shocked by magic darts again?" That won the conversation, and I cast a find magic spell. There was a faint orange glow.

I turned to Rory. "Didn't you come through the front door after I lowered you down from the spire window?"

"Aye." He snarled at the orange luminescence. "Maybe he set it after we left?"

That made sense. I searched for wards. Not finding any, I cast a dispel magic after everyone stepped back twenty paces.

Rory clambered back to the door and gave it a shove. It swung open. We stepped through.

The place was quiet...no sign of life. Nothing appeared amiss, but no one came to see what the noise was all about. There were no bodies on the floor and no tipped-over vases, so there hadn't been a struggle—not that I had expected one. The painting opposite the door still hung there. It didn't look like it had moved.

In short, everything appeared as we had left it.

A sudden clanging of pots came from down the hall and around the corner—the kitchen.

I shouted, "Jarl Retzlaff, we need to speak with you."

Silence.

Rory made to run forward, but I grabbed him by the belt. "We move as a team. No Rory heroics."

Still holding the sawdust in my other hand, I told Mick and Serafina to watch our flanks and to spread out behind us. We moved down the hall, past the parlor room, and turned the corner.

A stunted troll, about my height, looked up at us. It had brownish-green flesh covered in pustules and scabs. The thing looked odious. As a counterpoint, it had bright red strawberry jelly on its hands, mouth, and torso. Odder still, it had a third extra-long arm sprouting out of its spine.

The misshapen troll jumped at Rory, swinging its clawed left hand at him.

I shouted, "Look out!" But I should have saved my breath.

Rory danced and parried, drawing green-brackish blood. The human-sized troll swung with its right claw, which Rory dodged with ease. Trolls were dangerous because they were so hard to kill.

I darted in and slashed at the troll's right side. It twisted and flung its right arm to block the blow. I chopped off the claw at the wrist, spewing blackish-green blood all over the floor.

The troll yowled and swung its decapitated arm at me, spraying its putrid blood on my face and armor. As I wiped the goop off my face, the troll's claw regrew. The rearward hand reached around from the side and raked at me. But the arm's length proved insufficient, and it missed me by a foot.

"I hate trolls!" Mick shrieked. "And I's never met one before!"

Serafina said, "If you need aid, let me know."

"Fire darts!" Rory shouted at me as he hacked at the troll's head, scoring a gory hit and slinging grody blood over the kitchen walls. Greenish black blood drizzled down the troll's gangrenous face, mixing with the strawberry jam.

The head wound took longer to heal, but in a breath, the bleeding stopped.

Mick hit it with a round stone, about as big as a crab apple.

The troll howled and increased its pace of attack, throwing in a leg kick between claw-claw-claw sets of swipes. Its blows were predictable with an over-pronounced back swing. In my experience, trolls had two arms, but were smarter than most creatures. This one seemed half a serving shy of a full plate.

We held our own, avoiding the nasty swipes. But we weren't doing any permanent damage either.

Rory slashed and darted, using his magical gift of speed, avoiding an unexpected vicious bite from the beast's blackened teeth, spotted with red jam.

I waved my sword hand and uttered Varanusian to summon magic. I cast a series of magic darts.

Fire hurt the troll, and it was damage it didn't repair within a blink of an eye. Still, it could, over time, recover. What we needed was more firepower. Oil would have come in handy.

The troll turned to me. Maybe it had recognized its danger. Maybe it wasn't so dimwitted after all.

I rattled off a second spell. Right into its gut.

It clutched its wound and hissed like a svartkatt—not at all cute.

Fear sprouted in its eyes. Then a feral growl ripped the air, like a momma svartkatt seeing its baby hurt.

As it lunged at me, I let it have a third set of darts just as another stone from Mick clonked it on the noggin. From behind, Rory slashed at its spine.

The deformed troll slumped to the ground. I wobbled on my feet as I had cast four spells since arriving at Retzlaff's manor. I neared my capacity and would need healing soon.

With his sword, Rory stabbed the troll in the back, just below the third arm.

The troll wasn't dead though, just incapacitated, its body working on regenerating the wounds. Fire damage would take days to heal, while the blade through the heart would be repaired almost instantly once Rory pulled the sword free.

From behind me, Serafina chanted a series of Varanusian words, bit into a half-eaten Gravenstein apple—cheap, tart apples, used for cooking—waved a hand in a circle, and touched my shoulder with her apple-holding one.

After a deep draught of air, I felt better. "Thank you."

I yelled at Mick to find oil.

Leaving the sword in place, Rory and I dragged the troll outside. I stabbed the defenseless brute several times to keep it incapacitated and unconscious.

Mick and Serafina joined us. Mick doused the troll with a jar of clear, viscous liquid, and Serafina used a flint and striker to set the monster ablaze.

Rory dusted his hands. "Teamwork. I like it."

Serafina's mouth hung wide. "Wow! You two know what you're doing."

Mick swallowed, a hand tugging at his tawny hair. "I's never fought a troll before."

I winked at him. "Told you we killed two last year. With fireballs. But the kitchen is too small for such spells."

Mick stuttered. "I-I-I's never heard of them having three arms."

"They don't," Rory said. "This one is abnormal."

Serafina asked the obvious in her slow manner. "How does a troll get inside a house?"

The question was unanswerable. Not without finding Jarl Retzlaff.

Back inside, Rory asked, "Where is the jarl?"

We'd made plenty of noise. Yet no one bothered to show up.

Regrouped and checked for errant injuries, I thanked Serafina for her healing spell. "But I had one more in me."

"Don't wait till six," Rory said.

"I saw you teetering, so thought you were closer to your limit," Serafina said. "You have very good stamina. I know a sorceress in Vanaby. She can go five. But then she is like a spilled sack of beans. Down on the floor, gathering dust as she rolls around."

We took it much slower this time and searched the rest of the mansion. We first went to the man's bedroom on the odd chance the man was indisposed. I rummaged through the clothes drawer with Rory's help.

The topmost one held stacks of parchment. By the stamped icons, most had been delivered via hired couriers.

I glanced at one. "Ah, here's a note from Jarl Simmonson, demanding an explanation as to the irregular letter of credit." I read further. "Retzlaff would have had an overdrawn account, if the figure hadn't shifted. Simmonson demands the return of the purchase."

Mick growled. "He used the same chicanery like he did on me."

I shook my head. "This indicates Retzlaff didn't have as many funds as he wanted others to believe."

Rory pulled out a journal and unwound the string. He thumbed through pages. "This is a personal diary."

He got our attention, and we gathered around him. Rory jumped to the middle, then flipped pages.

"Ah, here's an entry from Spring Solstice. 'Made contact with the head of the Fraegah Temple. Implied I was interested in acquiring the family heirloom.'"

Rory turned more pages. "Dated two moons ago. 'With the return of magic, I solved the riddle left by grandfather. Now I know where the treasure is, but I cannot access it, as he warned of poison traps and magical wards. The wards I can dispel...I think.'"

"Treasure!" Mick lit up. "Ooh. I like the sound of that."

Rory turned more pages. He cleared his throat. "Met a thief yesterday. The fool tried to pick my pocket. I'll work with him to see if he has the talent. But he can't be too strong. Once he bypasses the traps, I'll have to kill him. And with me dispelling a ward, I won't have much firepower. Not without the ring."

I looked at Mick. His face lost what little color he had. But his spine stiffened.

"The rat bastard." Mick's jaw jutted forward. "I'll do him in before he gets me."

"Justice, not vengeance," I said. But I found it hard to take my own counsel.

Rory flipped pages. "The thief is flighty and while he has a soft touch, doesn't understand subtlety or the value of distractions. I had to save his ass by conking the target with a drowse spell. I don't think he'll be able to bypass the traps. But I have another idea to use his talents. I'll have to brush up on my beguile incantation. I'll have the kid stealing from his own mother."

Rory put the journal into his rucksack. "This is an admission of guilt."

"Finish searching," I said. "Rory and I will go through the rest of the clothes dresser."

Mick found the topaz jewel and the vial of healing in the nightstand drawer.

Rory closed the bottom drawer. "Which gives us five. And the vial and jewel are our payment." He looked up at me. "I'm done."

I nodded. "Me, too. Nothing in the middle one but underclothes and socks."

Rory stood and stretched. "Even if we don't have the ring, we have enough to swear out an arrest warrant with the...*ugh*."

"Order of Gixus," Mick finished.

"Except we can't visit them," I said.

Serafina scowled. "Why not? I thought you were bounty hunters."

We tried to explain Elise's limiting condition. In the end, Mick had to tell the story to spare our guts.

Serafina frowned. "She doesn't sound nice at all."

Mick chuckled. "Most days, you's right."

The half-alvae said, "I could go do it."

I looked at Mick, who looked back at me. His eyes were as wide as dinner plates.

"We can't," I said. "Mick would hang, same as Retzlaff."

"I could leave his name out of it," Serafina offered.

Rory groused. "Nah. We should find the, *ugh...*"

"The ruby ring," Mick finished.

"Which is worth what?" Serafina asked.

With the stolen item revealed, I found I could talk about it tangentially. "About two thousand to Elise. Close to four thousand was the asking price Elise had in mind. Jarl Retzlaff had expressed an interest in acquiring it, but stole it instead."

"How do I get paid?" Mick asked.

"We'll sell the jewel," Rory replied.

"Not the vial?" Mick asked.

"No." Rory sighed. "It, like the others, will come in handy. Whether here or elsewhere. The Shrine values them at a hundred silver. If one of us needs healing before we find the signet ring, then it's a party expense and no one benefits coin wise. If we make it to the end intact, then Ingefær and I will take them as our share."

We might have to make up the coin shortfall out of our own purse. But I smiled. He was thinking ahead of a life of adventure and bounty hunting.

Mick frowned, but nodded.

In a cloak pocket hanging in a side alcove near the bed, Rory found a scrap of parchment—a receipt from a furniture maker. "It's from Simmonson and dated five days ago." He flipped it over. "Delivery instructions say to leave everything at the spot where the path becomes paved."

The unspoken implication was the tracks we spotted two days ago were of persons moving the furniture through the hidden waterfall entrance. Which made no sense. "Why not deliver the furniture through the front door?"

Serafina said, "I'm confused. What are you talking about?"

Mick shrugged. "They's talk like that all the time. It's like a secret code between them."

I laughed. "We have been together for four years."

"Ingefær and I toured half and searched half of Hexerei Mansion two days ago. Every room was full of furniture. None of it looked new."

"Oh," Serafina said, as if she understood—though her furrowed brows said otherwise.

"Which doesn't answer my question," I said. "The new furniture, the front door?"

Rory shrugged. "We'll have to ask Retzlaff." He waved his free hand. "Come on, let's finish the search."

The two spires held nothing of interest beyond the views from the windows. From outside, the shutters appeared closed. Were the shutters the illusion? Or was it the panoramic scenery? I was tempted to cast a find magic on the windows. But Rory reminded me to pace myself.

Peering out, I scanned the neighboring landscape. The path by the stream leading to the waterfall remained hidden from sight. Which made little sense, as the spire could be seen on the path to the waterfall. Well, just in the one spot.

Jarl Retzlaff and Hexerei Mansion had a sneaky streak about them.

The servants' bedrooms behind the kitchen showed signs of personality. Dying flowers stood in dried-out vases. Coats, shawls, and other outer garments hung on coat racks. Shoes were stored beneath the edges of each bed, lined up in a row. The bedspreads showed a unique flavor in each room. But nothing revealed how many staff folk there were and, of the most import, where they were now.

We assembled downstairs before the wall opposite the main door and gaped at the lonesome wall hanging.

Serafina asked, "Why are we staring at the picture?"

"From our visit before, I believe there's a secret room." I took a deep breath. The search of the mansion had taken an hour. I was mentally tired from all the riding and worrying. Spell wise, I was raring to go. But what about the half-alvae? "How are you faring, Serafina?"

Rory asked, "How many of those healing spells can you cast?"

Serafina flashed what passed for a smile. "Uh, healing? Three."

Rory grimaced. "Three's better than nothing, and we have our vials. But, no offense, three's not a lot in the thick of combat."

She gnawed on her lower lip. "Aye. True. But then I can cast a stamina restoration spell instead of a healing one. Which is what I did on Miss Ingefær."

"Restoration?" I asked.

"If you're not injured, there's no need to cast the more powerful healing version. My restoration spell restores your stamina. It doesn't cure any injuries. My capacity, by trial and error, is three heal spells or four restoration spells. If I cast a restoration spell on myself after casting two heals or three restorations, I can get two more restoration incantations out of me. But then I am spent. Put a blanket on me because I'm going to sleep."

What an impressive description of her own limitations.

"What else can you do?" Mick asked.

"Oh, I can aid our morale or decrease an opponent's confidence. I've been working on a silence incantation. Self-taught." She laughed. "No one has agreed to my testing it on them. So I don't know what the effects are, nor how long they last."

"Could you silence Jarl Retzlaff?" I asked. Quieting a mage might be a battle changer.

"In theory." Serafina shrugged. "Never tried it in combat. Only on myself." She shook her head. "I don't recommend it."

"How did you gain the knowledge about your capacity with heal and restore spells?" Rory asked.

My husband knew how the Shrine of Eirene operated, having wooed my sister for a time. Each adherent would cast no more than one spell an hour, and never the last spell that would incapacitate them. It was very regimented, and it left a lot of potential untapped, for that's how I grew in power—by expending my strength and about passing out. It was the same as training with the sword by running, jumping, and slashing. Wear the muscles out, and they came back stronger.

Serafina gave Rory an irritated look. After a pause, she said, "At the piers on the Jernel River in Vanaby. I supported the army while they trained."

"What a coincidence," I said. "Rory and I got married in the Furæyar Shrine gardens last year. When were you in the city?"

"Uh, two years ago." Serafina's eyes darted toward the door, like she wanted to run.

I cocked my head at her. Her demeanor brought Rory's earlier suspicions to the forefront. *Why are you working with us? Why are you in Slangeh Buktah? When were you sick?*

Rory gave me a look. "Now is not the time. With Serafina helping us, we can find Retzlaff and the missing ring in short order."

Maybe he saw something in Serafina he trusted. I examined my feelings. It's not that I didn't trust her...she had just healed me. Yet there was a story she wasn't telling.

I nodded and stepped closer to the hidden door. The picture of a mountain scene hung in the center of the wide, bare wall. The painting was suspended by a nail, which had been pounded into the wood. I waved the others aside and cast a find magic and searched for wards. No white ward symbols appeared—just a rectangular orange glow defining the edges of a door. The picture hung right in the middle of it, so I took the picture off the wall and handed it to my husband.

With no sigils hiding behind the picture, I cast a dispel magic. At eye level, a round depression in the wall became visible. A perfect circle, two fingers wide.

"What's that?" I asked.

Mick studied it. "A knob?"

"But it's in the wall," Serafina said.

“Perfectly round,” Rory said. “Here, move off.”

With blade in hand, Rory pushed at either end of the revealed door’s edges until he was red in the face. Mick tried it, running his thin-bladed knife around the door cracks. He shook his head.

“There must be a mechanism,” I said, touching the depressed circle with a finger.

Rory bumped me to the side. “That’s my job.” He pressed down with his finger, and I heard the click. Rory opened the door by pushing in. It swung back and to the right with nary a sound.

The wood landing before us was small. Rory entered the space with me standing at his elbow. I eyed the metal spiral staircase, painted black, going down and down. *Narrow* came to mind—like single file wide. The staircase shaft was lit in a purple hue. It was comfortable for my eyes, but not very revealing, with lots of dim shadows.

“No way anything big is going up or down this staircase,” Rory said.

Which explained why the furniture had to be delivered through the waterfall. Except it hadn’t been, or at least not that we found. What furniture did Retzlaff need down below? Where had he put it? And where was he?

Rory glanced at me, and I nodded, casting yet another find magic, this time on the metal staircase.

Three spells in short order. I sensed we had a long way to go before we found our errant mage.

Not seeing an orange glow on the staircase, I informed the others, even though they could see it as easily as me.

Following Rory, I went down one metal step at a time. I focused my gaze on each step, ensuring firm footing before taking the next.

Assuming I hadn’t been turned around, we were facing west at the landing that marked the halfway point of the spiral stairs. Below me, more metal steps, beyond which there was a landing with more steps.

These were not metal, but stone—judging by the color. They led away to our right, which was north.

Rory led us down, step by careful step.

At the stone landing, we stopped. I huffed air. Then cast a find magic on the stone steps. Four in the last ten minutes. Yikes! The purple-hued walls wobbled before my eyes.

After my vision refocused, I gasped. The top and bottom step of the stone stairs glowed bright orange. But what got me was how both steps glistened with a bright white triangular sigil.

Wards. Rory had put a foot on the lower step yesterday and got jolted.

Rory said, "Great. Just great. The house is empty. He's down there after all."

"And we have to pass the deadly traps," I said.

Mick hiccupped.

Not waiting, I reached into my pouch for some vinegar-soaked lemon peel and cast a dispel magic, rubbing the air, mimicking the triangular shape.

Both white symbols winked out of existence, followed by the glow of the orange.

My world tilted. Rory hung on to me.

"Restore her, Serafina. I don't like the idea of five spells in such short order."

Serafina healed me all over again.

I murmured my thanks. When I felt better, I looked at her. "How are you doing?"

"Halfway for me," she said. "I'm feeling it. Would be nice to take a break and maybe eat and drink."

Rory said, "Not here. At the bottom. Maybe."

He hiked down the stairs, and crossed over the bottom step...even though the sigil had been dispelled. I couldn't blame him.

Rory said what I was thinking. "This here tunnel system—this dungeon—is deadly."

Mick hiccupped. "I wish I hadn't-*hic*-ever met the man. *Hic.*"

"Why did you call it a dungeon?" Serafina asked. "Are there jail cells down here?"

I sighed. "Yes. Well, one. So far. I think it's not far past these stairs. But it's worse than that. When we were down there yesterday, I felt trapped. Stuck and barred from the direction I wanted to go. I think there's but one direction we can go—the way the tunnels point."

Mick shrieked but stifled it half a second later. "Down. Deeper into the gloom."

I nodded, leaving the rest of my dark thoughts to myself. *Toward a certain death.* That was the effect the blue-lit tunnel had on me. We stood at the bottom of the stairs. Rory said, "I got lead."

I raised a hand. "Wait. We're right back where we left off. And except for retrieving the healing potion and the jewel, we're no wiser about Retzlaff and his location." I tugged at my husband's arm. "Serafina could use a break. Well, me, too. For water and bread. Or an apple."

Serafina asked, "Keep at least two of those for me. Mine is about gone."

Hiccupping, Mick shimmied past us. "Just not so close to them steps."

There was agreement all around, and we moved ten paces away.

As I sat in the blue-lit hallway with my back to a wall, I couldn't help but worry. We were back in the same damn tunnels. Were we equipped to handle what was ahead of us?

## Chapter Twenty-One

# TUNNELS, AGAIN

## RORY

Though we had a rounded-out party and had succeeded in bypassing the magically trapped steps, I felt my confidence leaking away. The others around me had dour looks on their faces. Ingefær was right. We were right back where we were yesterday. And not all that wiser.

Serafina had already proved her worth, having restored my wife's stamina. So, despite Ingefær's misgivings—I recognized her sideways glances at the healer—I took the half-alvae's presence as a boon.

Aye, we didn't know her. But she didn't know us. And I didn't blame Serafina for her down-turned mouth and sour demeanor. I suspected she had a good reason for it. Maybe she had a dark secret. Who was I to judge? I'd had several of my own for a long time. Ingefær had helped me to leave them behind.

I chinned at Mick. "Take a drink and stop hiccupping."

He nodded and did so. It seemed to help. At least the hiccups weren't so loud or as frequent.

Rested, we traipsed down the tunnel, scurrying past the jail cell and its torture implements. When we reached the door to the shaft leading to the waterfall, Mick confirmed it was the right place by checking for the piddle stains. They had dried and left a sticky-looking spot.

I led us through the flickering blue haze, past the passage with its eerie green light, and double-checked the rat-infested storage room. Beyond it, the tunnel ran on for another hundred strides before it came to a dead end.

I turned to the others behind me. "That's strange, don't you think?"

Serafina said, "A shaft running for a long way then abruptly stopping? It screams bizarre."

Mick stomped in a circle and clucked like a chicken. Serafina shushed him.

I said, "I thought you were over your roostering?"

Not that I blamed him for being scared. My hackles were up as well. Though, so far, all we'd done was reprise yesterday's trip. We'd just gone a bit farther down the blue-lit tunnel, where we came to a literal dead end.

Mick yanked at his tawny hair. He grimaced, swallowed a lump of something, and strutted about. At least he kept his mouth shut, squelching the steady flow of hiccups.

His antics made me feel antsy, bringing to life my own fears. What was down here? Where was Retzlaff? Why were there traps and illusions everywhere?

Ingefær waved at us to move behind her. She cast her magic. Bright orange, deep in shade like a fire's flame, outlined a doorway set into the stone—a door once hidden.

A pair of bright white glyphs appeared in the dead center of the door. One showed as a crescent moon, and the other as an eight-point star.

"Well, troll dung," I said. "Two glyphs on one door. They look dangerous."

Mick crowed like a rooster.

Serafina hushed him. "You'll wake the dead for sure."

That wasn't the best thing to say to calm him down. And I hoped there weren't any dead to wake. I bit my tongue, trying to keep my dark thoughts at bay.

"You didn't behave this way earlier," Ingefær said. "What's going on?"

Mick hiccupped, nice and loud. "I don't k-know. I guess it-*hic*-it's dawning on me, t-*hic*- this is a deadly place-*hic.*"

"Just now?" I asked. "Not when I got zapped by magic bolts?"

Mick shook his head.

"Or the troll in the kitchen?" I persisted.

Another shake.

Ingefær tugged at my jerkin. "Leave him be. At least he gets it now. The question is, do I dispel them?"

The incantation waned, and the two glyphs faded out.

"Can you do both at once?"

She shook her head. "That's not how the spells work. You dispel one, then the other."

"Which one first?" Serafina asked.

Ingefær tangled her short hair around her finger. "Knowing which is the trick."

I said, "But they look nothing like the wards we saw at the tomb."

Meaning they weren't complex. Meaning, they weren't as deadly—in theory. I chuckled at myself. I had almost died from the triangle ward.

Mick asked, "What tomb?"

"You don't want to know," I said.

Ingefær narrowed her eyes at me. "Even if the patterns are simple, they can kill." Her eyes flitted from me to Mick and Serafina. "My husband's referring to The Vala's tomb sigils, which were intricate—impossible to mimic and dispel."

I stood before the door. "Let's not go this way. I don't think guessing which one to dispel first is the right approach. I say we try the green-lit tunnel."

"He could be beyond this door," Serafina said.

In unison, Ingefær and I turned and looked back toward the dark outline of the green-lit shaft that led down.

Traveling with Vidarr, I had learned to trust my gut. Apparently, based on my wife's simultaneous motion, she had the same inkling.

"Possible, but like Ingefær, my gut says no." I heaved a breath. "He's down that way. Come on. Let's see what luck green can bring."

"Besides, we save casting spells," Ingefær said.

I led us back to the third tunnel opening. As I pivoted to my right into the brooding, green-lit tunnel, Mick ran in front of me. He lit his magic light stick and handed it over.

I thanked him. "Watch your step."

I noticed his hiccupping had stopped. Motion, or action, had a way of disrupting the mind from negative, and even hostile, thoughts.

A dozen steps later, the tunnel turned sharply to our right, and the slope sharpened. "Getting pretty steep."

Serafina said, "Aye. I feel it."

From behind me, Ingefær said, "Be careful."

The most careful I could be was to turn around and go home and yank weeds. But it's not what she meant. She was saying, *I love you.*

With a quick twist of my head, I winked at my bride.

I held Mick's artifact aloft, peering ahead as far as I could. This tunnel was narrower, and not as smooth as the first two...and it felt a lot...gloomier. I scanned high. No sign of spiders.

From behind, "These walls are cramping me," Serafina said. "I'm an outdoor lass."

Ingefær asked, "Are you afraid of dark, tight places?"

"Who ain't?" Mick retorted.

"If I'm lying on my back," Serafina replied.

I didn't ask how she came to her realization, as her description sounded like she'd been lying in a casket. With the lid closed. Had she tried that? And if so, why?

Several minutes later, we came to a landing made of planks. Wood over stone. I stopped short of it. "I think a detect magic is in order."

Ingefær shuffled forward and did her thing with a find magic incantation. We looked at the smooth wood landing and the stairs past it, continuing down. A soft orange glow covered it all.

As I studied the hue, the pattern of a crescent moon revealed itself. It wasn't bright white or carved or whittled. Instead, it was a pattern of somewhat darker orange knots cascading down the stairs, shaped altogether like a crescent.

Was it a ward? They always showed bright white, didn't they?

I glanced at my wife, arching my brows in question.

She shrugged.

If it was a ward, how complex would it be to dispel? Intricate patterns made of dozens of lines I'd seen before. But a barky knot pattern spread out across two scores of steps? I'd seen nothing like it.

In the dark depths, the light from Mick's stick mixing with the green light from the magic sconces cast sinister shadows flickering across the landing and down the stairs. As if ghosts were making a run for it.

I pointed with my sword at the guttering images and shuddered.

Mick clucked and yanked at his hair. "This place is creeping me out."

Serafina shushed him. "Not so loud."

Ingefær said, "Be ready to fight...or to run."

Mick hiccupped and moved behind the two ladies.

My wife cast a dispel magic at the steps. She waved one hand like she was washing a pot, while the other moved in a long and slow swoop, mimicking the arc of a waning moon. She assumed the sigil was one spell and not a series. The orange and knotty crescent moon disappeared.

And nothing bad happened.

"I wish I knew what the glyphs did." Ingefær stepped onto the platform and looked at the wood steps below. "I've never seen a ward that didn't glow white."

Her unasked question was...*what does it mean?*

I cleared my throat. "I don't know. 'Cause there's but one way to find out."

Mick clucked. "I don't want to find out."

I moved beside my wife. Beneath us, a few steps were wide, a couple narrow. By the shadows Mick's stick cast, some were tall, and others weren't. By my count, there were forty-four steps of various shapes and sizes; but I was at the max range of the white light, and some of the wider steps could have been two, not one. My memory of climbing the Temple of Fraegah's steps said there were around ten or twelve per floor. We were getting deep into the knoll.

The bad part was, I didn't know if we were heading east, west, north, or south. I thought west. But I doubted my senses. If we went straight—and not far—we would soon emerge out of the hillside. And that didn't sound right. I shared my thinking out loud.

Ingefær said, "The first tunnel from the waterfall ran south, and this tunnel, shifted over to the west, runs south as well. I think."

"But it had a sharp turn to the right, westward," I said. We should be close to the path we'd taken to get to the mansion. But were we?

Serafina said, "That can't be right. The knoll is rather steep. We would come out onto the paved stone path. Or close to it."

I paced on the wood landing. "We've twisted about. The tunnels we've been in had to have turned without us noticing. Or Retzlaff's illusion spells have us befuddled."

Serafina scoffed. "Not Jarl Retzlaff. He's not powerful, or so I've heard."

Someone had cast the spell covering the lever to the waterfall with a boulder illusion; somebody had done the shutters of the spires, too. Could a spell last for centuries?

"He's got me shaking in my boots," Mick said. "I wish I'd never met the man."

Wisdom comes at odd times. The young lad was figuring it out.

Ingefær played with her pearl-white snowflake. "These tunnels were dug way before Jarl Retzlaff's time. I think it's a predecessor's magic."

Wouldn't that make it worse?

Ingefær motioned me to move behind her. "I'm going to double-check these stairs. There is something off about them." She cast another detect magic on the stairs.

We were burning through magic at a fast rate. She'd cast four spells in less than a half an hour.

I steadied her as she wobbled on weak knees.

Serafina moved in, ready to cast a spell.

I said, "Wait. One more."

The half-alvae nodded.

Ingefær said, "We may need to rest up soon."

"Or drink a potion." I glanced at the stairs. "Nothing is glowing."

We debated moving on. I pressed to keep going. "We've made very little progress."

There were grunts and murmurs. No one said yes. But they nodded their chins.

With Mick's light stick, I led us down.

Midway, I stepped on a squishy step and about fell headlong down the stairs. For regaining my balance and putting my full weight onto the weirdly soft step, I was rewarded with a pair of metal-tipped darts shooting out from the walls.

The darts were fired with enough force to pierce my leather armor. "Yaggh!" Pain lanced my right arm and left shoulder.

I raised a hand to stop the others from running toward me. "A trap. I stepped on a squishy stair."

"But I detected no magic," Ingefær said, her red-tinted brows creating a deep furrow.

Standing there, I pulled one dart free, then the other. It hurt, but nothing like the fiery magic ones. I didn't remember how the poison one had felt. Studying the metal-tipped barbs, I tried to discern if they were coated with a substance. But they were covered with my blood, preventing any credible examination.

Mick crept step by step to move beside me. He asked for the light and inspected what I stood on with my right boot. He then moved over to study the holes in the rock wall.

"Ingenious," he said. "It's a wooden plank with a bag of air underneath. Master Belkin provided the pressure to trigger the firing mechanism."

"Great. Just great." I twisted and lifted my foot off the step—

"Don't!" Mick shouted.

But it was too late, and I was slow-witted to understand his warning.

Mick ducked, and I was struck by two more darts. This time, one in my back and one in my chest. Neither went deep, as the leather was thicker around my torso than my arms. Still. It stung.

Suddenly, I felt woozy. The light dimmed before my eyes and was replaced by sparkling stars. I lost my grip on my sword and heard it clang against the stone.

The stairs spun.

Words buzzed around me, but I must have had fabric stuffed into my ears. Twinkling stars made an appearance. When had I gone outside? When had it turned to night?

I felt like I was flying. Or maybe falling.

## Chapter Twenty-Two

# POISONED, AGAIN

## INGEF□R

I grabbed Rory by his belt and, with Serafina's help, jerked him backward. We sprawled atop the steps in a pile of arms, bodies, and legs.

The second set of darts must have been tipped with poison, because my husband lost consciousness. Again. I slapped his face and yelled at him, but all that got me was Mick shushing me.

*The gods! Not again. Please spare my husband...please save the love of my life.*

Recovering to our feet, we dragged Rory up the steps to the landing. I laid him down on the tunnel floor. Looking into Serafina's eyes, I asked, "Can you remove the poison?"

Tears threatened to overwhelm her green eyes. She shook her head. "No." She reached down and felt Rory's neck. "His heart beats." She placed an ear against his mouth. "He breathes. Not deep. But steady."

"You's have the slow poison potion," Mick said.

Serafina raised a hand to stop me from digging for it. "I'm not saying don't use it. I'm saying maybe wait. If it's a mild sedative, he just needs time."

Did Rory have time for us to figure it out?

Mick climbed up and kneeled beside me. "Pour water on him."

Uncorking my skin, I let a fair amount drizzle onto my husband's face.

No response.

*Come on, Rory! Fight!*

Serafina felt his neck again and bent over to feel his breath. "No change. I think he'll be alright. He's not spasming or frothing. I think it's mild. It may be designed for the individual to pass out and break their neck as they fall down the stairs."

I wasn't persuaded and reached for my hair, ready to mimic Mick's yanking.

She flashed a grim smile. "We should wait. See how his body deals with whatever is troubling him. We'll be able to tell if he worsens."

"I hate waiting," I said. Rory did too. But I remembered how Rory had looked after the first darts—pasty white and he'd felt hot. And she was right. I bent over him and kissed him on the lips. He felt...normal. "Don't you dare die on me? We're just getting started."

I turned to Serafina and hardened my voice. "If he worsens, we'll use the anti-poison potion."

Seeing her nod, I added, "I've cast four spells already, and you've cast two. We can rest while we monitor my husband."

Serafina's green eyes found mine. "Aye. A good plan."

"It's an hour, maybe two, after noon. Do we sleep now?"

Mick said, "I's thinks it's best. For you. I's can keep watch."

"Alright. We wait here." I pointed. "Mick, you check out the rest of the stairs. Be careful. Mark the traps so we know how to avoid them. Or, if you can, disable the traps altogether. Don't take any unnecessary risks."

Mick nodded and left with his stick light, leaving Serafina, myself, and Rory in a green gloom, with shadows dancing along the walls and down the stairs.

Serafina's breath grew harsh.

"Are you alright?" I asked.

"This odd darkness is pressing on me," she said. "Can't say I like this place."

I took her mind off it. "Check Rory, again. Please."

She did. "No change. He's stable."

I took it as good news.

I stood. "Let's set up camp so we can get some sleep. A place we can defend."

Serafina turned around. "There's nothing to do but put our backs against the wall. One person can face down the stairs and the other up the tunnel."

"I know where there are blankets and wood crates we can use to make a fire. But we'd need Mick's light stick."

We waited for Mick to return while checking on Rory at intervals. At least Serafina had it right. He wasn't any worse. He breathed slow and shallow, but steady. Rory would have to sleep off whatever ailed him. The alternative required forcing a liquid down his throat.

After a while, Mick trudged up the stairs and arrived with ragged breath. "That's done."

We questioned him.

"I's marked them all first," Mick said. "Then I's went back and disabled them."

"How?" I asked.

Mick rubbed the back of his knuckles on his blue vest. "Talent, is how."

I eyed him, not in the mood for wisecracks.

"I's got curious as to how they worked. It's a simple design...once I's figured it. I lifted the wood planks and poked a hole in the air bladder with my dagger." Mick shrugged. "Of course, now if anyone steps on one of them loose boards, they might stumble and fall, maybe break an arm or their neck as they tumble down. It's a long way to the bottom."

Serafina asked, "How many traps?"

"Seven," Mick replied. "Most were in the middle of a step, but there's one trap on the left and one on the right. I's used my knife to place an *x* on the wall. You's can see the marks with the glow stick, but not if you're walking in the green haze."

With Mick's light, he and I went back to the storeroom and retrieved four blankets. We emptied four crates, and after the rats had scurried to new homes, we dragged two of them back for firewood. On our second trip, we dug through two other crates and found sacks of grain, jars of honey, and bags of potatoes and carrots.

I had known about the honey. But the uneaten portions of grain about caused me to vomit, as rat droppings floated amongst the kernels. The potatoes and carrots were gnawed here and there, and rat scat dotted the russet skins of the spuds and the orange exterior of the root vegetable an oily black.

But the jars of honey were sealed well. After wiping one down with a wetted cloth, I brought it back with us, along with four of the cleanest spuds and a dozen carrots that appeared to be unsoiled.

After telling Serafina about the rodents, she had me gather everything into a pile and she cast a spell.

"What did you do?" Mick asked.

"I cast a cleanse spell to rid the items of whatever disease there might be." She half-smiled, half-grimaced. "We'll be resting, so might as well use up my spells."

I nodded. "Good idea." I eyed her. "Removing disease comes close to curing poison, no?"

Serafina narrowed one eye at me. "Aye. It does."

"You've been teaching yourself a silence spell. You think you could modify the cleanse disease spell to purifying poison?"

Serafina licked her lips. "You want me to use your husband as a test subject?"

She had a point. We had checked him after bringing the edible goods back, and he'd been no worse. "No. At least, I hope you never have to.

Let's rest. Recoup your stamina, as will I. And if he's not better by then, we'll use the vial first...and experiment as a last resort."

We got a fire going and passed out the blankets. I lay down next to my man and scootched close. His body was warm, and I invited myself to cuddle closer.

Through sheer experience of having journeyed with Rory for years, I didn't break down and cry. Though I wanted to. Losing my composure would be bad for Mick and Serafina. Besides, bawling over what I couldn't control wouldn't heal him.

I just had to hope he would be alright. Used to be I could pray. I missed knowing a greater power beyond me was there for help. It had always given me hope.

Some long hours later, Rory muttered under his breath as he shifted under the blanket, waking me from my nap.

I got water and helped my husband sit up and have a drink. After he took several bites of bread with honey, he worked himself into a standing position.

"You're wobbling," I said.

He nodded. "Aye. But I think I need to walk it off. You know, get my blood going."

"Well, don't walk near the landing." I helped him saunter up the tunnel and back. After the second trip, I asked, "Better?"

"Yeah. Thanks." Rory made for the bread and honey.

He was feeling better. If he was thinking about food, he wasn't hurting too bad.

Munching, he asked, "Did I miss anything? How long was I out?"

Serafina pinched a piece of bread and soaked it in the jar of honey. "I feel well-rested. Meaning, I think I have my full complement of spells. Which means I got at least six hours."

I nodded. "And you took a turn at the watch." I looked at Mick. "You watched us for six hours?"

Mick licked his lips, then shrugged. "Ain't got no spells to cast. Besides, I'm younger and just have more vigor...I guess."

The last part was said with a wide grin.

Serafina cleared her throat. "I'm not old. Well, I am older than you."

Rory said, "Thanks for watching over me. So, are we going down?"

Mick said, "I's defeated the traps. But watch out for them steps. There're a few rickety ones."

"You sure you're ready?" I asked.

Rory shrugged. "Don't want to stay here. Can't quit."

I wanted to argue. Twice, Rory had been nearly killed. And for what?

I looked into his eyes.

He shook his head. "We have to. Retzlaff is a bugbear. And there's no one else to do the job."

I growled, but nodded.

Serafina said, "The sooner we go, the sooner we get out of this place."

Mick, with a fistful of hair in his hands, asked, "Aren't you bothered by the lack of traffic? I mean, no one has come up or gone down. And we've been here for about eight hours."

Who would want to traipse across trapped steps? But he had a point.

Outside the mansion, we'd set the horses up for an overnight stay. And with our nap, it was the dead of night now. Mick's concerns were fair, but I didn't know how to answer him.

Rory stood and kicked the fire apart. "Get your light stick going, Mick. We're about to earn our reward."

That sounded like false bravado to my ears. But it beat pessimism. Hope kept folks alive in times like these. It's what praying to the gods used to do for me.

Mick lit his stick. "Careful, Master Belkin."

"You lead, lad," Rory said. "My head isn't quite right yet."

We gathered our gear, and I checked on my husband by looking deep into his dark brown eyes. He stared back. His pupils looked normal, and I saw anger there.

Yep. Retzlaff was going to regret his stupid traps.

## Chapter Twenty-Three

# SERAFINA REVEALS

## RORY

The effects of the poison were mostly gone, though my knees were weak, and my sense of balance hadn't returned in full, making me feel like a fishing bob on a windy day at the lake.

After drawing my blade, I followed Mick down the stairs. I stepped to the side wherever the young man pointed at a dodgy spot in the steps. At the bottom of the stairs was another wood landing, much like the top. The green-lit staircase turned into a blue-lit shaft, the blue and green mixing to light the planked wood in a sick hue, like that of a dead and bloated fish.

Why were the tunnels lit in different colors? Did it mean something?

With no answer, I turned to Ingefær. "Guess we have no choice."

She curled her lips in such a cute way that if Serafina and Mick hadn't been around, I would have kissed her.

I moved aside, and she cast her find magic spell. But instead of a moon sigil enmeshed into the wood, I made out a six-point star pattern formed by the series of glowing knots.

We all snarled our noses. There were but two options: dispel the ward or go home. I guess a third existed: scamper over it...and hope.

I knew what my bride would say. And after being jabbed and scorched by poisoned and magical darts—not to mention having to fight off a hideous troll and a phantom purple spider—I wanted to put an end to Retzlaff's vile ways.

After Ingefær cast the dispel incantation and air scrubbed the sigil away, the star-shaped knots dissolved into nothingness.

"I would like to know what those wards do," Ingefær said.

A growl resonated through the shaft. My years of hunting told me what it was. I whispered harshly. "A bear."

I took up a defensive stance, with Ingefær to my left. Mick scurried behind us.

Serafina said from behind me, "Don't hurt it."

I thought about laughing, but the situation was far too wrong. I glanced back at her, my brows knit tight. Was she loony? I licked my lips. "I won't if it doesn't attack."

Another growl. It had come closer, but was still obscured by the blue haze. I wished Mick's artifact illuminated farther down the shaft.

"Hold it higher, Mick," I said.

"You hold it, Master Belkin," Mick said, shoving it into my free hand.

The kid was right. Whoever held the light would be the primary target.

Ingefær said, "It might not be real."

A breath later, the massive brown bear appeared in the blue miasma, loping toward us. At seeing us, it sped up.

With my blade raised high, I stepped forward, telling my eyes they were lying to me. "Uh, I'm trying to not believe what I see...but it's not working."

Mick crowed. He wasn't having any better luck.

"Well, crap," Ingefær said. "I think it's real."

Serafina elbowed between me and Ingefær. "I'll deal with this." Then she looked over her shoulder at me, brandishing my sword. "I told you not to hurt it."

Yep, a confirmed loony.

The large brown bear, maybe as long as I was tall while it was on four legs, outweighed me and Ingefær combined. Its long sharp claws left etchings in the granite as it raced toward us. The beast would crush the waif-like half-alvae and leave a green stain on the ground.

With the shield in her left hand and her mace tucked into her pants, Serafina mumbled words and waved her hand at the charging bear.

There wasn't much of a difference between healers and mages. Mages needed some kind of material, while healers, depending on the spell, might need nothing—though it was said a physical component helped in all cases. They both had to know the language of magic, Varanusian, and have an ability to draw on the power of one or more of the four material planes, as well as the immaterial one—the Aether.

But healers were useful to society, and their spells were practical, like mending a broken limb. History said mages wrought destruction. Even the ones on the side of good weren't invited to dinner often, lest they set the kitchen on fire while showing a trick to the grandkids.

Maybe it was me who was loony for sharing a bed with one.

A dozen feet before the beast struck, it stopped with a skid...and lay down, resting its massive head on its humongous paws.

Serafina cooed at it like it was a baby and advanced. The bear whimpered.

My eyes about jumped out of their sockets. *What tomfoolery is this?*

She reached the brown bear, kneeled, and scratched behind its ears. Then she hollered at us. "Grab the jar of honey you found."

Ingefær rummaged through her kit and brought out a jar that shined gold under Mick's light stick. I pointed, open-mouthed. "There's another one in my rucksack."

My wife shuffled forward, but stopped short, eyeing the bear. Serafina closed the distance. With the jar of honey uncapped, the half-alvae poured it onto the ground. The bear lapped it up.

Serafina waved us forward as she rubbed the bear's fur. "Come on. He's a friend."

"It's a...he?" I asked. It was huge, but bears vary a lot based on their environment.

"Yep. I've named him Fudge. Doesn't he have the grandest colored fur? As dark as confectioner's chocolate." She rubbed him some more. "Who's a fluffy bear?"

Yep. Serafina had taken a blow to the head as a child. It was the lone explanation. I would have stayed put except Ingefær advanced. That wouldn't do, so I kept pace.

Ingefær asked, "What sort of spell did you invoke?"

Serafina shrugged. "Eh. I call it befriend animals."

*Oh?* I blinked several times. That was a mighty handy incantation for a hunter. Even though I lacked the ability to draw on the magical powers, I would have liked to learn such a spell.

Well, not here. But maybe later.

"What did you use for material?" My wife followed up.

Serafina's green skin darkened. "Uhm. Well, I don't want to say."

"Really?" Ingefær moved closer, to a stride away.

The bear growled.

Serafina scratched the bear again. "No, no. It's ok, Fudge. They're friends." She turned to Ingefær. "An emotion. My loneliness, to be specific."

My eyes narrowed. Was that even possible?

Ingefær said, "I've never heard of using emotion to power a spell."

A tingle ran down my spine. Serafina wasn't telling us everything. "How did you come to learn such a spell?"

Serafina sighed and stood, letting Fudge lick more of the honey off the floor. "I haven't been honest with you."

My jaw tightened.

My wife asked, "How do you mean?"

Mick was more direct. "What did you lie about?"

I definitely liked the lad.

Serafina said, "I am a trained healer recently working at the Shrine of Eirene. But beforehand, I was a healer in service to Furæyar."

He was the dreki God of Prosperity. One of the Væniere deities the alvaes used to follow.

She played with the ties to her studded leather armor. "I was assigned to an army unit. But got kicked out, which is why I am in Slangeh Buktah."

"Why'd they kick you out?" Mick asked.

"Because they said I practiced necromancy." Serafina patted Fudge's backside. "But making friends with animals isn't necromancy."

I couldn't think of a single mage or healer who talked to animals. Summoned them? Yes. Talked to? No.

Not that I knew many wizards or sorceresses. The stories I'd heard said that in the past, mages controlled their summoned animals—which, I suppose, implied they could talk to them. They summoned them to control them and wreak havoc. But those were thousand-year-old fables.

My gut told me Serafina was still leaving something out. "I'm struggling with why they kicked you out."

"Aye," she replied. "I understand."

Which was no answer at all.

"They just let you go?" I persisted. "As a suspected necromancer?"

"Well, not exactly." Serafina's eyes dropped to her boots and her fingers fidgeted. "You spotted it right away. My skin is gray because I was convicted of the crime and sent to the swamps. Alvae and marshes don't mix."

Neither did humans and swamps.

"You escaped!" Mick connected the dots.

Serafina looked up and nodded. "Aye. One day, they had us dredging near where the Jernel River washes out into the Mid Dreki Ocean. Most times, we work upstream a league or so. Anyway, while mucking the delta, I befriended a manatee who had gotten stuck in the bramble near the shoreline. She helped me swim free."

"And the Shrine of Eirene?" Ingefær asked.

"I arrived via a seafaring ship three moons ago. A week ago, I had drunk some wine and let slip the name of the Shrine I used to work at. Two days ago—three now—I learned the Shrine's lakare sent a letter to Vanaby asking questions." Serafina shrugged. "In another two or three days, they'll have their answer."

We stayed quiet. I didn't like the idea of traveling with a convicted criminal. But then, casting a befriend animal spell wasn't evil in my judgment. Necromancers did vile things with their incantations—like control people against their will or raise the dead.

Ingefær and I had an unpleasant experience in Vanaby when she was wrongly accused of setting the Furæyar Shrine on fire. So I was sympathetic to anyone subjected to false imprisonment. The lieutenant who'd headed up the entire ordeal was best described in polite company as a prejudiced simpleton.

"You don't think me a witch, do you?" Serafina asked.

Ingefær replied, "Of course not. We summon birds to send messages. Can't see why making friends with animals would be necromancy."

I nodded. And Raemoni had been playing with wyrms and spiders. But there was a line there...somewhere.

"That's what I said," Serafina half shouted, though a smile grew on her lips. "When I was convicted, I hadn't succeeded yet in my attempts. It was the senior lakare at the Shrine who overheard me trying."

"Did you say that was by the docks?" I was thinking of Arabella, who'd been the chief healer when we were in the city.

Serafina shook her head. "No. The Shrine up the river, just past the bridge connecting the center of the city and the farming fields. There are piers there for fishing. And a lieutenant had a company assigned to the eastern end of the city."

I didn't know the one she referred to, but there were five Furæyar Shrines in Vanaby. The eastern end of the city was mostly farming fields and farmers.

Serafina added, "I think she was threatened by my developing skills and got the lieutenant who oversees the eastern district to hold a tribunal. I didn't even get to say goodbye to my family."

"So, it wasn't a Lieutenant Smergasil?" I asked.

Or as I called him, Officer Dunderhead. Good fortune. He'd been stripped of his commission and was mucking the marsh himself today.

She shook her head. "No. Demperer was her name. But it wasn't so much her fault as it was the lakare and her friend. They lied under oath."

"How long were you in the marshes?" my wife asked.

"Two years." Serafina let Fudge lick inside the almost-empty jar.

I exchanged glances with my wife. She nodded. I agreed. Serafina's story sounded like the truth. And it also meant she'd had considerable power even before the return of magic. It was a conversation for a different time...and place.

I said, "I don't like being deceived. But I understand your reasons. And so long as you aren't a necromancer, you're quite handy to have around. Your befriending spell is mighty interesting. One I would like to learn after this adventure is over."

Ingefær relayed her experience with the dock leader—Lieutenant Smergasil.

"When was this?" Serafina asked.

"A year ago," Ingefær replied. "Captain Alvertos had several choice words for him when he found out."

"You know a captain in Vanaby?" Serafina's eyes widened.

"Yes. He's an acquaintance bordering on friendship," I replied.

Ingefær cocked her head. "He would have been a lieutenant when you were sent to the marshes. I don't know where he was based." She looked at me. "Maybe..."

I nodded. "Aye. Maybe we can get him to look at your conviction and set it aside?"

"But I escaped," Serafina said.

I shrugged. "Wrongly convicted. He looks at the first wrong, the event that precipitated the others. As long as the deeds don't escalate. He's fair. And smart."

Serafina smiled wide. "Maybe."

We stood there, lost in our thoughts. It sounded like Serafina had survived an injustice. That made her alright with me.

Mick brought us back to reality. "Can you's get Fudge to tell us about any more traps?"

Serafina squinted an eye. "Not in so many words. Wait a moment."

She closed her eyes, and I saw her lips moving, but she made no sound.

After a quick minute, Serafina said, "He doesn't know. He hasn't been here for very long. At least I think he knew what I meant when I asked. Animals don't have a grand sense of time."

"Can he come with us?" I asked. I'd gone from being terrified of a brown bear to wanting one of my own. Could I keep one as a pet? What would happen when Serafina's spell wore off? Or were the effects permanent? "How long does the spell last?"

"About an hour." Serafina placed her head against the bear's. She straightened. "But once an animal becomes a friend, it's unlikely they treat you as an enemy—as long as you don't hurt them. Fudge wants to go home. Doesn't like all this rock. No berry bushes. No water; no fish. If we know a way out, he will follow."

She touched foreheads again. "It has been a long while since he has eaten honey. I think a long while for him means more than a week. I can't be certain because Fudge's vocabulary is limited. And all I see are images." She touched foreheads again. "He thanks us for the honey and wonders if we have more." She giggled. "I have to think like a bear to make sense of his grunting."

Except I hadn't heard a peep out of Fudge.

Ingefær reached into my backpack and pulled out a second jar, the one I had eaten out of. She handed the two-thirds full jar to Serafina.

Once more, Serafina poured out the contents. "Fudge says he will guard our rears."

"Great," I said.

And I meant it. Nothing like a brown bear protecting your hide instead of swiping at it. We waited for Fudge to finish and hiked down the blue-hued shaft.

## Chapter Twenty-Four

# MONSTER MASH

## INGEF□R

After Fudge lapped up the last of the honey, I grabbed Rory's hand, and we hiked down the tunnel. Serafina and Mick took up the rear, with Fudge trailing behind.

At a turn in the tunnel, I stopped and asked Serafina, "Does Fudge know what's ahead of us?"

Perhaps it was foolish to rely on information from an animal I would normally run away from. Better to be prepared than proven a fool for not asking.

Serafina touched her skull to the brown bear. "Fudge does not. He was digging at a root when he, in an eye blink, found himself here."

My eyebrows climbed my forehead. "He was summoned?"

Serafina scowled. "I guess he must have been."

I scanned up and down the tunnel. No sign of scat or any other indicators that Fudge had been in the tunnel for very long.

Rory scowled. "By whom? And when?"

The tunnel remained cast in blue gloom. But with Mick's glow stick, visibility extended to thirty strides. "Retzlaff!" I called out. "Show yourself!"

Silence.

A sense of doom flitted around and through me. The blue haze here seemed thicker than it had been in the upper tunnel. The dim lighting was part of the problem. But another part was being far underneath the mansion. Where were those caverns the book spoke about?

With no answers to be had, we traipsed down an astonishingly clean tunnel.

So if Fudge had been summoned, who or what had done so? Glancing over my shoulder, I said, "I wonder if I dispelled the wards incorrectly."

After I'd dispelled the orange glowing crescent moon, Rory was shot with darts on the stairs. And after I dispelled the star-shaped orange ward, something had brought forth Fudge.

What had we gotten ourselves into? This place was a net of traps.

My suggestion had slowed the group to a halt. I gave my husband a gentle shove. "Lead the way."

Rory's brown eyes flicked at me, but he nodded. He held up the light stick, and we hiked down the shaft, arriving at the end of the tunnel. Set in the wall was a wooden door. Emblazoned on it was a slate blue six-point star, about a foot tall.

Why was this one visible while the others had been hidden?

I asked Rory to douse the glow stick. Sure enough, with the white light gone, the ward disappeared under the blue glow.

Serafina cleared her throat. "Could you please relight the stick?"

At my nod, Rory did so.

After a debate about moving on or going back—which rehashed the same arguments—I cast a find magic spell on the door before us. The star glowed orange, so I invoked a dispel magic incantation and was careful to wipe the sigil away, mimicking its pattern in the air. Nothing untoward happened as the star winked out.

Fatigue struck me and bowed my knees. I had cast four spells in a short amount of time. Again.

After passing the artifact to Mick, Rory grasped the door handle with his left hand while his right held his sword. He heaved at the door with his shoulder.

*Thud*! It didn't budge. It was stuck or locked.

Mick chuckled and squeezed in front of Rory. "Amateur."

The light stick found its way into my hand. Rory raised a threatening fist at Mick's backside. But only Serafina and I saw it.

Mick drew the thin piece of metal from his blue vest and poked and prodded while twisting the brass handle. A loud click sounded. "That did it."

With a grand sweep of his arm, Mick allowed Rory to step to the door.

Rory glowered at the tawny-haired young man, but turned his ire to the wood door blocking our progress. He twisted the handle and pushed hard. The door slammed against the rock wall, and the noise reverberated through the halls.

We lost our element of surprise. Assuming we'd had any to begin with.

The new tunnel ran straight, and along its way there were sconces which bathed the shaft in a jade-green light. Not candles, but magic, like the other tunnels. The white of the glow stick ate the green light for about ten steps. Visibility after another ten turned into pea soup.

The green light tugged at my senses; I felt like invisible ants crawled on my skin. Was the light a magic aimed at us? Or were my nerves just admitting the green hue was eerier than the blue?

After shaking off the sensation, we walked for thirty strides, then made a sharp right turn. I didn't know which direction we were headed—yet another element of disorientation causing my skin to itch.

One day, I would like to talk to an earth mage and learn how hard it would be to make something like this twisting, disorienting labyrinth. Which, again, brought to mind...where were the giant natural caverns the book talked about?

Rory rolled his shoulders. "I'm getting one of those feelings."

"What? You's hungry?" Mick asked, a grin on his face.

"No," Rory replied. "It's like I'm being watched." He doused the white light. "No sense in letting them get a good look at us."

Mick's smile turned into trembling lips, and his hand yanked at his hair.

Serafina hushed him before he screamed. "Wrong time for shenanigans, lad." Then, "Um, I like the white light."

Rory shook his head. "Maybe in a moment. Something feels off."

I took a hold of Mick's neck and squeezed. "Relax. Stay sharp and focus. I don't think we're done with the traps."

Single file, we hoofed it down the tunnel: Rory, me, Mick, Serafina, and the bear.

Forty strides later, a bright-white light sparked, and the tunnel filled with plumes of smoke, pulsing in shades of ash and vomited kale. Rory disappeared into the thick of it.

Coughing as the acrid smoke filled my lungs, I swung my sword into guard position; the wall to my right provided a sense of safety. I peered ahead but couldn't see anything through the billowing gray-green fumes.

Serafina bent over double and hacked her lungs out, while blindly swiping with her mace at the substance, trying to dissipate it.

Mick screeched as he stepped backward. With the smoke so thick, I lost sight of him.

"Argh!" Rory shouted from maybe five strides away, though my guess was based on the volume level.

I could hear his sword hacking at something. Branches? Metal struck wood...or bone. There was a brittle cracking now and then.

Fudge nudged my hip as he barreled past me and got lost in the nauseating vapors.

I couldn't see anything beyond ten feet. I debated edging my way forward when a bone-white figure stumbled into range, the green hue reflecting sickeningly off its skull.

The thing was without flesh and the bones were clean, as if they had lain in the sun to bleach for a century. I say *stumbled* because the creature walked in precarious fashion: leaning forward and snapping a leg under its body before it fell face—no, skull—first.

The skeletal figure, holding a four-foot hewed tree limb in both bony arms, swiped at me. A second skeleton appeared behind the first, angling toward the mace-wielding Serafina.

Fudge roared from somewhere ahead in the murk. Rory's sword hacks sounded like he was chopping dry twigs in twain and building a pyre.

I parried and slashed the skeleton's erratic swings. When it arched backward to club me again, I lunged and struck the neck bone with a solid thwack. The head lolled off, but the bony figure kept swatting its wooden limb at me. The blows became wild and errant, like it couldn't see. Which, I guess, made sense.

Serafina swiped her mace knee high and the skeleton lumbering toward her lost a leg and fell down, an arm limb separating. As the thing tried to rise, Serafina smashed the skull with her weapon.

A great tactic. The headless skeleton before me swung its tree branch, and I ducked, slashing at its leg. Its lower leg went flying, clanking off the stone wall. As soon as the skeleton fell, Serafina bashed the headless mass of bones with her mace, and the entire contraption crumbled.

I tried not to breathe in the pungent smoke, but it proved impossible. With shallow breaths, panting like a dog, I straightened and regained my composure. Such as it was.

I wanted to use my fiery darts, but my lack of vision beyond ten feet prevented the attempt. Serafina stood tall and mimicked my huffing.

Mick hiccupped behind me. I glanced over my shoulder and dipped a chin at him. He had moved back into view and wasn't screaming; but he hiccupped with each whirl of his sling.

Rory danced back to us. "Lokke's spawn! There's twenty more."

Up ahead, Fudge growled. Wood thudded. The bear roared, but it turned into a nerve-clenching whine that gouged me out from the inside.

"No!" Serafina pushed past me.

Rory grabbed onto her. "Don't be daft. I retreated because there's too many. It's a mash of monsters."

He jerked her hard and got her to look at his face. "I mean it. I have Roskva, and even with my fleet feet, there's no way to keep track of so many. An errant blow could kill you."

"But Fudge!" She wailed.

The smoke thinned a little, and three skeletons appeared, shoulder to shoulder. Seeing us, they lumbered forward in their spastic manner.

"Rory, take the left. I'll take the right." I put a hand on Serafina's shoulder. "You stay a step behind us. If any push through or fall down, you whack them."

From over my shoulder, a stone sailed straight into the central skeleton. The hollow *thunk* of stone on bone sounded, but no visible damage appeared. The skeleton rocked a little, then continued forward.

"Go," Serafina said, shoving at me. "Maybe we can push through and save Fudge."

With the skeletons advancing, I only needed to take two steps to get within range.

Parrying a wooden staff, I asked aloud, "Any chance they're illusions?"

Rory barked. "Damn that magic. I don't know. They were on me too fast."

Serafina sobbed. "That doesn't help Fudge. He's an animal. What he sees, he believes."

Rory slashed, his feet dancing. The skeleton to the left lost a bony arm, and the iron bar it had held clanked against stone.

Retreating a step, I said, "I don't believe they exist." I blinked.

A half second later, the skeleton on the right lunged, swinging its staff at me. I took the blow on the shoulder and careened off the wall.

"They're real!" I righted myself, lifting my sword into position. But had I disbelieved?

Mick smacked the one in the middle again with a stone. It distracted the thing for a couple of seconds. But then it resumed its advance.

Serafina clubbed the skeleton in front of me as it raised the staff high over its head.

Rory decapitated the skeleton before him as it reached for the iron bar with its remaining hand. His fleet feet took him out of harm's way as the skeleton in the middle swung its club.

The skeleton on the ground tried to get up but got trampled by another skeleton who took its place. The same happened on my side of the tunnel.

I stepped forward, stabbing at the next skeleton. The move struck bone, but the skeleton didn't care. It clawed at me with bony fingers. I avoided the raking motion, but got thwacked with a club strike from the skeleton in the middle.

The same shoulder, the same spot. It went numb from the armpit down. I huffed air, thankful it wasn't my sword arm.

Serafina reached out, using her shield to block a blow, and took another leg bone off at the knee. Yet another skeleton fell skull-first and was bashed until it lay still.

With a clutter of bones to shuffle through, the remaining skeletons advanced in erratic fashion, allowing us to defend against their wild clubbing. One by one, we dismembered them, then smashed them.

After a grisly few minutes, the last of the putrid smoke cleared, revealing all the skeletons to be dead. I stopped counting after twenty skulls.

*Where had these come from?*

Motion caught my eye. A dozen strides down the hall past the body of Fudge, a massive skeleton rose to full height. It stood eight feet tall and was wider in the shoulders than any two men.

It had lips. No, that wasn't quite right. More like a bony structure shaped like lips—and black as night. In the green hue of the hall, the mouth looked gangrenous, a sight I'd seen on a corpse two years ago.

"What the Hel is that?" I asked.

Mick hiccupped and hurled a stone. It smacked the big bony fiend in its oversized skull. The stone clanked off, and the thing tilted its head at us.

In a hissing whisper that raked the nerves of my spine, it spoke slowly and in a monotone, "Come. Kiss me."

With deliberate forward shuffles of its feet, it shambled through the bone detritus toward us, skittering the skeletal remains in its wake.

Rory flew forward, slashed at the thing's head, and connected with a ringing blow. He raced back.

The fiend shifted the angle of its skull. The slow, hissing whisper came forth. "You. Will. Be tasty."

I squinted, trying to see where Rory had struck it. Did my eyes and ears deceive me? "I thought you hit it?"

Rory looked at his blade. "I did."

The thing didn't act like it had been slashed at all.

Rory took off and swiped at the thing again, this time crouching to take a leg. Metal on bone. As clear as ringing a bell. Duller, drier, but the sound unmistakable. He retreated before the fiend grabbed his tunic.

The thing sloshed forward, feet sliding on stone, the bones of the dead skeletons rattling as they were kicked out of the way. "Hmm. Your aura. Is tantalizing."

Mick threw another stone. It bounced off.

Rory held out an arm toward Serafina. "Give me your mace."

With Rory's speed, he could evade the thing. So could we, if we ran away.

"Back up," I said. "Let Rory use his feet."

My husband wielded the mace in his right hand and the sword in his left. Once more, he flashed forward. He whacked the fiend on its skull with the mace and lashed at its neck with the sword.

With a lightning quick snatch of its fingers, the fiend clutched Rory's leather-wrapped arm.

Rory swiped upward with the mace and ripped himself free. In an eye blink, he was beside us. "We retreat. Our weapons do nothing."

His eyes found mine.

I nodded. Magic time.

"Be ready, Serafina," Rory said.

We stepped backward, getting distance.

I figured fiery darts wouldn't be strong enough. A fireball in such a confined shaft might kill us. I went with a lightning bolt. It was one of my slowest spells to cast, using air and the Aether.

I reached into my pouch with my left hand and pinched a fabric scrap from an old wool rug. Rubbing it between my fingers, my right hand—still holding my sword—made the motions. Varanusian flowed as I stepped backward.

I jabbed my left hand forward, throwing the rug fibers at the fiend.

Lightning ripped the air; the bolt flashed through the thing. The fiend stopped, the head tilting yet again.

My knees buckled, but I used the wall to keep upright.

It smiled. Well, the gangrene bony lips parted in what had to be a grin. "Oh. Such a feast. I shall have."

Rory and I exchanged looks. Mine, a grimace. We were over-matched. Nothing we had harmed this...this vile creature.

He said, "Heal her. Quick."

Serafina cast a restoration spell as we hobbled backward.

The thing resumed its foot-dragging advance. It had almost cleared the accumulated piles of bones from the *dead* skeletons.

We backed up some more. Rory took the front position, his arms held out wide. A mace in his right and his sword in his left, he warded us, giving us a chance to run away…if we wanted.

Mick shouted. "The dagger!"

I glanced behind me. "What dagger? What are you talking about?"

"The Fraegah Temple dagger I stole!"

Rory glanced over his shoulder. "Yeah. It's magicked."

We retreated as I rummaged through Rory's rucksack while it was still on his back.

The fiend reached open tunnel ground, and its feet slithered along, not lifting, not breaking contact with the earth. But it moved faster, doubling its prior speed.

I slapped the magic dagger into Rory's hand and handed Serafina's mace to her.

Rory faced the fiend, but spoke to us. "If this doesn't work. We run."

Beside me, Serafina mumbled a chant. "Please work. Please work."

I said, "Stab it in the mouth if you can. And if that doesn't work, stab it in its feet. Lift one up if you get the chance."

Rory half turned his head. "You want me to tickle its toes, too?"

Before I could glare at him, he flashed forward. He struck the thing's skull with the dagger. The blade penetrated bone and got buried to the hilt.

A surge of jubilation flashed through me. But then withered.

"Ow," it said. A pained look appeared on what passed for its face. It swiped at Rory, who ducked and sped behind it, racing to a safe distance.

*Safe* being a relative and hopeful term. Rory had, in fact, trapped himself. I knew why. He hoped to have the fiend turn and go after him, leaving the rest of us room to run.

The fiend, the magicked dagger still sticking out of its skull, stood there for a moment. Then it shuffled forward toward Serafina, Mick, and me.

"Holy Hel!" Serafina exclaimed. "Can nothing kill this thing?"

I asked for her mace. "I have an idea."

From behind, Rory slashed at skeleton's back with his sword, the clangs reverberating through the tunnel. It paid him no mind. Rory's sword may as well have been a feather by the way it reacted.

"Strike at its feet!" I yelled at Rory.

The fiend lumbered toward me as I took the lead position.

It smiled again. "You. I will eat. Slowly."

"Go goblin yourself," I said.

As Rory whacked at the thing's knees, I moved forward in a half-crouch.

The thing continued to advance without lifting a foot. It had to mean something. I hoped.

As it grabbed for me, I dropped to my knees and whacked at its forward foot.

I connected with the ankle bone. The mace bounced off, but the fiend's right foot slid sideways, the heel lifting off the ground a smidge.

From behind, Rory pushed or kicked—I didn't see—and the thing fell over on top of me.

A raucous noise echoed through the hall, piercing my ears. But it wasn't Mick. It was the bony fiend shrieking next to me.

I whirled around, sliding out from under, and crashed the mace down on the thing's oversized skull...straight into the gangrenous mouth.

The bones gave way...a little.

Screeching filled the halls. Bony legs splayed high in the air.

I smashed again, and again, and again.

The fifth time did it as the mouth structure caved in. The fiend's wailing screech ceased.

I kneeled there, panting, trying to gain my breath.

Rory slid beside me. He grabbed the hilt of the magicked dagger, put a boot to the thing's skull, and wrenched it free.

No blood, no sucking sound, just a...*CRACK*.

Mick and Serafina joined us.

Mick asked, "W-what is that t-thing?"

"I don't know," I said. "To me, it's a fiend from Hel."

Serafina nodded. "Aye. Undead. Summoned. Like the skeletons."

Rory straightened himself. "Summoned? By whom?"

A pop resounded. The air pressure shifted for a moment.

We looked up and down the corridor, now devoid of the skeleton gang's bones. Just those of the fiend remained. And Fudge, lying on his side in a pool of darkening blood that reflected the sickening cast of the green lights.

Serafina raced to him and kneeled beside him. "Oh Fudge. Why'd you run ahead?"

"Don't waste a heal spell," Rory said. "We may need it."

Serafina shot him a glare meant for the vilest of enemies. "Raising the dead is necromancy. I don't practice the dark arts."

Rory held up his hand, the one still holding the bejeweled dagger. "Sorry. Not what I was thinking."

"Look!" Mick pointed.

We followed his fingertip. The fiend's bones *brittled* before our eyes and turned to dust. The dust became finer and finer until it, too, was gone. Just a streak of white on an otherwise brown and gray stone floor.

Serafina got up and jabbed Rory in the chest. "If Fudge was still alive, and if I wanted to heal him, it's my right."

Rory's mouth tightened. His eyes searched mine for help.

I shrugged. We were in uncharted waters. It was her right, but then if she used up a spell we might later need, things could turn ugly between us. If we were alive.

Then again, Fudge had given us time.

Rory said, "Aye. If he was alive. But no way he was. Not with so much blood. Check your boots and knees."

Serafina did and scowled at the blood soaked into her clothes. "Oh. That's going to leave a stain." She looked up at me, her eyes watering over. Then she bawled, burying her face in my chest.

Rory said, "Sorry. I know it came out harsh. The circumstances had me riled up. I'm still quaking with battle energy."

Serafina's mouth pinched as she lifted her head. "Aye. Sorry if I lost my temper."

Rory gave her his boyish grin I so liked. "If?"

Serafina chuckled and spun about to face Rory. "I like animals."

I breathed a silent breath of relief. She wasn't blaming my husband.

Rory nodded. "I do, too."

I said, "Sorry, Fudge. And thank you for saving us."

Mick asked, "Saving?"

"Aye," I said. "He ran ahead. When the smoke cleared, the fiend was sucking the life out of the bear. I'm guessing, based on what I think I saw. There's a reason its lips were black and going on green. Fudge kept the fiend occupied while we killed its friends."

Rory nodded. "Yes. But back to the summoning part. Where did it and the skeletons come from? I didn't see any wards."

Mick took the light stick from Rory and flared it to life. We backtracked, peering at the floor and the walls. The young man pointed at the ground, past the spot where the first skeleton had struck at me. "There it is."

"A crescent moon," I said.

Rory jabbed it with his sword. "It wasn't there minutes ago."

"It was," Mick said. "You missed it." He raised his hand to stop my husband from yelling at him. "I'm not saying you missed it like that. Look."

He turned off the light and, sure enough, the crescent moon disappeared. Mick inflamed his artifact. "See. It's painted in a pigment that disappears in green light."

Rory nodded at Mick. "You're pretty clever. How about you walk up front with me?"

Mick shuddered. "No, thank you." He handed Rory the light stick. "I'll cover your rear."

"What? You'll scare off the monsters by screaming at them?"

I think Rory meant it as a joke, but it came out straight. Mick's face lost its pallor. He blinked a lot, his mouth hanging open.

"That's enough, Rory," I said.

His chest heaved. "Sorry, Mick. I'm mad at myself for missing the ward. And taking it out on you."

"The greenish-gray goop scared me," Mick said. "I's done nothing like what you's two have done."

Rory nodded. "Again. I'm sorry for my tone. This here escapade of ours is not at all what I expected."

Mick nodded. "Thank you. I'll try to do better next time."

Serafina elbowed the young lad in the hip. "We'll keep the white light on."

Mick nodded. "Aye. That's the trick."

He looked better, but I worried he'd been hurt past the point of repair with Rory. And I liked the young man. I put an arm around him. "We wouldn't have gotten this far without you. I'm glad you're here."

Mick's mouth dropped. Then he closed it. "You's warned me. I get what Master Belkin is saying."

"He can be gruff," I said.

Mick winked. "Can be?"

Rory put his hands on his hips. "Hey. I'm right here."

We got a chuckle out of that, and I whooshed air out of my lungs. We were in a maze of insanity and it tested our bonds. If we weren't facing traps, monsters appeared at random. Though it was probably not random at all. There were sigils we were missing. And Mick was helping.

I closed my eyes, and after another sigh, I said, "I tried to disbelieve they were real. And failed."

Rory's lips pursed, then flattened. "All too real."

Serafina said, "Based on what you said and what I've seen, the illusion spells are set in the upper tunnels. But ever since the stairs, the creatures appearing aren't illusions—they're summoned. From Fudge to the skeletons to that...thing."

Were we seeing Retzlaff's skills coming to the fore?

I said, "Summoning such a powerful fiend does not come from a weak mage."

There were murmurs of agreement, and worry shone in our eyes.

"Do we go on?" I asked. "We're battered and bruised. Both body and mind."

Rory looked at Mick, then Serafina. "I'm willing to go on if you are."

Serafina nodded at me. "You're healed up. I'm two into four. I'll take a vial of healing and keep it on my person, if you don't mind." Then a flash of a grim smile. "Besides, Retzlaff's minions killed my friend Fudge. I owe him."

Mick took a deep breath. "Aye. There's the ring to recover. And you's two can't quit without finding it."

True words that hurt. If not for the compel spell, would we have come this far?

I chuckled, in a dark sort of way. Not for a thousand silver. Hel, not for ten thousand. I had pushed us into this mess, and now we were left with no options.

## Chapter Twenty-Five

# PUZZLING BEASTS

## RORY

"Come on," I said, taking a hold of my wife's hand. "We're going to find Retzlaff and that damn ring."

Despite my earlier reservations about taking the job, I now wanted to see it done. Not just to recover the ring, but to bash Retzlaff's skull in. He had it coming.

We were close. I felt it. Though I didn't understand the traps or the tunnel design, except that it served one purpose—to keep trespassers out.

Mick pulled at his hair. "I's watch your backs."

Serafina asked us to wait a moment. Her hands waved, and she muttered too low for me to hear.

Mick's hands fell away from his hair. He stood straighter, his arms relaxing at his sides, the grip on his sling firm, like he was about to wring a chicken's neck.

"What did you do?" I asked Serafina.

"A bit of confidence enhancement," the half-alvae replied.

I could have used the spell myself, but there was no way I was going to admit it.

Mick's jaw firmed up, and his eyes gazed down the shaft.

I asked, "You ready?"

He nodded. "Aye. I's have a score to settle with Retzlaff."

Serafina said, "I may as well quaff a healing potion now. One more spell and I may not be able to drink it."

When she was done, I said, "Let's go."

I stomped off through the turns of the tunnel, holding the white light aloft and searching for glyphs on the floor and walls.

"I am eager to find Retzlaff," I said. "As I no longer have to be diplomatic. He's the, *ugh*, thief, and he has the ring."

*Stupid spell.*

"He's a murderer," Serafina said.

I didn't correct her about the law, as I was beyond angry. When I first feel the emotion, there's a sensation of heat flowing through my body. Now, I felt a cold resolve. Retzlaff was going to prison, or he was going to die. I preferred the latter.

I led us down the green-hued shaft to a set of stairs. Turning to Ingefær, I said, "So far, every staircase but the one from the waterfall has been warded."

"Do you see any sigils?" she asked.

"No. None."

She cast a find magic. For once, none of the steps glowed orange, and no knots appeared on the floor. The inkling crawling down the back of my neck told me I should find that very troubling.

I waved a hand at Mick. "Come here. You've got better eyes and a better sense of how traps work."

Mick shimmied his way forward, his head darting left and right. He inspected the landing and then took one step down at a time.

We followed a few steps behind him.

I pointed. "The light shifts back to blue at the bottom." Only the gods knew what it meant. Well, Retzlaff, too. But he was worse than a maggot.

At the bottom of the landing, Mick shouted as he ducked. "Yargh!"

A bolt ripped through Mick's tawny hair and shattered against the step I stood on.

I peered down the shaft lit by blue lights. "Stygg skapps!"

A quick headcount revealed there were a dozen of them, two of which had crossbows. "Take out the range weapons!"

I dashed down the tunnel to engage the hideous creatures. Roskva, my pinkish orange fylgjæ, popped into view, and I covered thirty strides in the blink of an eye.

Before reaching the first two, I skidded to a halt and gawked. Stygg skapps were the ugliest beasts in the Realm. And these were repulsive and huge—as tall as a troll.

Normal skapps had two eyes. These had a large, round third eye right smack in the middle of their foreheads. I had never seen a beast like it.

The books spoke of normal skapps being misshapen because of a cruel trick of the gods. One eye of their two was higher on one side and lower on the other, as were their ears. Their noses were bulbous and veered off at hard angles, giving their breaths a whistling sound. Each arm was of different length, as were their legs, which meant they walked funny. This was impacted further by the curvature of their spines. Despite all of their deformities, they were agile and strong.

Now I looked up at the grotesque hulk before me and into its third eye. I stood there, mesmerized, as the two beasts in front advanced. My sword hung from my hand at my right side, and the light stick hung from my left.

*Why won't my arms lift? Why do I feel at peace?* I remembered Ingefær's caution about disbelieving. I wanted to try—to blink—but I couldn't find the will.

A dagger flew from behind me, sailed above my head, and squelched into the big, rounded eye on the first skapp's forehead—the eye I'd been staring at. It flopped onto its back, spasmed twice, and lay still.

My eyes blinked, my gaze unglued. I refocused, and dashed three steps to the nearest lumbering skapp, keeping my gaze at its knees. "Don't look at their eyes!"

Using peripheral vision, I parried a rusty sword slashing at me and cut diagonally. Dark ochre blood exploded from the beast's chest, its leathery hide once a splotched mix of grays and browns. The creature fell face first and smashed its chin against the rock floor.

"Don't look at the third eye!" I engaged the next brute.

A trio of magic darts flew by and smote the crossbow-wielding brute in the rear of the group. The skapp tumbled to the ground. They were big, but they weren't as tough as the regular-sized ones.

Nine more to go. The trick to winning a battle was believing it to be possible. Sometimes, it meant I had to lie to myself.

The stygg skapp wielding the second crossbow loosened a salvo that would have hit me square in the chest, except I jumped and twisted with all my might. I should have leaped sideways. For my error, the bolt pierced the leather of my thigh guard and flew straight through the fleshy part.

I landed hard, but I didn't have the time or the luxury of feeling pain. I engaged the next skapp, deflecting the brutal smash of his club. Another series of darts took out the second crossbow-wielding skapp, who flopped onto his backside and lay still.

Moving with furious feet, one hobbling, I sliced lightning quick with my sword. The skapp before me fell with a thud, blood spurting from two deep stab wounds in its gut.

I learned long ago to avoid disemboweling. First, it made a Hel of a mess, making the ground as slippery as ice. And second, no matter what was killed, entrails stunk worse than anything coming out of a rear end.

A round rock, about the size of a small plum, slammed the next beast's third eye. It howled as it fell backward, cracking its skull against the ground. Ochre blood oozed out, forming a puddle.

I turned around at a grinning Mick. "Nice shot. The dagger was good, too."

His grin broadened.

No time for niceties, I dashed through to the rear flank and engaged the last two beasts. Their eyes turned toward me, surprised by my speed—which was my plan. By the time the second one thought to smack me, his friend had died on my blade.

In the blue haze of the magic light, I struggled to rip my sword free as the skapp towered over me, bleeding and leaking guts all over.

The second brute swung a heavy club and knocked the first one off me, taking my sword with it.

Sliding quick to the side, I pulled my dagger out of my boot. Club versus dagger was a terrible disadvantage. But with Roskva by my side, I darted and dashed, slicing at its legs.

The brute clubbed the air. I dodged under and looked up at its disfigured rear.

*I don't recommend the view. Not at all pleasant.*

I plunged my dagger into its back, in the spot where humans have kidneys.

A soft squelch was my reward.

The stygg skapp howled, and took a step as it swung the club around.

I ducked a second time, leaving my dagger stuck in its hide.

But I didn't need to worry. The skapp fell flat on its back the way a felled tree did in the woods. One bounce.

I looked up. Serafina swung her mace at the last stygg skapp's stomach. She hit, but the beast swung an arm at the same time and flung her to the side of the wall, where she flumped to the ground. She lay still.

I cursed. Where was Ingefær?

Mick slung a stone at the skapp. The moist squish was all I needed to hear. The enormous brute swooned onto its face...arms spread wide, chin shattering on the stone floor.

I checked the area. No upright skapps. Roskva popped out of sight, so I raced back on my own power, hobbling with effort. Pain jabbed my leg and shot up my spine.

Serafina clawed her way to her knees, shaking her head.

With frantic eyes, I searched for Ingefær.

A plume of fiery red flashed from underneath a skapp's armpit.

"No!"

I was at the beast's side, shoving it off of her. *Don't be dead.*

"What the Hel happened?" I demanded, getting the brute to slide off.

Mick shrugged. "I didn't see her get hit."

Serafina moved in beside me. She stretched her jaw like her ears were plugged.

Then she checked for my wife's breath. "As she cast her second set of fiery darts, Mick's stone felled a beast. I guess it fell on top of her."

Casting spells required concentration, so she wouldn't have seen the danger.

Hoping she hadn't been stabbed or clubbed to death, I scanned Ingefær's body. No wound was visible.

Mick came over and put a hand on my shoulder. "Sorry. I's seen it take aim at your wife."

Ingefær groaned.

I grinned at Mick. "Don't be sorry. You may have saved her life."

Serafina worked her jaw again. "She's alright. Well, she's breathing."

Grabbing a water skin, I dribbled liquid into my hands, then swatted my wife's cheeks. "Hey, lover bugs. No time for a nap."

Ingefær's eyes fluttered.

Mick chuckled. "Lover bugs?"

Serafina tittered along with Mick.

"Really?" I asked. "This is serious." I searched their eyes. "This stays between us."

Mick cleared his throat and nodded. Serafina grinned; her chin dipped once.

Ingefær raised her arms, and we helped her sit up. She rubbed her left arm, then her temple. "What hit me?"

"We think the skapp fell on you," I said. "Might have been a flailing elbow. There's a lot of heft to these beasts. You need healing?"

She shook her head. I helped her to her feet.

Ingefær worked her left arm. "No. This is from the skeletons earlier." She shifted her attention to her temple. "Is it bruised?"

I checked. "No. A little red?"

She massaged the area.

"You alright, Miss Ingefær?" Mick asked.

She nodded.

"Cuz it scared the you-know-what right out of me when I killed it with a stone and it flopped on top of you."

"No worse for the wear." My wife hugged him. "Thanks, though. I was so focused on the one in the back with the crossbow, I allowed the one in front of me to get too close."

I heaved a heavy sigh. We had to work on our battle tactics. Which presumed we knew what we would face. I suspected any plan made would perish at first contact.

Ingefær asked, "And how are you, Serafina?"

I glanced over. She looked her usual grayish-green self.

"I'm alright." She rubbed at her chin. "Tagged me good. I have never seen skapps like these."

"That and the three-armed troll tells me Retzlaff has been playing with things he shouldn't." I scanned the tunnel. "These bodies aren't disappearing like the skeletons. So, not a summoning?"

Serafina nodded. "Correct. It's a beastly crossover."

Ingefær nudged me on my shoulder. "What happened to you at the start? You stopped cold."

"It enthralled me," I said. "With its gigantic eye."

Nothing was natural down here. Serafina shuddered. Mick yanked at his tawny hair, but kept his mouth shut.

Ingefær chinned at Mick. “You’re quite handy with the sling. Where’d you learn to throw with such accuracy?”

“Me and my pals used to take old bread and throw it into a farm field. Then we’d take turns trying to smack crows.”

Serafina gasped. Her voice turned icy. “How cruel. Poor birds.”

I’d done similar things as a teen. To train up my skills and to eat. “When you’re hungry, a crow tastes good.”

Ingefær asked Mick, “How long ago?”

“It’s been a couple of years.” His brown eyes looked at Serafina. “I ain’t done it since.”

Furrows appeared between Serafina’s golden brows. “Well, then...see that you don’t. They’re not sport. Meals to eat, I understand. But no animal should be harmed for entertainment.”

I hobbled over and retrieved my sword, and rolled over another skapp to get my dagger. Pointing, I said. “These skapps have been made to amuse their creator. Same with the troll upstairs.”

Serafina scowled.

My wife said, “Yet another talent Mage Retzlaff appears to possess. Let’s see...illusions, animal summoning, animal transmutation, and undead summoning.”

Mick hiccupped.

We were up against a very potent mage. Elise’s information had been very wrong. Or had she lied to us?

I tapped Mick on his shoulder. “You sure you didn’t know Retzlaff could hurl so much magic?”

His brown eyes widened, and he shook his head. “No, sir. If he did anything, it seemed...minor. Dispelled the ward on the Temple and maybe made the targets sleepy. But now that you’s mention it, I was sure I’d flubbed the last job...well, the job before ma’s. Must have been Retzlaff who had cast something to keep the merchant from spotting me. Maybe it was an illusion spell, not that I’s see what they can do.”

We were back to the same dilemma. Go on, or turn back. Which wasn't a real choice. Not with Elise's conjuration upon me and Ingefær.

I took a deep breath, my hands going to my thigh. As my battle rage subsided, the pain in my leg increased.

Serafina caught the motion. "You're hurt. Why didn't you say so?"

I shrugged. Blood soaked my pant leg and pooled into my boot. Time for deflection. "Good teamwork."

Serafina grunted. "I'll cast a heal on you."

"Save the spell," I said. "A strip of cloth will stop the bleeding."

She tsked at me. "No. Down here, an open wound may get infected. And with you running like-like lightning—I've never seen anyone run so fast—you're bound to open the wound again."

Ingefær placed a hand on my arm. "It's why she's here."

My toes squished in my own warm goop. I closed my eyes. "Alright."

With her incantation, Serafina closed the wound in my leg. But it left a hole in my leather breeches. I counted our inventory in my head. "There're four vials of healing left."

In the blue cast of the tunnel, I dug into my backpack and handed Serafina one vial and Ingefær another. I had to dangle it for a moment before my wife rolled her eyes at me and took it.

"Serafina uses her powers to heal anyone injured. But, when she runs low, she quaffs a vial. You, my dear wife, are the most potent danger to another mage. You must stay clearheaded and, if possible, uninjured. Retzlaff is a terror."

Mick said, "Gosh, he really loves you, Miss Ingefær."

She grunted but put the vial into her pants pocket. "Nice speech."

I winked at her. Then I handed Mick a vial and pocketed the last one. "Don't use it unless necessary."

"What I want to know," Ingefær said, "is where is the glyph that summoned the skapps?"

I glanced at her. "We had the white light on."

She said, "Aye. Earlier we'd missed them because we weren't looking, missed another because we didn't have the right lighting, and I think I messed up once or twice with my dispel magic."

I followed her logic. "But this last time, it was none of the three."

We stood there in silence, eyeing each other.

Mick said, "I don't know where this batch of monsters came from."

Serafina shrugged. "Me neither. But it doesn't change our objective, does it?"

"No," I replied. "But if they weren't summoned, then where did they come from? I can't believe they sit in the shaft all day long hoping a group of idiots wanders down their tunnel. We missed something, and I want to know what."

"We may learn more if we go down the tunnel," Ingefær said.

"Aye." I sighed. "Let's search these things first."

We checked the skapps for anything useful and found nothing. Mick retrieved his thrown dagger. He left several of his sling stones buried in the stygg skapps' third eyes, too grossed out to dig for them.

I led us down the shaft. After a smooth but significant turn, we came to what I would call a room. A carved-out cave...with an iron door twice as thick as any normal wood one. It was swung wide open.

With sword at the ready position, I peeked around the corner.

The stench hit me hard. I moaned, working to keep my last meal where it belonged. My search revealed an empty grotto, maybe thirty strides around. It was full of debris, like torn clothing and a thigh bone—a human one—and scat. Lots and lots of scat.

Ingefær came up behind me and paled. "Ooh. Gross."

Mick moved to the door and inspected it.

Ingefær asked, "You're not going in there, are you?"

"No. Not unless you think we'll find something valuable."

"Over here," Mick said.

We turned around.

Mick was at the doorsill. He pointed high and low. Then manipulated the lower stone, waist high, shifting it outward. "These stones act as latches. And the door has prongs of the same height."

I eyed the door. "No handles."

Mick scanned the shaft. "There has to be a release mechanism back the way we came." Then he looked at me. "And I missed it when we came down the stairs."

Serafina said, "That makes no sense."

"I mean we—I—triggered the release of this door. Which released the skapps." Mick chewed on his lower lip. "I'll bet one step has a pressure pad. A subtle one."

Serafina asked, "So, to keep those three-eyed skapps locked away, you avoid the trapped step?"

Mick nodded. "Aye."

Ingefær jabbed a thumb over her shoulder. "There's a leg bone in there that once belonged to someone."

I growled. "Retzlaff has his own menagerie."

With the puzzle solved...maybe...I raised my finger. "We keep moving. Double your efforts to spot anything unusual."

Mick licked his lips. "Sorry I missed it."

Ingefær patted him on the shoulder. "We all missed something."

"Great job on figuring out the door, Mick," I said.

He beamed.

Mick was contributing. And he'd changed. He seemed more self-assured.

Was it the spell? Or had he felled enough skapps with his own abilities to build his confidence? Or maybe it came from knowing his thieving skills were solving puzzles.

I smiled. "You take lead, Mick."

The tawny-haired man shrugged and took the white light from me.

"Forward." I waved at the group.

## Chapter Twenty-Six

# INTO THE CRYPT

## INGEF□R

Mick led, holding his glow stick high. Rory and I followed, with Serafina in the rear. I kept a lookout at the left wall and the ceiling while my husband kept watch on the floor and the right wall.

Fifty strides past the stygg skapp jail cell, Mick stopped us with a wave of his hand. The reason was obvious: the shaft ended in an elaborate design that spoke of a door without actually being one.

We approached with soft steps and darting eyes.

Mick studied the floor, then the flat end of the shaft, then the tunnel sides. "There are scuff marks on the floor leading to this here...I'll call it an entryway."

Whatever it was, it was unnatural-looking, and huge. If it was a door, it stood twice as tall as any human and, counting the pointed arch it was ensconced in, it spanned the width of the tunnel. The door-looking part was made of some luminescent red stone that was also smooth. The arch was made of brownish-gray mortar and etched in strange runes. But ones I recognized.

I pointed. "Those are ancient Varanusian symbols."

Mick hiccupped. "How do you know?"

I said, "I traveled with Hombir Tramanek, a d'oglemann mage. He owns a few ancient tomes. I remember some of the writing."

Mick's hiccups grew louder and more frequent. "What does-*hic*-those symbols mean?"

I shrugged. "No idea. I can't read it. I just recognize it."

Within the luminescent red wall were veins of gold that formed elaborate loops, that, together, appeared to make the shape of a leaf.

Rory grunted. "And I supposed you don't know what that golden symbol represents?"

"No idea."

Mick pointed at a round, fist-sized stone sticking out about an inch from the wall on our left, waist high. "I's think this activates the jail cell lock. And disables it too. Either that, or it opens up this here glamorous entryway. I'd have to test it to make sure."

Rory said, "I don't think we want to be pushing at things at the moment."

Mick swallowed hard. "I'll bet it's warded."

My husband looked at me. "You're up."

I cast a detect magic spell, and the beautiful red door, along with the arch, glowed bright orange, brighter than anything we'd seen so far. Brighter than the door at the far end of the upper tunnel—the one past the crates and rats. A half second later, a big, bright white *R* appeared on the wall amidst the gold veined leaf.

"Great, just great," Rory said.

Which isn't what he meant.

We hadn't seen an *R* before. And this one was enmeshed in gold swirls and loops. Did this ward trigger something way worse than the star and crescent moon? I thought so.

I grimaced. "We either go through here, or we go to the tunnel with the crescent moon and star wards on it."

Everyone looked at the door before us.

Rory said, "This is too grand. We have to be close."

Which is what I had thought about a dozen spells ago. Without waiting for them to get ready, I dispelled the magic *R* on the door, being careful to wipe in short strokes, mimicking the gaps in the line where the gold veins crossed.

My knees shook, and the blue-lit tunnel flickered before my eyes. It wasn't the sconces.

Serafina came to my rescue, restoring my stamina. She'd been prepared.

"Look," Mick said, pointing as the orange glow dissipated.

An outline of a normal sized door formed in the wall, the gaps cutting through the gold-veined leaf. The door was the standard height and width for most. Why didn't I get a warm fuzzy feeling?

"Thank you," I said to Serafina. "Get ready to go in."

Mick said, "Nothing bad happened. Was that too easy?"

Rory said, "We have seen no sign of a living human, or alvae, or anyone else other than monstrous beasts. Jarl Retzlaff has to be past this here door."

Mick said, "I'll bet he doesn't walk this way. He's got himself a secret passage."

"I'll bet that's the door we turned away from," I said. The one with the crescent and the star.

There were murmurs of agreement.

No use blubbering over spent coins. We'd made our choices.

Serafina said, "Hindsight doesn't help. Time to finish this."

Mick handed the light artifact to my husband. "Master Belkin, would you do the honors?"

Rory flashed a smile, drew his blade, and approached the door. He pulled down on the now revealed handle and shoved. The door swung open with an enormous creak of the hidden hinges. "Crap. We've announced our presence again."

The new tunnel went straight, and the glow of the candle-less, magicked light shone blue, brighter than the tunnel we were in. Though not green, the eerie factor went up a notch. Why did brighter blue seem spookier?

What could be worse than one fiend from Hel? *Two fiends*. The thought came to mind all too quickly.

To Rory's right stood a set of stairs leading up. We inspected them without touching and found no visible wards.

"Do I check it?" I asked.

Rory shook his head. "No. We're going straight. I suspect Mick and Serafina are right. These stairs go up to the second tunnel. Well, first, if you come in through the mansion."

He turned and shuffled forward, stopping often to scout, presumably checking for sigils. I searched as well.

We turned a corner of the wayward, blue-lit shaft, and before us lay a vast cavern, all lit up like the sun, but in icy blues. It hurt my eyes, and I closed them to stop the throbbing in my head.

Rory took a step and stopped. "Crap. The stone I just stepped on sunk a smidge."

Mick scooted around me and went down to the ground to look. "Hold the light above me, Master Belkin."

Mick's fingers brushed loosed dirt. "Aye. You set a trap."

"Set?" Rory asked.

"Aye. At least I think so. Can't be sure until you move your foot." Mick chuckled. "Which I don't advise."

"We can't stay here," I said. "Try to disarm it."

Mick dug out his tool kit of various metal files and prongs. He poked and prodded. There was a metallic click.

"Oh, oh," Mick said.

A horde of shrieks came from the far-right side of the huge grotto.

Rory cursed and sped forward with sword in hand.

A score of goblins—greenish brutes with thick leathered hides and inch-long talons at the end of their toes and fingers—raced toward us. They gnashed their sharp teeth, all pointed for ripping and shredding flesh.

But these goblins differed from the standard ones I'd run into. These had a foot-long spike atop their heads. It appeared to be made of bone and cartilage...but I was guessing.

Just as my mind grappled with the monstrosity—for blinking and wishing them to disappear didn't work—the lead goblin lowered its head and charged at my husband.

Rory dodged and hacked, and the goblin went down, face first. I elected to save my magical prowess and joined the fray with sword in hand.

Goblins were nasty. Their taloned hands and feet, and the teeth in their mouth, were grimy and foul-smelling. Any wound they caused was sure to become infected. Death wasn't a certainty, but the odds of a high fever or a limb lost to gangrene ran high.

I skewered a goblin through the chest and pulled back, avoiding a raking claw from its friend to my left.

A stone the size of a peach pit flew by and rang a goblin's bell. With it stunned, Serafina clubbed it to death.

Three down, and seventeen to go.

We worked as a team. With Rory's blinding quickness—I never see his fylgjæ—he dispatched four more. Mick and Serafina downed another, and I decapitated one on my own.

The remaining eleven changed tactics, shifting into two ranks of five, standing shoulder to shoulder. The eleventh one gave guttural commands. Fighting typical goblins was a lesson in battle chaos, with them running in all directions at once. These goblins had a semblance of order and planning. Very unusual.

Advancing as a phalanx, they sneered and bared their pointy, blackened teeth.

Rory got in front of us. He used his magicked feet to dart forward, stab, then back.

The surviving goblins stepped over their two fallen comrades.

We backed up.

Rory, once again, dashed forward.

"Argh!" Rory shouted, sending a chill down my spine. I stepped forward as Rory ran back.

Blood ran down his right arm. The goblins had learned...and anticipated.

From behind me, Serafina said, "He's going to need healing."

"Give me a moment," Rory said. "There's seven left."

Mick said. "We'll be out of room in twenty feet. Unless you want to go back out the fancy door?"

"Or up the stairs?" I asked.

"No." Rory dashed.

The goblins raked at the sight of blurred motion. But two fell without Rory screaming.

Rory returned, grinning. "I ran in and slid low."

With five left, the goblins stopped their advance and looked at us, snarling. Inconveniently, they occupied the center of the cavern.

Could we bypass them? I didn't think so. No doubt they would follow and wait for us to make a mistake.

Rory said, "I'll go again."

I snagged his arm sleeve. "My turn. You've had all the fun so far."

I pinched sawdust and made my motions, uttering the incantation to a fireball. With the space the grotto provided, I could hurl the area spell, so long as I fired to their rear.

"When the pea flies, retreat to the door."

I waved both arms to summon a fireball and spoke Varanusian. I jabbed my left arm forward, thrusting the sawdust at the spot where I wanted the fiery bead to explode. The sawdust turned into a flaming pea and sailed over Rory's head.

My husband pushed Serafina and Mick away from the coming blast, while I shuffled backward, watching the pea fly.

The goblins cowered; one dropped to the ground, covering its head. But the bead sped past. The lead goblin showed me his dinner smile.

That's when the pea exploded.

I shut my eyes and covered my face against the flash of the heat. Hot air billowed through the grotto. When the roar of the fireball died, I surveyed the damage.

Not a goblin remained standing. The one who had crouched down smoldered from its backside.

Rory waved us forward. When we neared the burned goblins, the stench of the charred beasts turned my stomach. Burn wounds were unpleasant to look at, and smell, even on the enemy.

Mick fell to his knees and hurled.

Serafina turned so white, she could almost pass for human, if not for her eyes and ears.

Rory held the light stick high. With his sword in his right hand, he moved through the bodies and kicked and stabbed them, making sure they were dead. But before he got to the last one, they winked out of sight.

Serafina called Rory over to her. She took a swig of water and cast a heal spell on the gash in his arm. Using water for material meant she went for cleansing the wound as much as healing it.

Serafina said, "I'm going to cast a restore on myself." And she did.

Which meant she had two restore incantations available before it was healing potion time.

I checked everyone for wounds. Even the slightest scratch left untreated would be trouble. Rory double-checked me.

Gathering ourselves with Rory in the lead, we moved through the vast cave, searching. It had an oblong, egg-like shape. But it was devoid of anything. Not even scat. Well, after the dead goblins disappeared, I wasn't expecting any. We were trying to figure out a method to the madness. And failed.

We'd come into the grotto through the wide section. Now we stood at the natural opening at the opposite end. Out of the ice-blue area, we looked into a natural cavern. Other than the fact that it was lit up in hideous green. By appearance from our vantage point, it was forty strides in width.

In the middle of it, at an angle to us, sat a stone podium in the shape of a coffin...thrice as long as it was wide. Atop it, three feet off the ground, lay a naked dead man, his chest impaled by a black-handled dagger. The head of the man—I presumed based on the flat chest—had lolled away and all I saw was matted dark hair.

We crept forward, one hesitant step after another. I glanced left, then right. Nothing but green shadows.

My eyes tried to pierce the haze twenty strides past the dais. But all I saw was darkness outlining a jagged opening, maybe a foot bigger than I was tall and wide. How did I know it was an opening? Because it was as black as night.

At a distance some five strides from the dais, I stopped, snarled, and spat bile. Blood had dribbled down the man's sides and gathered at the base of his body. It had dried black where it hadn't pooled; but where the blood was thickest, it remained a deep currant red.

A pale Mick approached on tender feet and lifted the man's head. He screeched. "Agh!" Tugging at his own hair, he paced back and forth. "Yargh! Gagh!"

At least he wasn't clucking like a chicken.

Rory grabbed him by the collar and slapped him. "What's wrong?"

"That's...that's Jarl Retzlaff."

I stepped forward and studied the sheer white face. "Aye." I caught Rory's eyes. "The man's been dead, what, eight hours?"

Rory nodded and pointed. "The back of his head has been cut open. There's nothing inside the skull save dribbles of blackened blood."

"Oh, geez," Serafina said, turning as pasty as I felt. "Who does something like that?"

Why was the man we were seeking dead? What clue had we missed?

Worse still...what power had killed the man who appeared to have so much of his own?

## Chapter Twenty-Seven

# THE DEATH OF A JARL

## RORY

"Inspect his other hand," I said as I thumbed through the man's fingers on his right hand.

"Rory!" My wife chastised me.

"What?" I frowned. "We're looking for the ring."

She shuddered. "I find it unpleasant to rob the dead of their possessions."

Mick burst out with a booming guffaw. "That's the best way. No chance of getting caught or killed."

Serafina let the dead man's left hand flop to the dais. "No ring. One of his fingers is missing, though."

Ingefær's hands gripped the sides of her hips as she faced Mick. "It's the worst of ways. We should respect the dead."

"I respect them...and thank them," Mick said. "But they have no need for their trinkets where they's going." He pulled a black stylus and a tablet from his blue vest. He drew a straight line with the stylus across the tablet. "Got you."

"What did you just do?" I asked.

"Took Jarl Retzlaff out of my book of grudges."

I laughed. "Let me see."

"No, sir," Mick said. He tucked both items away.

The kid had an actual list. Should I be worried I was on it?

I sighed and turned to Serafina. "It's probably gone. But check Retzlaff's pockets."

We came away empty-handed. I did a slow circle in the green gloom of the chamber. "Where in the Realm is the ring?"

Serafina pointed rightward with a thumb. "There's more to this cave system."

She had it right. The grotto with the goblins had been the first section of the cavern, with a narrow passage connecting it to this one.

I scanned the ceiling. Lots of protrusions and jagged rock. "This wasn't dug out."

Ingefær pointed toward the dark spot in the cave wall. "Do we go on?"

I shook my head. I wanted to check the sides of our grotto, which were deep in dark shadows, as they weren't lit by the green sconces.

"We'll check the left side first," I said.

I shuffled into the darkened depths and hoisted Mick's glow stick high. The walls curved in, narrowing the space as I went.

At the left end of the cave, there was a desk with a chair, a dresser to the right, a cot, crumpled bedsheets and blanket, and a cupboard beyond at the end, all arranged to form an L taking up one half of the area. It was an odd set up. At least, I couldn't fathom why it was here, of all places.

We checked the desk first—not one scratch on its surface. It was clean and free of dust. That was true of the other pieces of furniture as well. I peered close. It all looked new.

We debated having Ingefær cast a detect magic spell, but I was adamant she save herself.

"I volunteer Mick to go through everything." I locked eyes with him. "Carefully."

Mick tugged at his mop of tawny hair but nodded.

He took his time, looking from above, then the sides, and even crawled under to study things from below, the light stick in his hand the whole time. Finished, Mick pulled at the desk drawer, and it opened with a soft whoosh.

He pulled out a stack of vellum papers and set them atop the desk.

"Keep searching," I said. "We're looking for the ring, or anything that tells us where it is—and for what killed Retzlaff."

Mick went through the rest of the desk and came away with two jars of ink, six quills, and yet more vellum, these blank.

The young man moved on to the dresser and repeated his routine. When he was sure it was safe, he pulled one drawer after another. "Clothes."

He shifted his attention to the bed. Mick checked under the straw-stuffed mattress and checked the planks from underneath. Finished with that, he ripped the sheets and blanket off and folded them nice and neat, setting them on the end.

Lastly, he moved to the cupboard. After concluding there were no traps, at least ones he could see, he opened one up. Four loaves of bread and a score of jars of honey. He opened the second cupboard, which contained six jugs full of liquid. Mick sniffed, then shrugged. He opened another panel. A sack full of light green Lodi apples, which ripened by summer around here. These were fresher than the ones we'd found in the storage room.

When Mick signaled he was done, I sighed my frustration. "No signet ring."

Well, I hadn't expected to find it. Whoever had killed Retzlaff now possessed the magic ring. And the finger that wore it.

I moved to the cupboard and picked up an apple and sniffed. Ripe and sweet was what my nose said, and I salivated. Instead of taking a bite, I sliced it open. It seemed real. No wyrms in it either.

I couldn't resist. I ate it, core and all. "Delicious. These are a week from being picked."

Ingefær frowned. "You and your stomach. One day...."

I grinned. We had ourselves a meal: bread, honey, and apples. We drank water from our skins, leaving alone what turned out to be a sweet red wine.

When we had finished, I waved my hand at the arrangement. "It's odd. He sets up living quarters down here, and yet we find him impaled."

Ingefær asked, "Is this the furniture delivered five or six days ago?"

Had we been on this job for three—no, four—days? It felt like a moon.

Ingefær said, "None of the rooms upstairs had any missing furniture."

"Meaning?" Mick asked.

"Meaning, he brought the dresser, bed, and desk in," she replied. "A week ago."

"Which explains the traffic by the waterfall," I said.

Serafina furrowed her blondish brows. "What waterfall?"

I caught her up on the exploring we'd done before she joined us.

"We're not leaving unless we get those draft horses," my wife said. Not all that deep down, Ingefær was a softie with animals. It was one of the many things I loved about her.

Mick scratched at his neck. "The spiral staircase is too narrow for this furniture."

He was right.

I thumbed through the stack of vellum with writing, skimming the first sentence or two of each page, then moving on. "Maybe this will help. It's a log; every page is dated."

I flipped to the bottom parchment and searched for the date. "Started a week after last year's Spring Equinox."

My wife and I exchanged wide eyes. The date was a week after Vidarr had saved the Realm from utter destruction—and when magic had returned in full force.

I read the top sheet with Mick hovering over my shoulder. "Dated seven days ago. Success is near at hand. I have the right ingredients now. But grandfather's notes about the incantation aren't quite right. The order has to be wrong. I need the heirloom ring the old man sold. I tire too quickly."

Ingefær snarled. "What was he doing?"

"I don't know." Splitting the stack into thirds, I handed two of the piles to Ingefær and Serafina. "Are you sure you don't want to read, Mick?"

"I's hold the light for everyone."

I kept the older entries, while Ingefær got the middle section, and Serafina the most recent. We thumbed through them, reading to ourselves.

Serafina gasped. "Holy Furæyar. I think…." She trailed off, her lips moving with no sound coming out as she read.

Ingefær joined her, her mouth dropping inch by inch.

"Well?" I asked.

Ingefær said, "He was trying to raise the dead."

"Most of his notes speak of failures, plus the incantations, materials, and motions he tried." Serafina set the pile of vellum on the desk. "The ones from right after this year's Spring Equinox complain of dwindling options."

"So, who killed Retzlaff?" I asked.

Mick nodded toward the opening we had yet to go through. "Whoever killed him must be through there. Or they went up the stairs we passed by."

Mick had it right. We had more cavern to search, and maybe our questions would be answered. No one was hurt, and both Ingefær and Serafina had spell capacity remaining.

Setting my stack of parchments down, I grabbed the magic stick from Mick's hand and waved at everyone to follow me. At the dais with Retzlaff's brainless body, I turned left toward the next opening—the one all blotted in black, like it ate up the green hue.

Approaching with care, I peered in. The light shifted to a bright red. By its glow and Mick's white light, I scanned the corridor. The shaft was a natural one, with plenty of twists and turns and jagged rocks all over. Except for the floor, which was more or less flat, but had lumps to it.

I scanned high. The ceiling was rough like the walls, and it was eight feet above us, about as tall as the tunnel was wide.

Ingefær said, “What makes something like this?”

Serafina replied, “Water. A river.”

“That had to be a long time ago,” Mick said.

“Thousands of years ago,” I said. And probably before the last Ragnarök. The first Divine Reckoning. Few would know about it, so I kept my mouth shut.

I whooshed air as I strode forward, my eyes searching for anything out of place. Anything that might indicate another trap.

After a hundred strides of twisting and turning, I stopped before the next cavern widening. A red hue, darker than the sheen we had walked through, seeped into our passage.

Well, we’d done green and blue several times each. What did the switch to red mean?

Peering past the glow of the white light stick, the space in the next area glistened crimson, at times flickering, like the air was on fire. Yet the light was too red, with no oranges or yellows. And I detected no heat. Instead, the stench of rotted flesh attacked my nostrils.

Ingefær sidled up beside me, a grimace on her otherwise beautiful face. “That doesn’t look or smell inviting.”

She had a penchant for understatement.

I said, “I’m guessing whoever...or whatever...killed Jarl Retzlaff is in there.”

Serafina blew a gust of air out that ruffled the collar of my shirt. She was a full stride away. “Oh boy. That smells worse than dead fish. And I know a lot about that.”

I flashed her a grin. We were comrades in arms. From false imprisonment to our dislike for fish.

Mick yanked at his hair, but nodded at me when I glared at him. “Don’t worry, Master Belkin. I know better than to scream here.” He faked a grin. “I hope there’s a lot of treasure in there, cause so far, this here adventure has been a bust.”

“Once we find the signet ring, I’m done with this place.” I wiped perspiration off my brow. The motion allowed me to smell an armpit. Ugh.

It wasn’t hot down here. The sweat was good old-fashioned trepidation. I called my fylgjæ. She rarely came when I summoned her, but this time, she appeared right away. She sensed my fears, too.

Her quick arrival confirmed for me big trouble lay ahead. I warned the others. Mick hiccupped, but took a deep breath and covered his mouth.

In single-file formation with Serafina in the rear, we entered the crimson cavern. I couldn’t gauge its size, as the red haze was too thick.

The grotto wasn’t clean like the rest of the tunnels. In the red pea soup, as we went deeper in, dead things along the ground appeared as if summoned.

I’m a hunter by training, but I couldn’t identify which animal or species the many piles of bones belonged to. A few carcasses gleamed clean white, but most had flesh rotting on them, with wyrms and maggots gorging.

Did Retzlaff use these remnants as material for his incantations, or were the remnants the result of his failed necromantic attempts?

I pointed at an organized pile of fully fleshed bodies, laid side by side. “This looks like the help.”

They were clothed as servants—a maid’s apron on two, a black jacket over a white shirt on one, and coveralls on two more. I didn’t see any blood on the bodies. But the tops of their heads, which were missing—just like the jarl—were black with it.

"Dead between one and three days." They were puffed up and were now decomposing, their limbs flaccid. It added to the stench of offal and the disfigured dead we had passed.

In other piles, there were rocks of various sizes, shredded clothing of different colors and materials—like linen and wool, and grayish planks of wood strewn in a separate pile.

Are the planks from a broken-apart casket?

A macabre laugh filled the cavern, sending shivers from my neck to my ass.

I may have farted.

## CHAPTER TWENTY-EIGHT

# THE FIRST JOHAN

## RORY

My eyes flashed into the cavernous depths as the red haze thinned, revealing a throne at the back of the cave. Its black stone was smooth, but instead of reflecting the unnatural light, it seemed to drink it in. The stone had to be made of polished obsidian, a rare lava-like rock found deep underground.

But my eyes were drawn to the man sitting on it. He wore no clothing, and if he hadn't moved, he would have looked *mostly* dead. Atop his disfigured skull—half covered in gangrenous flesh and half with weeping pustules of blackish blood—there was a bejeweled crown of reddish gold.

Was it the light or was it made of rose gold? An exceedingly rare and valuable ore.

I recalled the history we'd read. "Jarl Johan Retzlaff the first, I presume?"

The figure cackled again, and his bony chin lifted off his chest. The latter was a mass of black and frog-green muscle and flesh, minus the skin. His black heart pulsed, but I didn't see any blood swirling through, nor did his ash gray lungs move air.

"How hideous," Serafina said softly.

A blackish-blue strip of twisted flesh lashed out of his oversized toothless mouth. He lisped and mispronounced his words. "Oh good. I wash getting hungwy, and you bwought me my wunch." He cackled. "Ow ish it dinnah?"

I said, "I brought you cold steel. I can have you heated if you like."

Ingefær hissed. "Based on the other bodies, he wants our brains."

I nodded. "To eat."

Mick let out a high-pitched wail.

"Did you kill your great-grandson? Or is it great-great?" I asked.

The dry laugh ended in a cough. "He shevved his puhpush. And whined about me kiwwing the hep."

"Where's the ring?" I asked.

The rotted corpse's blue lips twitched. A finger atop the armrest moved as it tapped the stone chair to a song only he could hear.

From the decaying right arm, a flaming bead erupted.

A ball of fire.

With Roskva-imbued speed, I dashed left and forward, then dropped to the floor, covering my head.

The bead exploded; the fire sucked the air out of the cavern for a breath. My heart pounded. I'd survived thanks to my speed. The others hadn't stood a chance.

Rage took me, and I jumped to my feet, ready to skewer the once-dead man. But fear tinged with hope won out, and I glanced behind me.

Ingefær shook her head as she strutted toward the not-quite-dead man. She was alive! They were all alive.

Every other eye blink, I spotted a twinkling before her. I grinned. She'd gotten her wall of air spell up before the bead detonated. Or maybe she'd summoned it while Johan had yapped.

I raced forward and was rewarded with a stream of five magical darts of flaming energy.

Great. Just great.

I'm fast with Roskva around, and evaded two of the darts. Each blast hurt, stinging and burning, and caused my entire body to twitch.

The magic didn't incapacitate me the way the trap had with its poison. Still, I knew I couldn't take too many more of those from the not-quite dead man who sat before me.

Shifting her wall of air to the right—for I saw the sparkles in the red haze—Ingefær let loose with a bolt of lightning, which smashed into the seated corpse. Bits of rotted flesh exploded in flames. The obsidian throne crackled and arced with energy.

After it subsided, and the flames petered out, the living corpse crowed. "Oh yesh. Mowe pwease."

It stood, the blackened muscle rippling beneath the gangrenous tissue. Against all laws of the Realm—his parts somehow stayed assembled and in the right places. It was a hideous sight in the red glow of the cavern.

Hel, under any light.

In a way, his rotted flesh had healed—now grayer and with better definition. He was still a mottled mess of gray, black, and blue, just with an elasticity to him.

Mick stepped to the left, getting an angle past Ingefær's wall's edge. "Yaggh!" He let loose with a round rock. It shattered in midair four paces from its target. I never saw the once-dead Retzlaff twitch a finger or move his blue lips.

With Roskva, I dashed forward, my sword arm drawing back to slice the head from the corpse's body. And bounded into an invisible wall—face first. I spun in a half circle and about fell over. The cave tilted for a moment as my face and arms screamed at me to watch where I was going.

My chin bled. I wiped my mouth, getting blood on my sleeve. When had he summoned the shield wall spell?

Right! Mick's stone had disintegrated. The gods! The wall was huge, at least twenty paces in width.

The rotting man turned his attention to Ingefær, whose hands gyrated as she worked on a spell. Another stone hurled through the air.

A great shot. It left a divot, but no blood oozed out. Instead, it turned blue on black. Or black on blue. Either way, it looked purple in the reddened air.

*Am I concussed?*

With a flick of old Retzlaff's wrist and a word I didn't recognize, three wulvs sprung into existence just before Mick's third rock flew through the air, slamming into the man's forehead.

Ah, not so wide. He'd shifted it, same as Ingefær. Only I didn't see the outlines of his spell.

I reached out with my hands, moving to the right, trying to find the edge of old Retzlaff's invisible shield wall.

The wulvs ran at Ingefær, Mick, and Serafina.

Mick fired another missile. This time, it shattered midair, exploding against an invisible barrier well to my right. Retzlaff had moved the air shield again.

"Behind me!" Ingefær shouted. Her wall of air, serving as both a magical and physical shield, would block the wulvs until they figured a way around.

I had raced to the other side of the cavern to evade the fireball and to spread the not-quite dead man's attention. So far, the tactic had gotten me a bloody lip. With a hand before me and with cautious steps, I searched for the invisible wall of air, trying to find an opening. The maneuver brought me closer to the cavern's center.

"Dispel his wall!" I yelled at Ingefær.

Serafina waved her hands. What was she casting?

No time to figure it out as I had shifted too far right, and a wulv peeled off to lope toward me. Two wulvs snapped and pawed at Ingefær's wall, smacking into it, which only infuriated them further. Wulvs weren't stupid. They would find a way around in time.

The once-dead-man cackled. A finger of his left hand looped up and over, and I was bludgeoned by an invisible force—his air shield wall. Agony shot up my left arm, only to be silenced by a blow to my head.

Was it night out? Because stars twinkled.

The magic wall shoved at me, pushing me back, way left of the others. Fur flashed in my peripheral vision.

With Roskva-imbued speed, I created space between the magical wall and my wracked body. On instinct, I stabbed the wulv, who had found a seam in Retzlaff's shield...maybe because the necromancer had wanted it so?

The wall jerked toward me again, and I used my magicked feet to escape, racing for the entrance of the cavern. The wulv's dead carcass flew against the cave wall and got squished between a rock and an invisible, though very hard, wall of air.

I glanced at Ingefær. She needed help. The wulvs had split up, and she couldn't stretch her wall as wide as the thing on the throne controlled his wall.

I dashed toward her. But before I got there, one wulv stopped and bared its teeth at the other. With the first wulv winding its way around my wife's wall, the second one jumped on his summoned friend's back.

I knew what Serafina had done, turning the wulvs against each other, and raised a fist high in thanks. I glanced over to mouth a thank you, but her eyes were closed as she quaffed a potion.

Mick threw another stone at the not-quite dead jarl, conking him on the chin.

*Ha! That's what you get for trying to crush me!* He'd moved his wall too far.

The first Johan Retzlaff's gangrenous mouth twisted. He must not have been amused at seeing his summoned beasts fighting each other. Or perhaps it was the stone smacking him a third time.

He set off a stream of fiery darts.

Two struck Mick in his chest. He screamed in pain and flopped to the ground.

Three magic darts scorched Serafina, who fell to her knees, then face down. She lay still, while Mick crawled toward the cavern opening we'd come through.

Lokke's spawn!

Serafina had just quaffed her sole vial. If she was unconscious...or worse...

*Please don't be dead, Serafina. You've become a treasured member of the group.*

With the wulvs fighting each other, I turned my attention to the not-dead man. My luck held; his gaze focused on me. A black, toothless grin formed on his face.

I wanted to run forward again, but I searched for sparkles that might show me where his wall of air was.

Something had to change. One formerly-dead mage was holding off four living fighters.

Not seeing any sign of a wall of air, I darted forward, but at half Roskva's speed. It hurts to slam into a solid object. Especially invisible ones.

The man's right hand waved, and an invisible wall smashed into me from my left and from behind. I was thrown to the ground. Agony screamed from my entire body, overshadowed by the shrieks from my noggin, which had softened my landing on the stone ground.

Why is everything so red?

A sense of motion came to me, pain ripping at my shoulder as I tumbled over onto my backside. The invisible wall shoved forward, toward the cave wall behind the undead man's throne.

The pain brought focus. Alas, my sword arm lay beneath my butt, getting torn up by the rock floor. With the force of the air wall shoving at me, I couldn't get my arm free, nor find my footing.

Roskva raised her frond arms, like...*what do you want me to do?*

The cave wall approached at an alarming rate.

This was not how I thought I would depart the land of the living.

## Chapter Twenty-Nine

# A NECROMANCER

## INGEFAER

Rory was being plowed toward the wall by an invisible force. He wasn't running. He had to be dazed or otherwise restrained.

After shifting the air wall shield out of the way, I fired three fiery darts at Retzlaff the first. He may have grunted, as he turned to look at me.

The invisible wall slowed for a smidge, and Rory found his legs and ran behind the black throne. My husband staggered and moved at a sluggish normal-human speed. When he stopped, he shook his head as if to clear it.

The wulv who had attacked the other one, now had its jaw around its prey. There was whining and growling. Both wulvs were occupied.

I tread forward, shifting my wall of air a smidge to avoid disturbing them. A second flaming pea flew at me. It exploded maybe two strides before my wall. Flaming oranges, yellows, and reds obscured my vision for two eye blinks. The two wulvs, their fur charred and their skin blackened to a crisp, died in a heap, entangled with one another. Neither one had so much as yelped.

The heat of the fireball swooshed past the edges. But my wall of air held.

I had to be careful, for I had cast three spells. And without Serafina—who I had last seen lying on the ground—there was no help coming.

I did not want to pass out down here. I tapped the vial of healing in my pocket.

Rory waved his sword high in the air and growled. Like a grizzly bear challenging a rival. He shouted. "Fight me, you dead mass of pus."

What was my husband doing?

He'd wanted a dispel magic spell earlier. But I had been preoccupied. Old Retzlaff had an enormous spell-casting capacity and was so quick, too. A twirl of a finger and *whoosh*.

To dispel, I needed both my hands and my entire concentration, for it required me to draw on the power of the Aether in full. I shuddered, but let my wall down.

Standing thirty paces in front of the former jarl, my hands twirled, and I uttered the dispel incantation. "You're clear!"

Rory ran to the left side of the throne. The motion jerked the jarl's eyes to him. Rory stopped and sprinted back behind the throne. The mage's right finger lifted.

From behind me, a rock sailed and hit the mumbling corpse in the eye and stuck there.

I advanced, blade drawn, while Rory scooted in from the right, my side. "Keep throwing rocks!"

My plan? To engage in hand-to-hand combat—my husband and me against the mage. No way could old man Retzlaff get a spell off if we continually hacked at him and Mick plunked him with stones.

A sickening laugh escaped the gangrenous mouth. Old Retzlaff arched his rotted body and once more raised a finger.

And, once more, Mick plunked him with a stone.

Rory dashed back behind the throne and reemerged on the left side. He was playing a game of whack-the-troll, hoping to distract the necromancer.

Retzlaff waved both arms in huge sweeps, like he was swimming. I spotted the ruby ring. The old man could cast spells until we were all dead.

I didn't know what spell he was casting, so I hurried forward to close the distance.

From behind me, Serafina exclaimed. "Ha!"

Old Retzlaff jabbed with his hand at me—

—and nothing happened.

Did his spell fail?

Retzlaff went through the swimming motions again, while I advanced to meet up with my husband, who scooted around to the front of the dais.

By body posture and facial expression it looked like the mage was screaming at us, but there was no sound. The corpulent toothless mouth was wide open, and his head jerked forward as he poked his finger at Rory. Then at me. Not a peep emitted from his maw.

Old Retzlaff swung an arm in a wide arc, his other one aiming at my husband.

Rory swung his blade and severed the mage's arm. No blood erupted from the wound, nor was there any sound; no squelch or crunch as the arm hit the floor.

Sword in hand, I shifted to Rory's right.

Rory slashed his blade down from overhead; without a sound, his sword embedded itself in Old Retzlaff's shoulder area.

I stabbed. My sword wedged into his belly full of sludge, and I had to use both hands to maintain a grip as his remaining hand yanked at my blade.

Rory tugged at his blade, trying to loosen it, while I was doing the same. Somehow, Old Retzlaff kept our weapons lodged in his mass of...sludge and bones.

Mick came up from behind me...I never heard him coming...and leaped through the air, stabbing with his short sword and planted it in the dead man's darkened orb.

No squelch, no hiss, nothing.

Retzlaff's mouth opened in a silent scream, and his body released our swords. He swiped at Mick, then grabbed at the short sword in his eye.

Without a sound, Mick tumbled to the ground before Retzlaff's feet.

With my blade free, in Ære Warrior training fashion, I chopped at the old man's neck.

My aim was true, and the head rolled to the ground. Yet the body kept on struggling.

Rory jerked his weapon free, and we worked in unison to amputate the remaining arm and legs. The torso lolled off the throne to the floor, twitching.

Rory stabbed at the black pulsing heart.

Finally, the corpse was still.

I looked at my husband. Shivers ran down my spine. We'd survived. We'd killed the jarl. I smiled at him. Happy to be with him on this journey together.

He smiled. His mouth was all bloody. Was he missing a tooth?

I said, "        "

My mouth moved, and I felt my throat muscles twitching as if I were speaking. But no sound came out.

Rory helped Mick to his feet and grabbed me by the arm, and we walked toward a kneeling Serafina, bright-eyed and grinning.

When we reached her, Rory cleared his throat and said, "Great spell. Excellent timing."

Serafina mustered herself to her feet and dusted off.

Mick grinned. "Now that's teamwork."

Rory nodded at the half-alvae. "How many spells left?"

Serafina said, "Two. I drank the vial of healing a moment before he blasted me. So I healed myself as I lay there, pretending to be dead. Then I waited for the opportune time and cast my silence incantation." She grinned. "Handy, eh?"

I hugged her hard. "Grand. Simply Grand."

Rory squeezed Mick hard. "Your sling and stones helped save us all. At least once, you disrupted his spellcasting. And your timing with the sword couldn't have been better."

I walked over to the decapitated body parts and retrieved the arm with the magic band on the finger. As I brought it back, I worked the ruby signet ring loose and threw the rotted arm toward the throne.

Out of nowhere, a feeling of bulk evaporated from inside my stomach. It was as if I'd needed to evacuate my bowels, but abruptly, I didn't. The compel spell had vanished. I moaned at the sensation, even though I felt...better.

Rory whooshed air. "Wow. I didn't know I was feeling so weighed down. And here I thought it was all the bread and honey." He tugged his leather pants up. "I swear these were fitting tighter a minute ago."

Serafina chuckled.

I said, "Elise's compel spell has lifted."

I smiled and held the ring high. Holding it, I detected no arcane aura...my hand didn't tingle. But I was sure the ring was magical.

"Mighty powerful," Rory said. "He was casting spells with abandon."

"And so fast, too," Mick said. The lad waggled his brows at us. "Now we search the rest of the place for our spoils. Yeah?"

Pocketing the ring, I exchanged glances with Rory. Jarl Retzlaff the fifth, was a thief. A dead thief. His namesake, a necromancer.

Rory chewed on his lower lip. "Elise said he had no living relatives—he was the last in his line. We found the stolen ring. I think bounty hunter laws prevail."

I summarized the Realm law for Mick and Serafina. "When bringing a criminal to justice outside city walls, anything found on their person can be claimed by the retrievers...unless an obvious line of ownership can be established to said property." I elaborated. "It's written with thieves in mind. But necromancy is against the law as well, so by bringing Retzlaff the first—and his great-great-grandson—to justice, we can claim ownership of anything he owned...including the mansion. I think."

"You want the mansion?" Serafina asked.

"Uh, no," I said. "We'll have to check with the Order of Gixus. But if it's ours, we can sell it."

"Uh," Mick said. "Just don't say anything about me."

Grinning, Rory winked at me. "I think we can manage it. A new jarl and his family will live here. And pay us a large sum of silver to do it."

I chinned at Mick. "Let's search this place. Let's see what treasures the Retzlaff clan has amassed down here."

Mick tittered like a child who'd pinched two bites of his mother's freshly baked pie.

Rory said, "Remember, Retzlaff's notes said the treasure is warded and trapped."

We walked about the cavern, poking through the stacks of planks, the piles of bones, and then the clothes. We found about four hundred silver on the bodies. I placed the coins and the bejeweled crown of rose gold into an empty apple sack.

In an alcove—maybe forty feet wide and thirty feet deep—on the far right of the grotto, we found grave markers, with one grave dug out. Scanning the indoor cemetery, I saw every grave looked to have been recently disturbed. Like they'd been dug out and filled back in.

Rory toed the dirt mound beside the open grave. "This is where Jarl Retzlaff the first, was buried."

We investigated but found nothing of interest. Just a squirm of fat wyrms.

Mick pranced about, his head shifting left, then right. "Where's the treasure?"

I held up my hand. "Hold on. The obsidian throne is calling me."

It looked like the only thing that could hold both a ward spell and be trapped. If not, we would have to spend a lot of energy to find what Retzlaff the fifth had been hunting for.

We hoofed it back to the central area. I cast a find magic spell on the throne. And staggered.

Serafina scowled. "I can restore your stamina. But it would leave but one spell left for me."

"Drink the potion, my love." Rory looked at me with those soft brown eyes. The effect was dampened by the dried blood on his chin.

"You look like you could use it yourself," I said.

He shrugged. "I can wait."

Besides his bloody chin, he favored his left arm, holding it tight to his body. I felt bad drinking the vial of healing, but the others encouraged me.

Mick said, "There're more spells to cast." He pointed. "The throne is warded."

The base of the obsidian throne glowed orange and had a white crescent moon emblazoned on it.

"Hurry," Rory said.

I slugged the liquid like fermented cider. Except it didn't burn...it soothed, in a silky sort of way. Feeling refreshed, I dispelled the ward. Mimicking the crescent moon proved simple. Or so I hoped.

After the orange glow dissipated, we found an outline of a drawer beneath the seat.

Mick inspected it, using his handy flat piece of steel.

*Click.*

"Look out!" Mick sprung out of the way.

A long dart, as thin as a needle, shot under his shoulder and in between Rory's legs.

"The gods!" Serafina yelled.

Mick growled. "Not fair, Retzlaff. You's dead."

"Was that the trap?" I asked.

"He had a trap guarding a trap," Mick said, back down on his knees and poking away.

Rory motioned us to back off.

"You sure you want to be doing that?" I asked.

Mick grinned; his eyes were lit like two lamps. "Oh, this is living."

He went back at it.

*Click.*

I jumped.

Mick said, "That's that second one. Now the lock itself."

I shivered. "Whatever is in there, it better be good."

Yet a third *click*.

Mick got up and dusted his pants. "All clear."

"Pull it open," Rory said.

"Me?" Mick shook his head. "Nah. That's your job. I's did mine."

I nudged my husband with an elbow. "He did."

Rory rolled his eyes but squatted before the throne. "There's no handle." He wedged his sword into the crevice, levered it, and pulled. Then yanked. Then slashed at the black rock in frustration.

Mick laughed. "You're going about it all wrong. You're using force." Mick got down on his knees and pressed the drawer in.

The drawer popped out.

"See?" Mick stood and waved his hand in an overdone flourish.

Growling through a smile, Rory dipped his head, then got down on his knees to pull the drawer out.

A pile of old gold coins. And ten jewels on top.

I pumped my fist in the air. "Yah!"

Mick hugged Serafina.

"I wonder how long the treasure has been hidden down here." Rory inspected a gold coin. "I think the image on the coin is King Narek."

"We's got no king," Mick said.

"A thousand years ago, we did." I cleared my throat, the excitement of the find clogging it.

"A thousand years ago?" Mick half-shouted.

Serafina said, "Whoa. Old coins are worth a lot."

I said, "Jarl Retzlaff the fifth knew about the treasure, but feared the traps. Do you suppose, in order to get to it, he raised his great-great-grandfather? But then he was betrayed?"

Rory's brown eyes gleamed. "Maybe. The dagger in his chest says yes."

I nodded. *That's what you get for raising the dead.*

I smiled at our little group. We'd survived, and justice had been served.

And under bounty hunter laws, we were entitled to the spoils.

Chapter Thirty

# A RICHNESS BEYOND COIN

## RORY

I closed my mouth lest I drooled. Using my sword, I swished around the two-inch deep pile of treasure. I scooped and counted. My wife made four neat stacks.

When we were done, I smiled. Big. "Four hundred forty-four pieces of ancient gold. That's almost nine thousand pieces of silver at current rates."

A man could live for a year on three hundred silvers—and call it a good year.

Mick gawped. Then closed his mouth. "And they's a thousand years old?"

I nodded. "Maybe nine hundred. I don't know when they stopped stamping gold with the king's image. Might be worth twice what I said."

Ingefær plucked a gem. "And three rubies, three sapphires, two emeralds, one yellow stone—I think citrine—and a diamond."

"We're rich!" Mick half-shouted.

Rising, I placed an arm around Mick and Serafina. "We're rich because we have each other." I patted Mick's back. "You did good. You have a useful set of skills." I winked at the lad. "I could do with less screaming, though."

Mick blushed. "I used my thieving for good, huh?"

"You did." Ingefær looked at me with raised brows. "I think I want to buy Jarl Retzlaff's ring. It'll come in handy for our future endeavors."

I nodded. "You know what else we need?"

The three shook their heads.

I looked into Serafina's green eyes. "We need a healer to join us."

"What about me?" Mick asked.

"I assumed you were already a part of the team," I replied.

Ingefær said, "It's important to ask, not assume."

I bowed my head. "My apologies, Master Mick. Would you join us on our future assignments?"

Mick looked me in the eye. "Equal shares?"

"Yes, I think so." I stood straight. "This job, too."

I checked with Ingefær. She nodded.

This treasure was enough to pay for five homes if we wanted, and I wasn't counting the value of the jewels, nor the crown made of rose gold. Ingefær's share should cover the cost of the ruby ring and leave extra.

Mick thanked me with a big hug. "I knew joining up with you was a brilliant decision."

Serafina said, "I'm intrigued. The treasure helps ease my primary concern, which is shelter and food. But once the army learns of my whereabouts...they'll send a bounty hunter after me."

"Because you befriend animals?" Mick asked.

Serafina moaned as if in discomfort. "It's not necromancy, I assure you. I don't summon them." Then she smiled. "Not yet."

"So, are you an adherent of the Eirene Shrine?" I asked.

"You mean, do I follow the healing precepts?" Serafina asked in return.

"Aye."

"Yes." Serafina adjusted her leather armor. "But there's more to me than healing. I feel a pull in a different direction. I think about trees and animals all the time."

Laughing, I said, "Me too. I'm a woodsman at heart."

Ingefær put a hand on Serafina's arm. "Remember. We're friends with Captain Alvertos."

Serafina's mouth hung open. "You weren't just saying that, so I wouldn't quit?"

I smiled. "It's true. He and I met before the drekis returned. And again afterward, at our wedding."

Ingefær added, "We solved a mystery involving a Shrine fire."

Serafina's head bounced between us. "You...you would put in a word for me?"

I beamed. "I would. But I'm not sure my word is worth more than a pile of troll shit."

I was underselling it...just in case. Necromancy was a crime in every city-state. Befriending animals shouldn't be one, but those kinds of decisions were made by the power structure. At best, all I could do was suggest.

"Rory." My wife's tone chastised me. I wasn't sure if it was because I swore, or because I downplayed the worth of my word. "He's right. We have no power with your military, legally speaking. But perhaps the subject of summoning and befriending should be brought before Tyrrby. A discussion with the various city-states may provide a solution."

I nodded. "What an excellent suggestion. Maybe we can get your sentence commuted."

"How long would it take?" Serafina asked.

Ingefær shook her head. "No idea."

I shrugged. "Never done anything like it, so I can't say. I would venture a year, maybe two. One worry—Vanaby isn't a signatory with Tyrrby and their justice warriors. At least they weren't last year."

Serafina pursed her lips. "Won't those Tyrrby folks care that I've been cast out by the alvae army and convicted of a crime?"

Ingefær sighed. "If they agree to get involved, they'll want to cast a truth spell on you. So, unless you think it's a problem, I don't think they will. Intent is important to them."

Serafina smiled, her green eyes shining. "It's the truth. Thank you. Yes, I will join up with you."

"Alright," I said. "Let's move on. Everyone's healed."

"You're not," Ingefær said. "How hard did the wall hit you?"

"Eh," I smiled. "It's more of how hard I hit it." I rotated a shoulder. "A good night's sleep will fix it."

Mick said, "I took two darts, you know."

My eyes swiveled to him. "And how do you feel?"

"Good enough to move on." He rubbed his chest, then grinned. "Those things hurt. But if there is another load like this, I would gladly take two more of those fiery blasts."

We laughed.

We loaded up the treasure using more emptied apple sacks. And we ate our fill of the fruit and the bread and honey. I also gathered up Retzlaff's log of his necromantic attempts.

Ingefær and I huddled over the dead servants. There wasn't anything we could do, but leaving them lying there didn't seem right.

Mick said, "Can't bury 'em. Their kin might want to put them in a family plot."

I nodded. "Alright. Ingefær and I have to inform the Order of Gixus anyway. They'll bring the bodies back to the city."

We'd been going for hours, and a fifteen-minute skirmish took a lot out of folks, me included. For an hour, we took turns catnapping or engaging in quiet conversations. There were horses to check on.

I washed my bloodied face, wincing as the pain in my shoulder told me there was more damage. When we reached the surface, I would ask to be healed.

## Chapter Thirty-One

# NO ESCAPE

### RORY

I sharpened my blade while the others rested.

After an hour, Ingefær fidgeted. "The horses have been out there all alone. For what? Two days?"

"A day and a half." I cleared my throat. "But by the time we surface...aye, might be two."

We debated retracing our steps, but it would leave a section of the dungeon unexplored. So we moved up the stone steps without a door—after Ingefær checked for magic and wards. Going up, Mick spotted two dodgy steps. They weren't magicked, just a bladder-and-dart setup with pressure pads. Mick diffused them with a deft flourish of his dirk.

We climbed and climbed and climbed some more. As we neared the top landing, I slowed. "I don't think there's magic here, as I think this staircase and whatever is beyond the door is protected by the warded door we avoided. But I'd hate to be wrong."

Mick studied the last step and the landing. "No traps that I can see."

Ingefær had us back up while she cast a find magic. The top step glowed orange.

"Who wards their own secret passage?" I asked.

Mick shrugged. “The caster doesn’t have to dispel the ward, they can just provide the password and stroll on by.”

I checked with Ingefær, who nodded. I turned to back to Mick. “And you know this how?”

“Ma has been teaching me off and on, hoping one of her lessons would take.” He smiled, but the longing showed in his eyes.

I, too, longed for a little of the arcane power. The idea of befriending animals, summoning messenger birds, and similar spells was tantalizing.

Ingefær dispelled the crescent moon ward. And wobbled.

I tapped Serafina on the shoulder. “Drink a potion. Then heal my wife.”

“I’ll do it the other way around.”

She healed Ingefær. Then, shaking on rickety legs, the half-alvae took a vial and guzzled. It left us with one vial of healing. It had to be enough to get us out of here.

With everyone at full capacity—well, not me—we hiked past the once magicked landing, and five strides later, stood before the door.

“Lokke’s spawn.” My empty hand clenched into a fist. “Is there no escape? How many spells do we have to cast to get out of here?”

I turned to Ingefær. “You’re up. Again.”

She cast a find magic, and for once, the door didn’t glow.

I moved to the door and tried the handle. “Locked.” I checked the seams. “It swings this way, so barging in won’t work.” Not even if my shoulder wasn’t sore.

Mick moved to the keyhole and pulled out his implements. He had me hold the light behind his head, at door handle height.

He picked and prodded. “Ow!”

His hand jerked back and he put a finger to his mouth. Then he rolled backwards.

I caught him before he smashed his head on the rock floor.

His eyes were glazed over already. He breathed like he was gagging. His hands began trembling, soon followed by his feet.

"Quick, the remove poison potion." I reached out a hand while steadying the young lad. "Don't you dare die on me. Not now. Not after we became friends."

Serafina slapped the vial into my hand. I uncorked it with my teeth and gripped Mick's jaw, opening his quivering lips.

Slowly, I poured the liquid into his mouth.

He gagged and sputtered half of it out, the magic fluid dribbling down his chin.

I tilted the vial again. This time, I clamped his mouth shut. He would either swallow the magic or he would drown.

His legs quit quivering, then his hands.

I opened his mouth and peered in. Not seeing anything, I dumped the rest of the vial's contents.

Mick swallowed, but his eyes remained closed and he didn't move.

I got up. "Your turn, Serafina."

She kneeled beside Mick. First, she listened to his chest, then his mouth. "He's still with us." She made her motions and cast a heal spell, using water for material.

We waited and watched. Mick's chest rose and fell in a steady rhythm.

I wanted to slap him awake, but restrained myself. I exchanged worried looks with Ingefær.

She asked, "What do you think, Serafina?"

"He'll be alright. Was a potent poison, though." She rose. "Give him another minute."

After the minute was up, I asked Serafina if she could cast another spell.

She shook her head. "He's out of harm's way. And I don't want to deplete myself. We've but one vial left. We may have to rest down here."

Mick groaned.

Ingefær moved beside him, checking his forehead. "You're alright. It's safe to wake."

Mick moaned louder, this time rotating his body and curling his legs to his stomach. It took a dozen minutes, but we got him to sit up and drink water. Finally, he stood. He trembled, and he was pale, but he refused aid in walking.

When we were ready to go, I asked, "Which way?"

Mick said, "Try the door. I think I got it to unlock."

I hesitated, my hand not wanting to touch the handle.

"The gods!" Mick stepped by me and yanked the door.

Which opened.

The room beyond the door contained a library, laboratory equipment, and storage shelves.

One wall was lined with books, eight feet high. A rickety ladder leaned at one end. On the other side was an oak desk, and beside it was a ten-foot-long bench. Atop the bench were a pair of pestle and mortar sets, a distillery with what looked like copper tubes, and a set of glass bowls filled with liquid. I suspected it was some kind of lamp oil, as each bowl had a wick.

Beneath the bench top were pails, and an assortment of wooden limbs of various thicknesses—several oak, most elm, and one walnut. Off to one end was a stack of blank vellum.

Ingefær cast a find magic spell on half the room. Nothing lit up. But now she was halfway into her spells.

I said in a loud voice so all could hear. "No more spells in here. Save yourselves for the door we want to leave through."

Mick shouted as he pointed. "Hey!"

We looked at the desk and the drawers on one side. The tiniest seam of orange peeked through.

The drawer itself wasn't magicked. It was something inside. I shooed everyone out of the room. Then I pulled very, very slowly.

Inside, I found four scrolls and a wooden rod, about eighteen inches long. When I say rod, I mean a whittled, sanded, and polished thin branch, made from an aspen limb. It was straight, and there was one knot about five inches from the end.

I called the others back in and pointed. "Scrolls, and I think a rod with magical powers."

Ingefær unfurled a scroll.

"Don't read it aloud, or even mumble to yourself," Serafina warned.

"Aye," Mick said. "Ma always said to read it backwards. That way, you won't set off a spell by accident. Unless it's cursed."

We all looked at him.

"What?" He pleaded. "I paid attention...some of the time."

Serafina said, "He's right. Scrolls don't need material, they just need to be read. And a few, not even aloud."

Ingefær inspected, then set the first scroll down. "I can't be sure, but I think it's a wither or emaciate spell. The sense I got is you kill a person, or maybe a lot of individuals."

Even I shuddered at such evil. If I had to die, I wanted it to be quick.

Ingefær went through the other scrolls and announced, "This one is a mass heal spell. Everyone in range is healed."

That sounded useful.

Serafina shook her head. "No. Doesn't sound right. This man, the necromancer Jarl Retzlaff—whether the fifth or a prior generation—he was evil. He liked to harm what he couldn't control."

"What do you think it does?" I asked.

"Maybe the opposite. Instead of healing, a mass wound incantation."

Ingefær glanced through the scroll. "There's one Varanusian word I don't understand. So maybe Serafina is right."

"What's the other two do?" Mick asked.

"A fireball spell and an invisibility spell." She tucked the scrolls into her backpack. "That, I think, is useful."

"Ma will check it out for us." Mick looked around, his jaw set firm. "Free of charge."

His mother was going to get a talking to. A compel spell without full consent was an improper use of magic.

"What about the wand?" Serafina asked.

"No idea." Ingefær gripped it between her thumb and forefinger. "Don't want to grab a hold of it. It, too, may be cursed."

"Ma will check it out."

Mick was generous with his mother's talents. But I figured he was right. Elise owed us big for her dirty trick.

We packed the magicked items away, using a cloth to grasp the rod, and searched the rest of the room.

I found two drawers full of notes. Parsing through them, I said, "This is a journal of an elder Retzlaff. Here it talks about an old ward failing and having to replace it with one of his own."

Ingefær said, "Pack it all. We'll read it when we have time. Maybe those notes explain how and why the tunnels and wards were designed the way they were."

I knew why. "Evil needs no design. Retzlaff the first, second, third and more each protected their home and dabbled in necromancy. The tunnels and wards were to keep their secret while they pursued their wicked ways."

Ingefær grunted. "Put the documents into my backpack. I think your rucksack is full of coins."

While Mick and I stuffed papers, Serafina and Ingefær salivated over the wooden cases containing all manner of herbs and exotic materials.

Having finished with the chore, I moved beside them and held a glass vial high. "Really? You want to take the toes of a toad home with you? Where will you put it? In the kitchen?"

"For you, my dear, I will gladly put it on the nightstand by your side of the bed." Ingefær smiled at me. "A once-potent mage had it for a reason. It has value."

"I want half of everything," Serafina said.

I looked at Mick. "We'll carry up the loot, and let the ladies carry their precious trunks of herbs."

"Hey." Ingefær scowled at me. "That's not the man I married."

I stifled a retort. She was right. "I beg your pardon, pretty lady. I will be happy to carry your treasures."

That earned me a grunt. "It's alright. I wouldn't want you to get too tired. I might need you for another task."

"Gross," Mick said, blushing.

When we figured out a system to carry everything—for I got the others to agree to never come back down here—we advanced on the door I hoped led to our escape.

I stood behind Ingefær as she cast a find magic spell. The door didn't glow.

"But it had from the other side," I said.

Mick looked through the keyhole and the side jambs. He nodded. "Looks clear."

Ingefær shrugged. "A directional ward? Stops folks from entering, but not leaving?"

All eyes turned to me. Sighing, I advanced on the door, hoping hard it wasn't locked. Or trapped. Or warded.

Turning the handle, it moved.

*Click.*

But that was it. Nothing shot out, nothing stabbed me. No plume of vile smoke filled the air.

I pulled the door open.

A blue light radiated throughout the shaft before me.

A quick scan down the tunnel revealed a dark opening on our right with a bit of green gleaming from it.

We were at the second tunnel—or the first one below the mansion's spiral staircase.

"Time to go home," I said, hefting the heavy and jingling sack over my shoulder.

## Chapter Thirty-Two

# CONJUROR ELISE

## INGEF□R

When we reached the outside—the glorious, but dark outside—I tended to Thunder and Muffin. They were happy to see us, but then mad. Thunder shifted his head away every time I tried to nuzzle with him.

"Sorry, boy. I'll make it up to you." Scratching at his neck, I pulled out a Lodi apple. "I know grass isn't your favorite."

As Thunder munched, relief swept over me; nothing had happened to them. No carnivorous critter or gang of humanoids had come along. Maybe Retzlaff had an outer ward, and it kept the beasts at bay?

We watered the horses, and refilled our skins, using the jarl's hand pump in the kitchen. After feeding them the last of their oats, I gave them each another apple, including the donkey. I got a wet nose in my ear from the ass.

We loaded up. Rory and I led our steeds as we hoofed it down the trail from Jarl Retzlaff's Hexerei Mansion.

"We can't forget the two draft horses in Retzlaff's stable," Rory said.

"Ugh," Mick said. "Back through the waterfall."

Rory nodded. "Aye. But we know the way is safe."

The moon was dim, hiding behind thin clouds, making for a murky trip to the waterfall. Rory and I moved through the levers and the waterfall entrance, Serafina's wide green eyes following us the entire way. We found the two Shire mares standing in sodden straw. The grey had kicked at its stall enough to rip a hinge off the gate.

Armed with apples and sweet whispers, I convinced them to follow us out. With two draft horses, we rearranged saddle bags and hiked down the trail. By the time we arrived at the Temple of Fraegah, the sun peeked over the eastern horizon.

We tied off the horses. Mick knocked and spoke under his breath as he waved a hand over the handle.

"What did you do?" I asked.

"Oh, it's a ward passkey incantation." He shrugged. "I told you's. All you need to know is the password. Even usable by those without the talent. I's bet a fortune Retzlaff's wards are set up the same way."

While it sounded true, I wasn't so sure Mick didn't have a channel to the arcane planes. He'd waved his hand and uttered words. He had to have some aptitude. Maybe he was hiding it, or maybe he didn't realize it, attributing the skill to bland explanations.

"Maybe your mom can teach me how to cast wards. We're having a home built."

I was trying to think nice thoughts about Elise. But deep inside, I was livid with her.

Rory raised his brows. "Impressive what magic can do."

Good and bad. I said, "You, young lad, are full of surprises."

Mick rolled his eyes at me. "It's the lone door that works for me. Don't you think I've tried?"

We followed Mick in and went past the burgundy drapes. He went to the door that was off to one side and knocked softly.

A moment later, Elise came out and waved a hand in the air, lighting the candles above us with a word. She wore a beautiful purple shawl and robe combination. Her tawny-blonde hair was matted on one side.

She hugged her son. "You've been gone so long...I worried myself sick."

Mick endured for a breath, then squirmed out of the hold. "We got it, Ma. We got the ring back."

Elise straightened her clothes. "I knew Retzlaff had it. Did you—"

Rory interrupted. "He did. For a while. But one of his antecedents took it from him. Jarl Retzlaff the fifth is dead."

"We found him," I added. "Stabbed with a knife as he lay on a raised platform in what looked like a ceremony."

Come to think of it, we had left the black-handled dagger in Retzlaff's chest. It might have been magical. Then again, it had been used in a dark ritual. I shivered.

"Necromancy." Elise pursed her lips like she'd tasted vinegar. "Magic comes back and straight away there are necromancers plying their evil."

Rory said, "Jarl Retzlaff the first is dead, too. Again."

We told her of our escapades, with Mick filling in details about all the traps he cleared.

I sighed. "We have a problem, Elise."

Her eyes searched mine.

"You compelled us without our consent," I said.

"You consented." Her arms crossed under her bosom.

"Not to the full spell you cast." I stepped closer. "To stay quiet about your son and not visit the Order of Gixus...that's what we agreed to."

Her lips tightened.

Rory joined me at my side. "To be forced to retrieve the ring...Elise...my wife, was almost killed."

I clasped Rory's hand. "My husband, too. Twice if not thrice. And your son would have died if we hadn't had a vial of cure poison."

Mick moved to stand on my right, then Serafina stepped up to Rory's left.

Elise's shoulders sagged. "I had to have the ring."

"Why?" I asked.

"I'm in danger of losing my position." She rubbed her palms together. "At the last conclave, Maerek requested a change in leadership. He demonstrated a higher ability with the elemental planes. But the elders wanted to wait before making any changes. After the ring went missing, Maerek had given me a week to get the ring back, and then he would inform the Fraegah Order hierarchy."

"They would fire you?" Rory asked. "Or just demote you?"

Her lips pushed in and out. "Probably just demote."

I shook my head. "Even a firing wasn't worth our lives." I glanced at Mick. "What do you think is a proper punishment for abuse of sorcerous powers?"

Mick scratched at his neck. "Well, I suppose Ma can divine all the stuff we found. For free."

I nodded, a small smile appearing on my face. We hadn't discussed it beforehand. I was testing Mick's judgement...his desire for vengeance. I didn't think he'd rat his mother out, for abuse of a compel spell would get her banned from the Fraegah Temple. Going after people's jobs crossed a line if all I was doing was satiating my feelings of injustice.

"Well?" Rory asked.

I wanted to see the contrition on Elise's face. If she showed us a little, then she was someone we could work with in the future.

Elise searched our faces. Then her chin dipped to her chest. "Aye. That's fair. I'm so sorry the job went goblin on you. I didn't think Retzlaff was at all powerful." Her head lifted. "I swear, all he could do was a couple of mild incantations, relying on the Aether."

Her eyes were puffy and red, so I believed her.

Pulling the ruby ring out of my pocket, I hoisted it before her. "What will you sell this for?"

Elise paused, her eyes widening. "You want to buy it?"

"As long as it's not cursed," I replied.

As good luck would have it, the *R* suited me: Ingefær vod Renku.

Elise shook her head. "No. I checked. As did my predecessors. It is a powerful trinket. Gives you stamina to cast unlimited spells as long as you have material."

We'd learned about stamina the hard way.

I said, "I didn't see the risen Retzlaff use any material at all. In fact, his hand machinations were subtle and quick. For most spells, his finger twitched. At the end, his arms waved. But he never had to repeat the design three times."

Her mouth dropped. "I-I don't know how he did that."

Neither did I. "Maybe because he'd been raised from the dead. Maybe it eased his spell-summoning tasks."

Or maybe the ring would do that for me, too. Tingles ran down my leg at the thought.

"You said you wanted three thousand six hundred silvers from Retzlaff," Rory said.

"I think I can get more for it since magic has returned," Elise retorted.

Mick jabbed her in the hip with a finger, glowering at his mom. "Don't push it, Ma."

Elise chewed on her lip. After a moment, she nodded. "Alright, I'll sell it to you for that price."

"Along with the password to activate it," I said.

Elise shook her head. "I'm sorry, I don't know it."

Serafina scoffed. "Then how will she get it to work?"

Elise raised her shoulders to her ears. "No idea."

"I think the price just dropped," Rory said. "It's worth the thirty-six hundred with the command word."

We haggled. She was a hard woman—from almost being reported for abuse of sorcerous powers, she was right back to being stubborn.

Voices rose with heat.

Mick screeched. "Dammit, Ma. We saved the Temple's reputation. We saved your job. Either provide the command word or cut the asking price."

Cowed by her son, she relented and reduced the price to three thousand silver coins.

Rory touched me on my arm. "What good is spending three thousand if it never works?"

Elise said, "There may be a few sorcerers or sorceresses who could divine what I and my colleagues here cannot. The most powerful sorceress of our order resides in Jernel Drakken. And there's always the city library. The command word may be as simple as saying *Retzlaff.* But the records I have said it's been tried."

Hoping to reduce the tensions further, I said, "How about this? I will pay you three thousand. But if after a year I cannot use it, you agree the Fraegah Temple will buy it back."

Rory said, "Your word is not good enough. Call in Raemoni and Maerek as witnesses."

Elise scowled at my husband.

Serafina said, "You said he knew about the theft."

Elise sighed. "Aye. He does. Maerek is giddy with it." She flashed a smile that wasn't. "I'll be right back."

While she was gone, I said, "Mick, you're doing great. Thanks for helping with her."

Mick gave a cockeyed grin. "Aye, well, I's been dealing with her all my life."

After we stipulated the deal before Maerek and Raemoni, the groggy mages went back to bed.

Before Elise, we separated the remaining treasure, counting out gold coins and taking turns picking jewels out of the pile.

Rory showed the conjurer one of the stamped gold coins.

Elise gasped.

"How much do you think it's worth?"

Her eyes went round and wide. "I don't know. Maybe forty silvers a piece."

The amount Rory had thought.

Rory said, "If you're willing to take the risk of its value, we'll pay you with seventy-five gold coins."

Elise sputtered. "This will attract all sorts of brigands." But a silly grin had lodged itself on her face.

I made a mental note to ascertain the stamped gold's value before we spent more of it.

"It's all we have to cover the cost," I said. I didn't want to hand over the jewels, as I didn't know their worth. "There is also the matter of the wand and the scrolls we found."

"Ma. As part of your punishment for your compel spell, you agreed to perform the divination free of charge."

Elise narrowed her eyes at him for a moment. "Hmm. Maybe I'll stop paying for your room and board." She softened her countenance and winked at him. "Ah, it's alright, you didn't know. And, as you say, I crossed the line. You watch and see if you learn anything."

I moved to her elbow. "Can I watch too?"

"Can you pull on the golden hues from the Aether plane?" Elise asked.

I nodded. "I can, but the find and remove magic spells take more concentration than air and fire. And it takes longer, too." And I needed both my hands.

Elise got a kerchief before she took the wooden wand. "The Aether is my specialty." Then she added, "I can cast but two spells today."

"Lighting the room didn't take a spell?" Rory asked.

"No. It's an heirloom incantation placed on the chandelier." Elise smiled, this time genuinely. "It just needs a command word."

After I told her I wanted to learn how to discern magic, I listened in to her divination spell.

"Each artifact is based on a different substance. This one is wood."

She fumbled with her mage belt and pulled a splinter of wood. Holding the rod in her right hand, she waved it in a big circle three times. She used her left hand to grip the splinter as she appeared to write, like she used a quill. Varanusian flowed, the equivalent of *reveal your true powers*. Then she touched her head with the rod.

With eyes closed, Elise took a deep breath. "It is a wand of summoning animals."

Her eyes flashed open, and she studied the rod. Seemingly satisfied, she nodded. "If it had been related to the undead or something otherwise vile, I would have to destroy it."

Rory said, "So, you agree summoning animals isn't necromancy?"

"Of course not. Almost all mages summon messenger birds." Conjuror Elise's lips twitched. "The summoned animal is under the direction of the mage. So, unless the mage directs the creature to attack, the spell won't harm anyone."

Unlike fireballs and other violent spells. Those incantations were designed to harm and kill, with the mage's intent clear from the outset.

I sighed. The law and magic never meshed, even before its return. Then again, Serafina had said her superior hadn't accused her of summoning animals, but of necromancy.

Serafina asked, "I wonder if you would permit me to claim it as my share?"

That seemed like a reasonable suggestion, so I handed her the wand.

"Thank you."

Elise said, "You will have to practice with it. I suspect, like most wands, it will summon what it has been designed for without the need of material or pulling power from the magical planes."

"And the command word?" Serafina asked.

Elise replied, "The command word is *innkalle.*"

"And you know this how?" I asked.

"It's scripted just below the knot." She pointed at what I figured was the handle end.

"I didn't see it before," Rory said. "And I checked."

"Uh, no. My divine spell revealed it." Elise flashed a smile. "The etched word will dissipate in a couple of hours."

Rory asked, "Will using it tire her?"

"It shouldn't," Elise replied.

Serafina bowed her head. "Thank you. All of you. You are very generous. I will practice."

"Not with me around, I hope," Mick said, eliciting a group chuckle.

Elise turned to the other scrolls and, one by one—without using a spell—she confirmed my interpretations. The healing scroll was, in fact, a wound scroll. She pointed at the deceiving word and scowled. "Necromancy. I will destroy it."

We agreed.

"But for education purposes," I asked, "What does it do?"

"Without divining it, I'm not sure how much it hurts the target. Whether the power is imbued into the scroll already, or whether it depends on the thoughts and power of the caster, I don't know. It is a weapon, like a sword. Of that, I'm sure."

Serafina asked, "How do you destroy it?"

"I'll use it as a fire starter," Elise said. "Nothing bad will happen, unless the scroll is warded. And I think you would have discovered that when you unrolled it."

Which left the fireball and invisibility scroll. Elise confirmed they appeared normal.

Rory asked, "What's your pleasure, Mick? Fireball or invisibility?"

Mick eyed his mom. "Do I have to cull the powers of the planes to use the scrolls?"

"No. Just read the Varanusian, son." Elise eyed him. "You remember your lessons, don't you?"

He nodded. "I'll take the invisibility spell."

Rory said, "True to form."

We laughed.

I nudged Mick. "Now it's time to talk about the light stick."

"Aw." Mick shuffled his feet.

Elise's mouth dropped. "Maerek has been missing one for over a moon. Did you—"

"Aye, Ma. I took it. But I's willing to pay for it."

Rory asked, "How much?"

Elise nibbled at her lower lip. "Seven hundred silver."

I nodded at Mick.

"I will pay for it out of my share." Mick flashed a smile at his mother. "Sorry. I don't do that no more, Ma. I promise."

Rory cleared his throat. "I'd like to buy one as well."

Elise stopped glowering at her son. "What? Oh, yes. I can arrange it. Might take a while."

I said, "We'll pay for it in advance; you can let us know when it's ready."

The four of us held a conference, as I had an idea of how to deal with the rose gold crown. "We have the stamped gold coins, the ten jewels, and a rose crown weighing nigh on a pound."

Taking a cleansing breath, I said, "I want to gift half the rose crown's value to the care of Elise and the Fraegah Temple. We'll have a trust drawn up by a city magistrate. The funds will be used to train mages."

Rory nodded. "What about the other half of its value?"

"That's for us." I grinned.

"And the mansion?" Rory asked.

"I have no desire to live there." I scanned Mick's and Serafina's faces. "You?"

Mick guffawed. "No way. There're creepy things crawling all over, and maybe they's come out of the tunnels while you's sleep."

Serafina shook her head. "It's on the road to Vanaby. I need to get farther away from the city. And quick. The messenger bird from Vanaby is bound to have returned by now."

I nodded. "We'll keep you out of sight after we leave here." To the group, I said, "From the mansion sale, we'll set up another trust whose proceeds will feed and house the poor."

"Which presumes the Order of Gixus agrees with our interpretation of the law." Rory said, but he was smiling.

We returned to Elise and told her of our plans regarding the rose crown.

Elise's eyes widened. "How can I say no?" Then a genuine smile softened her brown eyes. "I have a sense my job is no longer in jeopardy. Thank you."

We shook hands all around. Elise wasn't my favorite person in the world—dealing with adversity in an underhanded way—but she'd owned up to it. Not that she had much of a choice.

Rory said, "It may take us a couple of days."

Elise nodded.

A warm sensation filled me.

We had completed our first real job. And came away richer than I ever envisioned. More importantly, Rory and I had two new friends, each with their specialized skills. We were better off for knowing them. I couldn't help but feel proud.

## CHAPTER THIRTY-THREE

# FINAL BUSINESS

## RORY

After leaving Elise, we grabbed breakfast at a nearby tavern. Serafina worried about going to the Order of Gixus, so we first marched to an inn near the north gates and secured three rooms.

Leaving Serafina in one of them, Mick, Ingefær, and I hiked to the Order of Gixus and informed them of our findings at Hexerei Mansion. As proof, we handed over Retzlaff's notes to Captain Ambliss. Which led to a host of questions about why we had gone there. I avoided a discussion of the Fraegah Temple and Mick's theft, citing instead vague complaints and then Ingefær and me being unjustly imprisoned.

The process proved laborious, but when we finished, we moved on to the documents we had brought back. We went through one painstaking parchment at a time. We learned why some tunnels were green lit and others were blue. And why some of the summoned monsters were half as difficult as the skeletal fiend.

Thank the gods some of the heirloom spells had failed a generation ago. Those were the tunnels with the blue sconces. Something much fiercer would have ambushed us than spike-headed goblins and three-eyed stygg skapps. And we'd almost died there.

The documents revealed the Retzlaff clan's obsession with animal transmutation. They also identified where the traps were, and the fifth

Retzlaff's work journal documented his necromantic attempts—and eventual success. The plum atop the pudding was the complaint from a jarl about a funny letter of credit. Apparently, the jarl had filed a formal complaint.

As we wound up, I said, "By the laws of the Realm, and by our bounty hunting license as provided by the Tyrrby Order, we lay claim to the Hexerei Mansion."

Captain Ambliss, who I knew from his days in Hjulstadt, snarled. "That's bold of you."

Ingefær asked, "Does the law say different? We're reliably informed there is no next of kin."

Ambliss chewed on his tongue. "We'll have to check it out. And make sure it's as you say."

"I expected no less," I said. "We know it will take time. Bring mages and healers with you when you go. Don't rely on the document trove. There are dead at the bottom of the next-to-last cavern whose kin need to be notified."

"It will cost quite the coin," Ambliss said.

"I expect so," I said. "Your costs will be reimbursed from the sale of Hexerei Mansion. Just don't get anyone else killed. Any deaths are on you."

We haggled. He wanted half of the value of the mansion for doing his job, which was worth a tenth. In the end, to speed things up as there were other things to do, we agreed to let the Order have twenty-five percent.

Papers were drawn up and signed.

After eating lunch, we went about the process of selling the stamped gold, the jewels, and the rose gold crown. At Mick's suggestion, we sent messages to the jarls and wealthy merchants in the city—names we got from an artiste-turned-vendor selling custom carved marble statues—announcing our find, and inviting them to an auction to be held at noon, a few hours shy of three days away.

We returned to the inn and brought Serafina up to date. We cleaned up, took care of the horses, and turned in. Battles and adventures wore folks out. The comedown from fighting life-and-death battles, surviving poisoned needles, and finding a life's worth of treasure had us sleeping most of the following day away.

The morning after—with two nights of rest behind us—I pocketed ten pieces of the stamped gold and one emerald. "Mick and I will make the rounds. You two stay and guard the rest of it. We won't come back until an hour before the auction, which is scheduled for tomorrow."

Ingefær kissed me warmly and fully, on the mouth. "Do be careful."

Mick and I rode through the city, advertising our goods to the wealthier merchants and the jarls we had informed two days ago. I referenced the rose-gold crown and the other valuables and told them where the auction was to be held. In between visits, we hired an auctioneer.

For the rest of the day, Mick and I drank sherry and ate cucumber sandwiches with the high and mighty, and organized the auction. At night, we boarded with the Order of Gixus, paying Ambliss a silver for the privilege.

It was a very miserable night for me. First off, the cots were hard. And I missed my wife. Since half a dozen moons before Ingefær and I were married, we'd never been apart more than a day...even when she was imprisoned.

Finally, the day of the auction arrived. Bringing the goods, Ingefær joined us, and we had a great time watching the elites shout at each other, cursing whenever they were outbid by another. Based on the advice of the auctioneer, we broke up the stamped gold into ten lots. It garnered us a lot more than forty silvers per coin. Then merchants clamored to provide their services, citing their esteemed letters of credit.

Ingefær and I already had an account, but Mick enjoyed himself being fawned over. When he picked a merchant, he told the man, "Don't want no disappearing words. My friends have friends in Tyrrby."

Serafina's share we kept in silver, as per her wishes. We bought a small trunk and a hefty lock for it.

After the auction, we spent a long hour with a solicitor. Aye, my skin crawled.

But he served a useful function, drawing up a trust agreement. We bequeathed the promised coins to train mages in care of the Fraegah Temple.

Mick left to inform his ma about the trust documents and about his decision to join up with us.

Ingefær and I made the rounds, visiting the dock merchant and confirming our order had been sent two days hence. We stopped by the carpenter and upgraded our house plans.

We met up with Mick at the Temple. He had yet another sack full of his stuff. "Cleaned out the boarding room I's staying in."

As we made to return to the north-side inn, an alvae stopped her black gelding before us. She picked at her teeth with a toothpick and motioned at me. "Greetings. Are you the one they call Belkin?"

I narrowed my eyes at her. With long, flowing, silver hair, the alvae possessed a lithe body and wore two long blades at her hips.

"Who wants to know?" I answered her question with a question.

A flicker of a grin. "I'm Melinda. Charged with the retrieval of a half-alvae called Serafina." She sniffed, her chin high in the air. "Last seen at the Shrine of Eirene." She pointed the toothpick at me. "Which is where I picked up your tracks."

Her green eyes locked on mine. "I'm told you were healed there five days ago."

"So?" I said. I looked at Ingefær, then at Melinda, a smile on my lips. "I'm sorry. But I don't remember much. I'd been poisoned."

Melinda eyed my wife, the toothpick pointing. "And you?"

"Sorry. I was so wrapped up in seeing to my husband's care, I remember little." She cleared her throat. "I remember seeing a half-alvae. Is she no longer there?"

I smiled. My wife had learned to lie. Not to be devious, but to save a life.

"She went missing the morning after you left," Melinda said, her green eyes narrowing at us.

Mick said, "We've been busy. We hunted down a necromancer at the Hexerei Mansion."

*Nice deflection*, Mick.

Ingefær added. "We're bounty hunters, too."

Melinda's eyes flashed between us. Then she frowned. "Aye. I've heard a lot about you the past two days." She nodded. "Congratulations. If you spot the half-alvae healer, send a bird to the Shrine. They're taking my messages while I search the city."

Melinda had arrived as fast as a bird, and I wanted to know more. But that would be a strange question to ask. "How much is the reward?"

Melinda downright scowled at us. "Don't be taking my bounty. You have plenty, if what I heard is right."

I shrugged. "Old habit."

Melinda flicked her toothpick and wheeled her gelding about, trotting off to the east.

I blew air out. "It's a good thing Serafina wanted to hide out."

Mick said, "She got here fast."

As we rode off, Ingefær said, "I don't believe Melinda arrived with the messenger bird, or even a day behind it. No way. She must have been in town already. And got a messenger bird from Vanaby."

*Ah, that made sense.*

Taking a circuitous route, with me checking over my shoulder often—now not just for cutthroats, but also Melinda—we returned with Serafina's share just as the sun set.

She hugged us all. With a thin-lipped smile, she said, "I was getting worried you lit out of town."

"Nah," Mick said. "That's now how partners are treated."

Ingefær told Serafina about the bounty hunter. She frowned, closing her eyes as her gray-green pallor lightened.

"You're still joining us?" Ingefær asked. "I hope so. Because you're a valuable part of the team."

The half-alvae smiled, though it didn't make it to her eyes. "Aye. Best if I get out of the city. I need you to send a bird to your Captain Alvertos."

There was more of an urgency to the task now.

In the morning, over breakfast, Mick asked, "You's think I can learn to ride a horse?"

Ingefær said, "Nothing you can't do if you put your mind to it."

On our way out of the city, we stopped by the stables recommended to us, and we bought Mick a roan mare named Cinnamon. Serafina got a grey mare and renamed her Silver.

We rode off with the two Shire draft horses in tow. They'd be perfect on our farm.

I sat tall in the saddle. "We have three days of dusty riding ahead."

I held my bride's hand as we clopped for what would soon be our home—and our base of operations. My head swiveled left and right, searching for bandits and a bounty-hunting alvae.

My wife had been right to take on the job.

We had righted an injustice, and it wouldn't have come to pass if not for our efforts. Hel, what would have happened if the undead Retzlaff had ripened in his powers?

I shuddered.

Thoughts of farming and weeding floated in, but were shoved aside by the prospect of future adventures. Endeavors I now looked forward to.

I smiled. We had a good team. The news of our escapades would bring more adventures.

THE END

# Also by Rene Vecka

The following books have been published by the Author as of July 2025.

<u>Mid Dreki Realm series</u>

In Search of Justice https://books2read.com/u/3koB78

In Search of Kin https://books2read.com/u/4jNrYo

In Search of Gods https://books2read.com/u/49dnrw

In Search of the Rod https://books2read.com/u/b5w9BG

At Searches' End https://books2read.com/u/m2nZYr

<u>Madcap Adventures (standalone novels)</u>

Not for the Faint of Heart https://books2read.com/u/31o8jW

Deadly Dungeon https://books2read.com/u/3JAePX

Death, On Ice https://books2read.com/u/4E172z

<u>Short Story Collection</u>

The First Viking, and Other Grim Dark Short Stories https://books2read.com/u/bQAN9P

# Afterword

I hope you enjoyed dungeon crawling (brought me back to my days of D&D dungeon mastering) along with Rory and Ingefaer. Mick and Serafina round out the Madcap Adventures team nicely, IMO. If so, would you be so kind and leave a review wherever you buy books? A star rating is all that is needed—but a short blurb is incredibly generous. Thank you.

Each novel in the Madcap Adventure world is designed as a standalone novel and, in theory, you can read them in any order. That said, I'm pretty sure the current 'final' book, Laehvateinn, will need to be read last.

The next installment is titled *Death, On Ice,* where Rory, Ingefær, Mick, and Serafina visit the Ice Plains. Things definitely take a dark turn. I still inject humor and the first hint about the last novel is laid in here. It's written, just needs editing. I expect it will be published in July 2025.

The other six novels are laid out chronologically and book 4, *Pirate Problem,* is half plotted, as is book 5, *Sorcerous Favors.* Then there's *Trouble in Paradise, Monster Hunt, Dvaerven Depths, Dragon Deals,* and the aforementioned *Laehvateinn (Lokke's Sword).* And if you haven't read *Not for the Faint of Heart,* now is your chance.

If you're into epic fantasy, I have a pentalogy titled Mid Dreki Realm. The first installment is *In Search of Justice.* Vidarr Allefar is a chosen one who doesn't know it. He grows in power as he bounces from one godly assigned task to another until the finale, where he's tasked with saving the Realm from a divine reckoning (destruction of the world…even the gods).

Check out my website renevecka.com for more information or if you want to join my newsletter. You can also find me on Facebook: facebo ok.com/czechveck. Alternatively, if email is your gig, you can reach out to me at rene@renevecka.com. If you're interested in seeing your name in print, as a bad guy or a side character, let me know. Melinda is a dear friend of mine.

Thanks again for reading.

René

# Acknowledgements

A novel comes together through the hard work and support of many individuals.

First, there's my wife who supports me all day, every day. I am a blessed man. There're the folks at Apex Writers who chip in with weekly writerly advice. Then there're the Superstars Writers Conference folks, where I learned things about the business of becoming an author. There's Colin, who helped me with my website SEO. Thank you all for your support.

Regarding this novel, Tom, James, and Paul read the first draft and provided immeasurable aid. There's my book coach, Nicole, who helped me get deeper into the characters' heads and heightened the suspense throughout.

Mandy provided copy editing services. Any mistakes remaining are my own.

Thank you!

René

# About the author

Rene Vecka is mostly retired from financial services and spends much of his time imagining new characters in new worlds. He's a reader of mystery, science fiction, and fantasy. He writes what he reads. Mr. Vecka has published five novels in the Mid Dreki Realm series, and a short story collection titled *The First Viking and other Grim Dark Short Stories.* He's also written a modern day murder mystery and thriller titled *Queen Sacrifice*, which is currently being solicited to agents. Mr. Vecka also has two sci-fi novels drafted in near time and near space, preliminarily titled *Blade Foxxe.*

The Author lives in the foothills between Denver and Colorado Springs. He lives with his wife, two dogs, and two cats. Occasionally, his three children stop by. He's a chess player, reader, and writer, and Christian.

You can contact him:

www.renevecka.com

www.facebook.com/czechveck

www.instagram.com/czechveck

https://www.bookbub.com/authors/rene-vecka

email: rene@renevecka.com

www.ingramcontent.com/pod-product-compliance
Lightning Source LLC
LaVergne TN
LVHW091111080826
845145LV00008B/1876

* 9 7 8 1 9 5 8 0 4 9 1 8 1 *